"Cruz, would you please tell me what's wrong?"

Ally asked. "Are you mad at me?"

"Why should I be angry at you? If I'm angry at anyone, I'm angry at myself, because of what I put you through. Because I treated you like a criminal."

"You were trying to be evenhanded. You can't blame yourself for that."

"Yes, I can! I was trying to be fair, but I ended up coming down hardest on you. I was kidding myself, pretending—"

He broke off, and she frowned. "I don't get it. What were you pretending?"

He looked at her, a muscle jumping in his jaw. "Don't you know?" he asked in a husky rumble. "Don't you know?"

His fingers tightened on her shoulders, and Ally could feel the effort it cost him to control himself. And then, with a muttered oath, he abandoned the attempt, pulled her into his embrace and took her mouth in a hard, hungry kiss.

Dear Reader,

Once again, Silhouette Intimate Moments has something new in store for you. This month we both begin a series that will carry you into the future *and* bring you a book by one of your favorite authors that, for some of you at least, will awaken memories of past pleasures.

Let's start with the new: Lucy Hamilton's Dodd Memorial Hospital Trilogy. Set in a fictional Los Angeles hospital, these three books are all connected by their setting and their cast of characters, but each one also stands alone as a completely satisfying romance in its own right. And who better to tackle such a project than Lucy Hamilton, a former medical librarian who just happens to be married to a doctor? We think these books will excite you so much that once you check into Dodd Memorial, you may not want to check out!

And what about that favorite author we mentioned? Of course she's none other than Nora Roberts. And the book? It's *Irish Rose*, and if that title sounds familiar to some of you, it's because Nora's very first Silhouette Romance was a heartwarming story called *Irish Thoroughbred*. For those of you who recall that first book, this one should provide a welcome trip down memory lane. And for those of you who met Nora through her later works, we think this book will show you why she charmed so many readers right from the start.

Don't miss our other offerings this month, either, because once again we're introducing some new authors you'll be hearing more from in the future. And, as always, keep your eye on the months ahead, when authors like Parris Afton Bonds, Emilie Richards and Linda Howard will be coming your way.

Leslie J. Wainger
Senior Editor
Silhouette Intimate Moments

Lucy Hamilton
Under Suspicion

Silhouette Intimate Moments

Published by Silhouette Books New York

America's Publisher of Contemporary Romance

The Dodd Memorial Hospital series is dedicated
to my grandmother, Thelma June Wheeler Sargeant.
For all the stories you told me,
and for teaching me how to tell stories, thank you.
These are for you, Grandma.

This book is for Lynne. Thanks for being there.

SILHOUETTE BOOKS
300 East 42nd St., New York, N.Y. 10017

ISBN: 0-373-07229-5

First Silhouette Books printing March 1988

America's Publisher of Contemporary Romance

Printed in the U.S.A.

Books by Lucy Hamilton

Silhouette Special Edition

A Woman's Place #18
All's Fair #92
Shooting Star #172
The Bitter with the Sweet #206

Silhouette Intimate Moments

Agent Provocateur #126
Under Suspicion #229

LUCY HAMILTON

traces her love of books to her childhood, and her love of writing to her college days. Her training and the years she spent as a medical librarian translated readily into a career as a writer. "I didn't realize it until I began to write, but a writer is what I was meant to be." An articulate public speaker, the mother of an active grade-school-age daughter, and the wife of a physician, Lucy brings diversity and an extensive knowledge of the medical community to her writing. A native of Indiana, she now resides in Southern California with her family and three friendly felines.

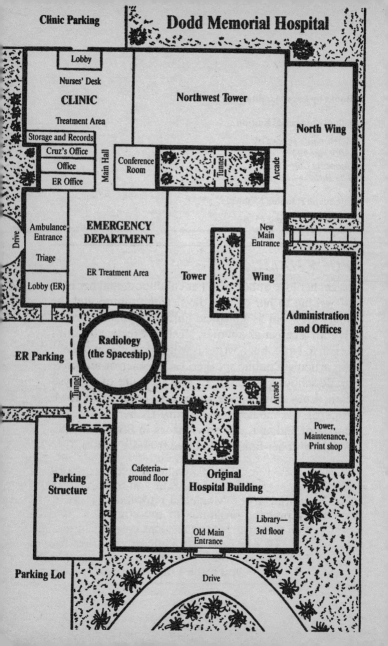

Dodd Memorial Hospital

Clinic Parking

Lobby

Nurses' Desk

CLINIC

Treatment Area

Storage and Records

Cruz's Office

Office

ER Office

Main Hall

Northwest Tower

Conference Room

Tunnel

Arcade

North Wing

Drive

Ambulance Entrance

Triage

Lobby (ER)

EMERGENCY DEPARTMENT

ER Treatment Area

Tower

Wing

New Main Entrance

Administration and Offices

ER Parking

Tunnel

Radiology (the Spaceship)

Arcade

Power, Maintenance, Print shop

Parking Structure

Cafeteria— ground floor

Original Hospital Building

Old Main Entrance

Library— 3rd floor

Parking Lot

Drive

Prologue

Memorial Hospital?"

"Yes, Memorial. Is that so surprising?"

"Well..." She hesitated. "Actually, it is. I didn't think you'd want me to do my training there."

They faced each other across a small dining table, the elderly man and his beautiful granddaughter. Allison Schuyler used a black jasper Wedgwood coffeepot to pour for them both. The table was spread with a snowy linen cloth, the china was antique, and the silver glowed with the soft patina that comes from years of daily use. With silver tongs, Ally added sugar, then passed the cup to her grandfather.

"Thank you, sweetheart." Randolph Schuyler sipped his coffee, frowning. "Of course I want you to do your training at Memorial. Dodd Memorial Hospital has one of the best family practice programs in the country. You'd be working with the cream of the resident crop, including our chief resident, Dr. Gallego. He's a talented man and a good teacher. At Memorial you'll work with, and be taught by, the best. Why would you think I might suggest somewhere else?"

"Because you're Memorial's chief of staff." Ally selected a flaky apricot pastry from the porcelain-and-gilt cake stand beside her. "It will look as if I've been admitted to the program because of your influence."

The light gleamed on Randolph's still-thick silver hair as he looked at her. "The fact that you're ranked third in your medical school class and have excellent test scores might have something to do with it."

Ally's smile was rueful. "*I* know that everyone at Memorial gets their residency position on their own merits, but that's not how it's going to look. People will assume I got in because my grandfather is chief of staff."

"My granddaughter is afraid of a little idle gossip?" He shook his head sadly. "Who'd have thought it?"

"It may not be a little gossip. It may be a lot of gossip."

"And if it is? You hold your head up high and ignore it. It will pass."

"Granddad, you know—"

He lifted a hand to silence her. "Think about your training, Allison." He used her full name only when he was very serious. "At Memorial, you'll get the best. Are you willing to settle for second-best because of a little gossip?"

Chapter 1

Y ou don't deserve to be here."

The cold, uncompromising words hung in the still air.

"I don't?" Ally bent over a cart piled high with library books, and her hair swung down to screen her face behind a blond curtain. When she looked up, her deep blue eyes were grave.

"No, you don't," was Stacy Alexander's blunt reply.

At five feet, five inches, Ally had a slender figure that curved in all the proper places and a classically lovely face. Stacy was taller and slimmer, with an interesting, angular face and thick, wavy brunette hair. She carried an ebony cane slung over her wrist.

"They say the only reason you were admitted to the family practice program," Stacy went on, "is because your grandfather is chief of staff. You don't have brains enough to find your way home, much less to be a resident here. The program's tough, and you'll be lucky to last three weeks."

"But my grandfather's not chief of staff anymore. He's not even in town," Ally protested. "He'll be celebrating his retirement on that round-the-world cruise for the next ten months."

"What difference does that make? He was chief when the committee selected you. It doesn't take a genius to figure out why you got the position."

"And I'd be wasting my breath saying it's not true?"

Stacy's only reply was a cynical snort.

It was six in the evening on the last day of June. Outside the hospital, the palm-lined streets of Pasadena were clogged with rush-hour traffic, and the late-afternoon air was smoggy and hot. It was quiet in the hospital library, though, with only the faraway hum of the air-conditioning system and the occasional turning of pages to break the silence. A nurse and a medical student were sitting in the reading room, and an exhausted resident snored softly on a deep leather sofa in the browsing corner. The stacks in the back room were empty of patrons. Between the tall ranks of shelves, the two old friends continued their chore.

"I knew there was going to be gossip," Ally said softly, "but I didn't think it would be this bad."

"There's a lot of talk, Ally, but idle gossip is all it is. Can you hand me the liver-disease book?"

Ally passed the book over, and Stacy slid it into the correct spot on the shelf.

"Are there any more in this section?" Ally asked.

Stacy shook her head. "Next aisle." She let her cane slide down her arm and into her hand. She'd used a cane since a severe skiing accident had nearly cost her her leg in college. The cane she carried now was of beautifully carved ebony, a gift from Ally when the future had seemed too bleak for Stacy to face. She led the way, steering the front end of the cart with her free hand as Ally pushed from behind.

"You make a good library assistant, Al." She grinned over her shoulder. "If you ever decide to give up medicine, I can offer you fifty cents over minimum wage."

"You're all heart, Stace."

Ally grinned and maneuvered the cart around the corner. If family tradition and personal inclination hadn't sent her to medical school, she might well have become a medical librarian like Stacy. Sharing the chore of shelving books had begun years before, when they had been college roommates and Stacy had worked part-time as a library assistant. She was now the medical librarian at Dodd Memorial Hospital, but the tradition had continued. It relieved the tedium of the chore and gave them time to talk.

"I know." Leaning on her cane, Stacy turned to grin at her friend. "But if everything I've been hearing is true, you'll never make it through your internship, much less the whole four years of residency. You might as well have something to fall back on."

"They're really saying all those things about me?"

"I'm afraid so."

Ally sighed. "I hate this! I wasn't even going to apply here because Granddad was chief of staff."

"So why did you?" Stacy slid a massive brown volume on the circulatory system into place.

"He talked me into it. He asked me if I was really going to settle for second-best training just because of gossip."

"He was right, Ally. Hospitals are such gossip mills, you can't take it seriously."

Ally reached out to hug her. "Oh, Stacy, thank you. I'm glad there's one person in this hospital who doesn't think I'm a spoiled rich brat who used her grandfather's influence to take a job that should have gone to someone more deserving."

Ally's gratitude went deeper than her words conveyed. She'd been a lonely, withdrawn child and still found it difficult to open herself to another person. Stacy understood her when no one else could, and Ally treasured their friendship.

"There's no one more deserving," Stacy said stoutly. "You're smarter than any ten people I know, and I watched you work like a dog through eight years of college and medical school. You earned the position." She took Ally's shoulders and gave her a little shake. "Remember that."

"Yes, ma'am," Ally said meekly, then sobered while Stacy laughed. "You know what worries me?"

"Hmm?" Stacy slid another book onto the shelf and pulled the cart farther along.

"The people I'll be working with, the other residents and the staff. Have they heard this stuff?"

"I'm sure they have, but that doesn't mean they believe it."

"What if they do?"

"Cruz Gallego wouldn't let them." Stacy shook her head firmly.

"Gallego?" Ally remembered that name.

"He's the chief resident of Family Practice. He's a sweetie, and he's always fair. He even makes the FP residents return their overdue books."

"Granddad said he was a good teacher and a good doctor. You don't think he'll believe the gossip?"

Stacy shook her head, and her thick, wavy red-brown hair bounced. "Cruz wouldn't listen to that garbage. You'll see when you meet him tomorrow." She grinned. "Did your grandfather mention that he's gorgeous?"

"Hardly."

"They coined the phrase 'tall, dark and handsome' for him."

"Sounds like you've got a crush on him."

Stacy grinned and shook her head. "We're just friends."

"I hope you're right and he'll keep an open mind. Right now, I feel like I could use an advocate."

"You've got one right here," Stacy said stoutly. "And once you start working, they'll see how good you are and this will all be forgotten."

Cruz was plowing his way through a pile of paperwork when a knock on his office door interrupted him. He muttered an irritable oath and raked his hand through his hair, ruffling the jet-black curls. He hated paperwork.

"Yeah?" It wasn't a welcoming response.

The third-year resident who had knocked stuck his head in the door. Charlie Parsons had a puckish, slightly wicked smile and a halo of frizzy brown hair and wasn't cowed by Cruz's bad temper.

"If you're going to do your head-honcho number, Cruz, you'd better get out here. It's eight o'clock, and the new troops are waiting for the chief resident's words of wisdom.''

''All of them?''

''If eight is the magic number, they're all here.''

''Okay.'' Cruz scrawled his name on a form and moved it from one pile to another. ''I've got to sign these. Five minutes.''

''I'll keep the wolves at bay.'' Charlie backed out the door.

Cruz bent over his forms, grinning to himself. Those interns wouldn't be hungry wolves when he walked into the conference room. They'd be scared to death, and he planned to scare them a little more. None of them would dare take their work for granted after his speech, and by the time they relaxed, the habit of hard work would already be ingrained.

These interns were the best, bright and talented, the fortunate few who had gained admission to Dodd Memorial's family practice residency program. The only fly in the ointment was Dr. Schuyler's granddaughter. Cruz's grin faded. The paperwork wasn't entirely responsible for his bad mood.

He'd heard the gossip and discounted most of it. She couldn't be as dumb or as ugly as they said. Allison Schuyler *was* Randolph Schuyler's granddaughter, though.

He couldn't ignore the fact that little Miss Schuyler had been born to money and privilege, that she'd never wanted for anything in her life.

As a child of poverty who'd fought his way out of the barrio to stand at the brink of the career he'd always dreamed of, Cruz couldn't help but resent that. And he couldn't help but suspect that her connection to Dr. Schuyler had smoothed her way into the program, just as it had undoubtedly smoothed life's other bumps from her path.

It galled Cruz to have a spoiled rich girl on his resident staff. He hadn't chosen her, but he was stuck with her, and he didn't like it. His lips tightened into a hard, thin line. He had to live with it, but he was going to lay the rules out for her very clearly. Money and connections cut no ice with him. If she didn't keep up her end she'd be out, grandfather or no grandfather.

He signed the last of the forms with an angry flourish and added it to the stack, then dragged on a white lab coat with an identification pin that read Cruz Gallego, M.D.: Chief Resident—Family Practice. Dressed and ready to strike terror into interns' hearts, he picked up a thick stack of handouts to distribute to the new people. They would read the handouts, but it was his speech that they'd remember.

Ally sat at the conference table with the others, all of them a little nervous, a little eager, as they waited. There were eight of them, five men and three women. She could tell who had heard the gossip and who hadn't from the way they reacted to her. The ones who had heard were cool and reserved; those who hadn't were willing to be friendly. They shared a certain fellow feeling, though, for they were all facing the same challenge.

At 8:05 the conference room door opened and they turned as one to see Cruz Gallego enter.

Stacy was right, Ally thought as she watched him walk to the head of the conference table with an easy, graceful stride. He set down a stack of handouts and leaned forward to brace his hands on the scratched Formica tabletop. Stacy was absolutely right. He was gorgeous.

He was six feet tall and solidly built, and his strength was obvious, despite the ill-fitting lab coat. He wasn't musclebound but deep-chested and broad-shouldered, his legs and arms strong. His face was square and strongly carved, with high cheekbones and a strong beak of a nose. His lips were slightly full, with an almost sensuous curve, his teeth a flash of white as he smiled at the assembled group.

It was his eyes that held her attention, though. Very dark, so dark they were nearly black, they were deep-set and heavy-lidded, almost sleepy-looking. She suspected that sleepy look was deceptive, hiding his thoughts as he looked slowly around the table.

"Good morning," he said when his survey was completed. His voice was deep and rich, smooth as melted chocolate, with the merest trace of a Los Angeles Hispanic accent. "I'm Cruz Gallego, your chief resident, and this morning I'm going to talk about what you can expect during your first year of training."

He spoke for half an hour, and by the time he'd finished, a palpable tension filled the room. Ally glanced around and saw the apprehension she herself felt mirrored on the other faces. For her part, Ally was calling on everything she had learned at Miss Pinckney's School of Charm about concealing one's emotions behind a calm and pleasant facade.

Dr. Gallego's remarks had not been encouraging. He'd reviewed the schedules they would follow, which were similar, despite the fact that each of them would be assigned to a different service for the first rotation. Ally was to begin her internship in the hospital's Clinic, which was run by the Family Practice Department.

Her feelings were mixed. The clinic rotation was the one that most closely approximated the actual practice of family medicine, with all its variety and challenge. It was also acknowledged to be the most difficult rotation in the FP program.

Ally knew it would be fascinating; she hoped it wouldn't be overwhelming. Dr. Gallego had kept his eyes on her while he'd outlined the schedule, and she had felt something more than simple interest in his gaze. Did he have doubts about her ability to cope? She swallowed the lump of tension in her throat and kept her face impassive.

When Cruz was finished speaking, he looked around the table, studying the reactions on the faces there. They looked suitably scared, and he was confident that his intimidating message had been heard and understood.

Allison Schuyler returned his gaze calmly, though, her Dresden-doll face serene, her clear blue eyes untroubled. She didn't appear to be scared of him or anything else, and that placid lack of reaction infuriated him. Was she so sure that her grandfather's name would smooth her way?

Something dark and angry in him wanted to shake her confidence, to knock that arrogant, privileged poise aside and see what was underneath it.

God, but she's beautiful.

The thought came unbidden and lay smugly in his outraged brain, undeniable in its truth. With an effort, he pulled his gaze away, staring down at the page of notes in front of him. But he didn't see his scrawled sentences, only her face.

Allison Schuyler wasn't merely pretty, she was beautiful. Her hair was thick and glossy, the color of ripe wheat, and it swung just above her shoulders. Cruz knew it would feel soft and would smell of flowers. Her eyes were a clear cornflower blue, large and round, fringed with impossibly thick, dark lashes. Her features were fine and aristocratic, with high, arrogant cheekbones and a straight, narrow nose, a firm, even stubborn chin and a hint of passion in the soft pink mouth.

He looked away, but he could see her in his mind, her small hands folded in her lap like a little girl in dancing school. Her linen dress clung lightly to her curves, and if Cruz let himself, he could imagine how beautiful she would be if he undid those buttons and very slowly slipped the dress off her body.

Stop it! he commanded himself. What Allison Schuyler looked like, with or without her clothes, was of no interest to him. And you're a liar, said a little voice in his mind.

He looked at all of them, but it was Allison Schuyler he saw. She made a note on the pad in front of her, and he watched her small hands and fragile wrists. She was slightly above average height and elegantly slim, but Cruz saw the gentle curves beneath her expensively simple dress. The skin of her throat was thin and fine, and he knew it would feel like satin under his fingertips. Her lips were pink and soft, and they would taste sweet, like warm honey.

He swallowed, his mouth unaccountably dry. When he looked up, she was watching him, those china-blue eyes holding nothing but mild curiosity. She didn't look as though she'd ever had an original thought in her life, Cruz thought with a sudden anger he didn't really understand. Oh, he had her figured, all right. She was cotton candy, soft and sweet and empty.

Ally met Cruz Gallego's dark, hostile gaze with all the poise and self-control she could muster. She was more scared than she wanted to admit, but she was also growing angry. He kept staring at her as if he was deliberately trying to intimidate her. She'd be damned if she would give him the satisfaction of seeing that he had.

When Cruz finally looked at someone else, she sighed with relief. Now that he wasn't watching her, she could watch him, and she did. She watched his hands as he gathered his papers. They were tanned and strong, with long, straight fingers, and they moved with a deft economy of motion. Beautiful hands.

"That's all for today," he said as he slid the papers into a folder. "Pick up your patient assignments in the FP office at the end of the hall. You'll find the charts on the units where you're working. Be ready for rounds in the morning, and the other residents and I will see you at seven."

There was a general shuffle and clatter as the eight interns pushed back their chairs and rose.

"Dr. Schuyler?"

It wasn't until he spoke her name the second time that Ally realized Cruz was talking to her. She'd only been Dr. Schuyler for three weeks, and she still wasn't used to the title. She kept expecting her grandfather to answer.

"Yes, Dr. Gallego?" She kept her face under control, but there was a knot of ice in her stomach.

"Would you stay a moment? I'd like to speak with you." The words were polite, the voice civil, but his eyes were cold.

"Of course," she replied in her best charm-school voice, and sat down again, folding her hands demurely. If she kept her hands in her lap, he couldn't see them shake. And what was she so scared of, anyway?

The last intern shuffled out of the room, clutching his fistful of handouts as he mumbled goodbye. Cruz closed the door firmly behind him and turned back to Ally.

She looked up at him, waiting patiently for him to speak, but he stood motionless by the door, studying her. It was an uncomfortable scrutiny. The seconds ticked past, and she felt more and more like a specimen under a microscope.

She let her lips curve into a small smile, hoping to ease the tension that hummed between them. It didn't help. A muscle tightened along his jaw, and he pushed himself away from the door to walk back to the table.

"Were you listening, Dr. Schuyler?" His voice was soft, with an edge like a well-tempered blade.

"Listening to what?" She wasn't sure what he was referring to.

"To the things I said in the meeting just now."

"Yes, I was."

"I wonder if you understand what kind of program you've managed to get yourself into."

The edge had grown sharper, and Ally didn't like it. She was beginning to see where this conversation was heading, and her temper was rising.

"I understand quite well, Dr. Gallego." Her voice was soft as warm butter, but her eyes were chips of ice. "You made your points with a fairly graphic clarity." She smiled, cool and amused. "Am I supposed to be terrified?"

"I wasn't trying to terrify anyone," he retorted.

"Weren't you?" She lifted one elegant eyebrow. "I got the impression that the point of your remarkably pessimistic speech was to strike terror into the hearts of us poor interns."

Ally noticed with satisfaction that his lips tightened and his nostrils flared in anger. She was beginning to enjoy herself. She hadn't expected the great Dr. Gallego to get rattled.

"Evidently you're not terrified."

"I knew what was involved when I applied to this program."

"You think so?"

He walked around the table, grasped the back of her chair with one hand and planted the other on the table beside her. Trapped, Ally could feel the heat of his body as he bent over her. She stiffened her spine, sitting very straight, her eyes glittering with anger.

"I doubt if you have any idea at all how hard you're going to work over the next four years," he said softly. "Especially since your admission had nothing to do with your qualifications."

Ally gasped and jerked around in her chair to look into his face. "I beg your—"

He cut her off. "Don't bother begging my pardon, Dr. Schuyler. Frankly, I'm not interested. I wanted to speak to you alone because I want to tell you that I've heard a great deal about you and your admission to the program."

"You can't seriously—"

"I don't ordinarily give credence to gossip," he said, rolling right over her protest. "But it's obvious that your grandfather's position had a lot to do with your admission."

"My grandfather wouldn't do that!"

"No, he wouldn't. But he was chief of staff, and he had a lot of clout with the members of the admissions committee. That must have had some influence on them."

He stopped, waiting for a response Ally wouldn't give him. He was baiting her, but she refused to be drawn out.

"Nothing to say?" He smiled, but it was the cold smile of a predator watching its prey. It was his conversation now, and her moment of advantage was gone. "Good, because I have a great deal to say. You don't belong here, Dr. Schuyler, and, frankly, I'd be just as happy if you quit right now."

"I won't!"

"Your decision." He shrugged. "And, I suspect, the wrong one. The Schuyler name and your grandfather's influence got you into this program, but that's as far as it goes."

He leaned closer, his face grim. Ally wanted to slap him, wanted it so badly her palm itched.

"I have a warning for you. If you don't carry your weight, nothing and nobody on this earth will keep you in."

He stared at her for a moment, then turned on his heel and strode out of the room.

Ally sat frozen in fury as the door slammed closed behind him. The hand she lifted to brush her hair off her brow was shaking, not with fear, but with anger.

She didn't give a damn if the high-and-mighty Cruz Gallego worked her into the ground. She'd work harder than he did, longer than he did, and she'd show him how wrong he was.

Furious, she zipped her papers into her briefcase and gathered her belongings. She would make him eat every one of those words or she'd die trying!

From the opposite end of the corridor, Cruz watched Allison leave the conference room, outrage in every perfectly sculpted line of her body as she slammed the door with a reverberating crash and stalked away. Grinning, he watched until she'd disappeared around the corner; then he unlocked his office and went in.

Small and chaotically overcrowded, the office was furnished with a battered desk and chair, several file cabinets and a straight chair in front of the desk. Every horizontal surface in the room was piled with papers, files, medical journals and books. A dead fern in a pot shared the windowsill with a stack of library books. Cruz didn't even see the disorder. He shoved a stack of reports away from the center of his desk and dumped the papers he'd been carrying in the newly created space, but his mind was on Allison Schuyler.

She was a surprising young woman. Cruz dropped into his chair and swiveled around to gaze past the dead fern at the courtyard outside his window. He'd thought he had her all figured out, but she'd proven him wrong. He didn't like that. He'd been comfortable with his mental image of her as a wealthy, shallow dilettante. He wasn't sure what to make of the icily outraged woman in the conference room.

She didn't look as if she was capable of more than a delicate blush or a genteel swoon, but when he'd delivered his parting shot, she'd been practically smoking with rage. On the surface she was all gloss and money, beauty and sophistication, but Cruz was far more interested in what that surface concealed.

Interesting, Cruz thought, unaware that he was smiling. It would be very interesting to peel back the layers and see the real Allison Schuyler.

Chapter 2

"Here you are!"

Stacy startled Ally out of her grim absorption in the pile of notes that lay beside her bowl of the cafeteria's beef stew.

Ally jerked her head up to see Stacy and a small, pretty, dark-haired woman standing by the table. The movement dislodged several sheets, which drifted to the floor. Ally smiled weakly at the two women and bent to pick them up.

"You scare me to death when you sneak up on me." Her complaint was muffled by the table.

"I never sneak. You're just so deep in whatever that is that you wouldn't hear a brass band coming." Stacy and her companion sat down. "Where have you been all morning?"

"I was hiding in the FP clinic chart room. The catacombs. It's perfect—low ceiling, dim lights, lots of dust." Ally surfaced, her hands full of papers. She looked at Stacy's companion and smiled. "Hi. I'm Ally Schuyler."

"I'm Thea Stevens." She reached over to shake Ally's hand. "Glad to meet you."

"Thea's the new media coordinator, and since we're both in the education department, I'm showing her the hospital."

"Congratulations on your new job." Ally grinned. "How are you doing at finding your way around?"

Thea laughed, her dark eyes gleaming in her perfect oval face. "I'll never figure this place out! I get lost as soon as I leave my office."

"We all do. This place is a maze, just one addition after another for sixty years."

"With no planning or forethought whatever." Stacy grinned around a bite of turkey on rye. "You'll get used to it, though." She turned to Ally. "What were you doing in the chart room?"

"Reading charts. I start in the clinic tomorrow, so I've got a bunch of patients to research before their appointments."

"You start in the clinic?" Stacy was suddenly serious. "That's too bad."

"Oh, come on! You're supposed to say something bright and bracing about how it'll be a challenge but I'll do great."

"It'll be a challenge but you'll do great," Stacy parroted mechanically, and Thea chuckled.

"Is the clinic that bad?" she asked.

"It's got a reputation as the toughest rotation in the family practice program," Ally replied, "because it's the most like actual practice." She took a mouthful of stew. "I don't mind. I'm here to learn." Her voice hardened. "And I will, and serve him his words on a silver platter!"

"You're going to serve who what?" Stacy asked.

"Dr. Gallego." Ally bit the name out with icy distaste.

"Cruz?" Stacy straightened in her chair. "Are we talking about Cruz Gallego?"

"We are if we're talking about that arrogant, judgmental, obnoxious, megalomaniacal..."

"Wait a minute! Cruz?"

"...high-handed tyrant of a chief resident," Ally finished, rolling right on through her list of adjectives. She'd been mulling them over as she worked, and she didn't want to leave anything out.

"Arrogant, high-handed tyrant?" Stacy shook her head. "You left out obnoxious and megalomaniacal."

Thea looked from one to the other. "Who are you talking about?"

"I'm not sure we're talking about the same guy," Stacy said.

"We're talking about the chief resident in family practice." Ally gave them a quick synopsis of the morning's events. When she'd finished, Stacy was staring at her open-mouthed.

"The Cruz Gallego I know wouldn't do something like that."

"Maybe you don't know the Cruz Gallego I met today." Ally pushed her bowl away. "I've never been so mad in my life."

It wasn't simple anger, though. A lot of other, less definite emotions were mixed in. She was starting a new phase of her education and her life, and she was a little excited, a little nervous, a bit eager and just a touch scared, even without Cruz Gallego.

What if he was right? The residency was going to be difficult, so how would she handle any extra pressure he put on her? There had been a definite threat in his promise to watch her every move. She swallowed, her throat oddly dry.

"I can see how mad he made you," Stacy said, "but did you notice that the man is gorgeous?"

"I didn't pay any attention." Her tone was coolly dismissive and, to her relief, the subject was dropped. It was only when Stacy and Thea Stevens left her to continue their tour that Ally let herself think about it again.

She'd lied to Stacy.

She had paid attention to every devastating detail of Cruz Gallego's appearance. The boxy lab coats seemed to make everyone look like a sack of potatoes—everyone, that is, except Cruz Gallego. Nothing could hide the deep chest and broad shoulders, the strongly muscled arms. His legs were strong, too, and his flannel slacks had strained over muscular thighs as he perched on the edge of the table.

His hair was raven black, thick and glossy and neatly cut, brushed back in crisp waves and echoed by black hair curling at the base of his throat, where two buttons had been undone on his pale green cotton shirt. His eyes had fascinated her, deep-set and heavy-lidded, a brown so dark they looked black. Ally had been unable to read anything but hostility in them, but she'd wanted those eyes to match the beauty of his face and especially his wide, slightly full mouth.

A sensuous mouth. It had thinned to a hard line when he had delivered his warning, but it was a mouth made for kissing, for driving a woman mad. And his hands, square and strong, moving among his papers with a deft economy of motion. He would have a light touch, a gentle touch. He would caress a woman's body surely and lightly—

"No!" She shoved herself back from the table. She didn't realize she'd spoken aloud until she noticed the curious stares. Heat rushed to her cheeks as she bent over her papers again, but she could still feel the staring eyes. She rubbed the back of her neck, where small hairs prickled.

The feeling didn't ease, and she looked up after a moment to meet a pair of eyes trained intently on her. It was rude and annoying, and Ally stared back at the tall, silver-haired nurse. After several seconds the woman flushed and looked away.

Ally watched for a moment to make sure she didn't start staring again, then let her gaze slide idly over the steady stream of people moving through the cafeteria. They were a colorful blur, a background for the one man who caught her eye.

Cruz Gallego walked into the big, noisy room, laughing with a pretty woman in a white uniform. Ally could see the warmth in his eyes. When he'd looked at her, they'd been cold and opaque, like chips of onyx.

She bent her head again, letting her hair screen her face until Cruz and the woman walked into the serving line and out of her sight. Before he could emerge from the other end, she scooped up her notes and hurried out of the cafeteria.

She thought she was prepared. She really, honestly thought she was well prepared for her first day at the clinic. She walked in the staff door shortly before the 8:00 a.m. opening time and realized how wrong she was.

The clinic, shoehorned into a suite of rooms that had originally been a laboratory, was always crowded. Nurses, nursing aides, technicians and others bustled through the cramped little rooms and hallways that radiated from a central lobby and nurses' station. They were stocking supplies and readying things for the day's work while the residents clustered at the nurses' station, reading charts and appointment sheets and grumbling good-naturedly about the day's schedule.

Ally stopped just inside the door. She had no idea where to go or what to do first. She was the only intern assigned to the clinic; the rest of the residents were in their second and third years. Except for Cruz Gallego, of course. She knew how closely he'd be supervising her, looking over her shoulder, waiting for her to slip up, while she tried to figure out what on earth she was supposed to do.

"Oops!" A tall, thin nurse carrying an armload of folded patients' gowns brushed past Ally, nearly knocking her back out the door. "Sorry about that, Dr.—" She peered over her armload of linen to read the plastic name tag pinned to Ally's white coat. "Dr. Schuyler." She smiled in recognition, her slightly worn face warming into prettiness. "You must be Dr. Schuyler's granddaughter."

"Yes, I am." Ally couldn't resist the warmth in the nurse's smile. Here was one person who didn't resent her presence. "I'm glad to meet you—" she leaned forward to read the nurse's name pin "—Miss Clark."

"It's Ms., and call me Barbara, please."

"I'm Ally."

"Glad to meet you, Ally. I won't keep you. You'll want to read the appointment list like everybody else." She jerked her head toward the cluster of residents. "See you later." She grinned and went on her way.

Ally crossed to the nurses' station, still smiling.

"You look pretty cheerful."

Cruz spoke from just behind her, and she stumbled slightly on the smooth floor. He caught her arm in a gesture that she would have considered courteous if it had come from anyone else. His fingers bit into the soft flesh just above her elbow; she freed her arm with a jerk but kept smiling.

"Yes," she told him smoothly, "I'm feeling cheerful. I'm ready to start work."

"Are you?" He looked her up and down, taking in the designer skirt and blouse, the smoothly styled hair and carefully applied makeup, the snakeskin pumps. He smiled as if something amused him. "Have you signed in?"

Ally hadn't known she was supposed to sign in, but she hid her dismay. "No, I haven't. Where do I do that?"

"On the clipboard over there." He pointed. "Then check your list of appointments. There may have been some changes since last night."

"All right." Changes? Her heart sank, but she kept her voice level. "Should I pull my own charts?"

"No need. The aides put the chart in the exam room when they bring the patient in. They've stocked supplies, but if you need something else, just send somebody for it."

"I can get my own supplies," she offered quickly. "There's no need to send somebody else."

"There's every need. You have just fifteen minutes for each appointment, and you can't spend that running up and down the halls looking for tongue depressors while your patients are waiting. You aren't a medical student anymore, *Dr.* Schuyler." He edged her name with ice. "Quit thinking like one."

He turned on his heel and started away.

"Very good, *sir*!" Ally muttered under her breath. A resident standing beside her muffled a snort of laughter. Cruz halted and turned back.

"Did you want something else?"

His gaze impaled her where she stood, but Ally didn't flinch. If this was a contest of wills, she wasn't about to fold at the first skirmish. She blinked guileless blue eyes at him.

"Oh, no. Nothing at all."

His gaze narrowed on her for a moment; then he turned and strode away. Ally watched until he entered the hallway that led to his office, then let out the breath she had been holding.

Beside her, the resident chuckled softly. "Don't worry," he said. "It'll get worse."

Ally turned to see a man of about her height, stocky and solid, wearing rumpled chinos and a nondescript gray shirt beneath his lab coat. He had the square, cheerful face of a cynical elf, with bright brown eyes, ruddy cheeks and a thick mustache that echoed his cap of unruly curls. His grin was wicked and irresistible.

"Thanks a lot!" She grinned back at him. "Are you always so optimistic?"

"I try. I'm Charlie Parsons, third-year."

Ally smiled. "I'm Ally Schuyler, lowly intern."

"Yeah. And you need to sign in." Ally was relieved that he didn't feel compelled to discuss what had passed between her and Cruz Gallego. "You do that over here." He pulled over a clipboard chained to the desk. "When you leave for your lunch break, you sign out with the time you leave and then sign back in. That way everybody knows where you are."

"Thanks." She scribbled her name and the time. "What do I do first? I'm all ready to start practicing medicine, but I don't know the mundane details, like where to put my purse."

"Well, I don't know where to put your purse, but Karen will." Taking Ally's hand, he pulled her toward the only other woman in a resident's white coat. "Hey, Karen! We need a little information over here."

Karen was tiny and dark-haired, with a pretty, pixielike face. She'd been laughing, but when she saw who Charlie had with him, her smile stiffened into something polite and cool.

"Yes, Charlie?"

"Karen, this is Ally Schuyler, the new victim...er, intern. She needs to know where to stash her purse, and since I left mine at home, I can't help her out. Ally, this is Karen

Willis, M.D. Second-year resident and clinician extraordinaire.''

"Charlie, you're an idiot!" Her laugh was natural and her smile warm when she looked at Charlie. She turned back to Ally, and the chill set in again. "You mustn't pay any attention to him, Dr. Schuyler. He talks a lot of nonsense."

"Call me Ally, please. And I don't mind Charlie talking nonsense." She grinned. "It takes my mind off the fact that I'm scared to death."

Karen studied her for a moment, and her smile slowly returned. "I know that feeling. The first time I walked into this place I had no idea what to expect."

"What should I expect?" Ally asked. "I'm dying to know."

"Bedlam at first, but you'll work yourself into the routine. You leave your purse and things in the locker room. It's down this way." She led Ally into a hallway connecting the clinic and the ER. The women's locker room was halfway along on the left side. "Just pick an empty locker and bring in your own lock. You can put your stuff in my locker today."

"Thank you. This is awfully nice of you." As they put Ally's purse and briefcase in the locker, they could hear an increase in the noise level behind them.

"Don't worry about it." Karen glanced at her watch. "It's time to open the store, so we'd better get in there. Yell if you need a hand, okay?"

"I will," Ally assured her with fervent honesty. "Promise."

Karen hurried back through the swinging door, but Ally hesitated. The people moving around in there all seemed to know exactly where to go and what to do. She only hoped she could figure things out quickly. Ally took a deep breath, gathered her nerve and waded into the chaos.

She didn't have to worry about signing out for lunch, because she didn't get to eat lunch. Her fifteen-minute appointments stretched to twenty and twenty-five as she tried and failed to keep up with the other residents, all of whom were more experienced and more efficient. She had to work straight through her lunch hour in order to finish her morning appointments before the afternoon patients began arriving.

By 2:30 she was behind again, with no end in sight. She was examining a cranky, feverish two-year-old with a suspected ear infection when she discovered there were no more ear speculums in the drawer. She pushed her disheveled hair off her forehead and closed the drawer.

"I'm sorry, Mrs. Baker, but I have to get a little funnel to look in Jamie's ear. Do you mind waiting for just a moment?"

"Oh, no, ma'am." Jamie's mother absently fended him off as he tried to climb onto her shoulders. "I don't mind at all."

While Mrs. Baker, pale and wrung out, with a kind of downtrodden stoicism, was in the examining room with Jamie, the receptionist out in the waiting room was wrangling with his two brothers and one sister, aged fourteen months to four and a half. Ally looked out as she passed the door and saw that they were systematically dismantling the toy corner. She shook her head and rounded the corner to the nurses' station. One nurse was there, writing in a chart.

"Excuse me."

The nurse glanced up, and Ally recognized her as the woman who had stared at her so rudely in the cafeteria. She was tall and slim, with silver-gray hair pulled back into a tight bun and a face set in discontented lines. She scowled at Ally and returned to her notes.

"Excuse me," Ally repeated, "but I need some ear speculums. The pediatric size."

"Congratulations." Head down, she kept writing.

This was deliberate rudeness. Ally's soft lips firmed into a line. "Dr. Gallego told me to ask for supplies if I ran out. Would you bring some speculums to room 6, please?"

"I have things to do. Get your own speculums."

"Dr. Gallego said—"

"I don't care what he said!" The woman looked up, her face set in a sneer. "You may think you're better than the rest of us, *Dr. Schuyler*, but think again! I have things to do.''

While Ally watched in disbelief, she stalked away.

"I'll get those speculums for you, ma'am.'' The offer came from a young man in a white uniform who was approaching from another hallway. "Don't let Miss Mott bother you. She's not a very cheerful person.''

Ally couldn't argue with that. Miss Mott was rude, unpleasant and downright nasty.

"What size speculums do you need?''

"The small pediatric ones. The patient is two.'' She tried to discreetly read his name tag, and he grinned as he held it up.

"I'm Ray Walcott. I'm a nursing aide. Where will you be?''

"Room 6. And thank you.''

"No problem.''

She watched as Ray hurried away. He was a plain-looking young man in his mid-twenties, with thin, rather lank brown hair and scars from teenage acne on his face. In high school they would have called him a nerd, but he'd been pleasant and helpful to her. She was prepared to like him, especially when he brought her a pack of speculums about six seconds after she got back to Jamie and his mother.

Her problems were far from over. Though he looked like a chubby, dark-haired cherub, Jamie didn't feel good, he was in a bad mood, and he didn't want *anybody* looking in his ears.

Ally crooned soothingly as she picked him up and laid him on the exam table, but he was having none of it. He kicked and flailed and squealed like a little pig, and though she struggled valiantly, she couldn't get the otoscope into his ear. In her efforts to be careful, she managed to get herself kicked in the nose so hard she saw stars.

She jerked away and shook her head, blinking back tears of pain. "Wow! Jamie, you sure are strong for such a little guy!'' He blinked owlishly at her, momentarily silent, and his mother smiled proudly.

"He is, isn't he? I knew he was going to be strong because he kicked a lot before he was born."

"He's certainly a vigorous little boy," Ally agreed tiredly. "Okay, Jamie, do you think you might let me look in your ears now?" She bent over him again, and Jamie resumed shrieking.

"How are you doing in here?"

The question was shouted so that it could be heard over Jamie's furious yelling. Startled, Ally jerked around and froze as the final straw fell on the camel's back. Cruz Gallego stood in the doorway, smiling as he surveyed the scene.

Ally knew why he was smiling. She was frazzled, and it showed. Her hair was a mess, her lipstick long gone, and a streak of cherry-red cough syrup adorned the front of her raw-silk skirt. She was still in there slugging it out, but she was nearing the end of her rope.

Cruz's smile widened as he walked into the room. Ally knew he was going to read her the riot act for her incompetence, and she waited stoically for the blast. He surprised her.

"What's the problem, pal?" He moved past her to pick Jamie up. The boy stared in fascination at this new face.

"Suspected otitis media," Ally said quietly from behind him.

"Have you had a look in his ears?"

"I've been trying, but Jamie doesn't like the idea. I don't know how to do it without hurting him."

"That's where you're having trouble." Cruz laid Jamie down and picked up the otoscope. Jamie promptly began yelling again. "You're being a little too gentle. Kids are sturdier than they look, aren't they, Jamie?" He bent over the little boy, using his arms and body to block kicks and punches while he held Jamie's head immobile and peered into his ear. "Mm-hmm. No wonder he's not too happy. Take a look at this, Dr. Schuyler."

Ally moved into place. Cruz stayed right behind her, and their bodies brushed as he showed her what to do. His face was next to hers, his breath warm on her cheek, and he smelled of shaving lotion and hospital soap and man. He was standing so close that he was practically holding her in an embrace. Ally could feel herself flush.

She looked through the otoscope and saw what she'd expected, an obviously inflamed eardrum. When Cruz was satisfied that she knew what to do, he stood back while she examined the other ear. With his body no longer pressed against hers from shoulder to thigh, she could breathe freely again.

The rest of the exam went quickly. Ally wrote a prescription for antibiotics, which Cruz cosigned, and showed Jamie's mother how to give the medicine. Ally and Cruz finally escorted mother and son to the reception desk, then walked back into the staff area, where Ally sagged wearily against the wall.

"Thank you," she said quietly.

"What for?"

"For helping me with Jamie." She leaned her head back against the cool tiles and closed her eyes. "I didn't know how to look in his ears. You probably think I'm an idiot, but I needed the help and I want to thank you."

"*De nada.*"

Her eyes were closed, but she could feel Cruz's scrutiny. She knew she looked like the wrath of God, but she was too tired to care. It would be enough if she survived this day.

"Parsons!" Cruz shouted, startling Ally into opening her eyes again. Charlie looked up from the chart he was reading. "Take Dr. Schuyler's next appointment, will you?"

"No sweat." Charlie snapped the chart closed and grinned at Ally. "What exam room are you in?"

"Room 6, but I don't—"

"Got it." He gave her a grin and a thumbs-up sign, then headed off toward the waiting room.

"Charlie, wait—" But he was already gone. Ally looked after him, then turned to Cruz, her brows knit in a puzzled frown. She couldn't read his thoughts in his face. "Why did you do that?"

"Because you need a break. Come on." He strode away, Ally in his wake.

The staff lounge was a small, cramped room furnished in a style that might have been called "institutional castoff." There was an uncomfortable two-seat sofa and two equally uncomfortable vinyl armchairs, all in shades of mud. A coffee urn stood on a table in the corner, and there was a soda machine in the hall outside. Ally followed him in and stood awkwardly in the middle of the room.

"Sit down," Cruz ordered her, and he disappeared into the hall again, to return moments later with two cans of soda. "Go on, sit down. The machine's out of cola, so I got orange and root beer. Which would you like?"

With a feeling of utter unreality, Ally sank to the sofa. "Orange sounds good, thank you."

He popped the tab and handed her the can, then drank thirstily from his own. Ally took a long swallow and leaned back, stretching her legs out in front of her.

"I know this isn't what you're used to," Cruz said, grinning wryly at his can, "but the machine was out of champagne, too."

She laughed softly at the idea. "Champagne makes me burp. Cream soda and tortilla chips got me through those long nights of studying in med school."

"The princess doesn't mind drinking soda from a can?"

Ally opened her eyes and found Cruz watching her. His scrutiny was unnerving and made her feel like a specimen under a microscope. Why was he staring at her that way, asking those silly questions? And what was this "princess" business?

"Not a princess," she said, her expression deadpan. "A countess, maybe, or a duchess at the most."

He was silent for a moment; then he laughed, full-throated, in honest amusement. It was a wonderful sound, deep and vibrant and utterly masculine, without the hostile tightness his voice always seemed to have when he spoke to her.

"Okay, Countess." He shook his head. "The pediatrics department prints a pamphlet on exam techniques for infants and kids. You can stop by my office when the day is over and pick one up."

"Thank you."

He glanced at the clock on the wall and made for the door. "Time to get back to work."

"Dr. Gallego?"

He stopped and looked over his shoulder. "Hmm?"

"Why did you do this?" she asked. "Give me a break, I mean, and buy me a soda."

His gaze slid away, and when he spoke his voice was rough. "You can't practice good medicine when you're out on your feet," he said, though he knew that was far from the whole truth, and vanished around the corner.

Ally finished her soda thoughtfully and went back to work.

It was after six before she knocked on his office door.

"Come in."

Ally entered the office hesitantly. It was tiny and cluttered, with papers and journals piled on every surface, including the seat of the side chair. The only thing that redeemed the room was the window, which looked out on a lush lawn and the mountains beyond the hospital walls.

She stood before his desk like a schoolgirl waiting to be chastised. "You said I could pick up that brochure from you this evening."

"Yeah. I've got it right here." He retrieved a pamphlet from beneath the pile of forms he was working on. He looked up at her and waved toward the chair. "Sit down, please. I know you must be tired."

"I'd love to sit down." She glanced down and grinned. "But have you looked at this chair lately?"

He looked over the desk. "Oh, sorry. Hand me that stuff and I'll stash it somewhere."

Ally passed him the stack, and he added it to a pile on the floor behind his desk, then turned around again, smiling.

Ally caught her breath. The smile transformed him from an angry ogre into the hunk Stacy had described. He leaned back, linking his hands behind his head, stretching his shirt across the muscular breadth of his chest. Ally's mouth went dry, and she pulled her gaze away, staring blankly out at the view.

"Thank you," she said to break the silence. "It feels good to sit down."

"Are you on your way home?"

She shook her head. "I'm on call tonight."

"That's right. I'd forgotten. If you survive this, you can survive anything."

"You can't imagine how much better that makes me feel."

Cruz chuckled at her dry tone. "Supper would make you feel better. Why don't you come to the cafeteria with me and eat while you have the chance?"

Ally was so astonished that she missed the look of surprise Cruz's offer had brought to his own face. She waited for a moment, fully expecting him to come to his senses and retract the offer. He didn't. One second stretched into two, and then she decided.

"Thank you," she said politely. "I'd like that."

Chapter 3

Confused and not liking the feeling, Cruz held the door politely and allowed Allison Schuyler to precede him into the cafeteria. What the hell am I doing here? he asked himself almost angrily.

Ally was too hungry to worry about his motivations. She chose her meal quickly, carried her tray to the first empty table and dug in. Cruz sat more slowly, eyeing her salad, extra-hot chili and cupcake skeptically.

"Are you going to eat all that?"

She looked up and grinned. "I'm starving, and I love their chili."

"You got the extra-hot, with the jalapeños?"

"Yeah." She plucked one of the innocent-looking but fiery pale green peppers off the bowl of chili and munched it with relish. "I love 'em."

Cruz sampled his beef stew and shook his head. "It's hard to picture Dr. Schuyler's granddaughter eating junk food with extra-hot peppers."

Ally studied him for a moment, then put down her spoon. "I wish you'd quit that," she said quietly.

"Quit what?"

"Looking at me and seeing somebody called 'Dr. Schuyler's granddaughter.' I don't know who she is, but I don't think I'd like her. I'm not her, I'm me, *Ally*, and I like junk food and hot chili and even disgusting stuff like this store-bought cupcake, which is what I plan to have for dessert." She indicated his plate. "I didn't say anything about the fact that your name's Gallego and you're eating mulligan stew."

Cruz frowned. "I didn't mean to prejudge you."

"Didn't you?" She returned to her chili.

Thoughtful, Cruz watched her eat. Was he making unjustified assumptions about her? He didn't think so. Maybe she liked junk food, but the rest was still true.

She was Dr. Schuyler's granddaughter. She had grown up rich, and the finishing school gloss showed. It was true that she'd surprised him today. She'd worked hard, and she hadn't been a complaining prima donna, but it would take more than one day to convince Cruz that she belonged here.

They ate hungrily and talked little. Ally was far more relaxed in the presence of the ogre when he didn't talk, and she'd just as soon he kept his opinion of her to himself. She watched him through the screen of her lashes and wondered what his thoughts might be.

He had finished his stew and was cutting an apple into pieces. She watched his hands as he worked at the small task. They were man's hands, strong, but they would be gentle hands. They would touch a woman's body with delicacy and skill....

Ally brought herself up short. She wouldn't let her thoughts wander along that track! But she had to agree with Stacy, Cruz Gallego was an enormously attractive man. He was her chief resident, though. He was off limits.

She forced herself to concentrate on her supper. She'd nearly finished when the intercom speaker above her head crackled to life.

"Dr. Schuyler," the tinny voice intoned. "Dr. A. Schuyler to the emergency room. Dr. A. Schuyler to the emergency room."

"I don't get my cupcake after all." She picked up her tray, then looked at Cruz. For a moment the finishing school facade slipped. "I wish I wasn't scared to death."

"You'll do okay."

"I hope so." She forced a smile. "Well, thanks for the supper. I wish you'd let me pay for it."

He waved that off. "Go on. They're waiting for you."

She went, hurrying to the ER, which was at the opposite end of the hospital, where a young man who had injured his arm in a lathe accident was waiting for her.

Her job when she was on call was triage and immediate care. She saw the newly arrived patients, assessed their injuries or illnesses and either treated them or referred them to the proper specialist. Cruz had told the new interns that the most important thing a family practitioner could know was when to refer. He'd said they would get plenty of practice in the ER.

He'd also mentioned that they would get very little sleep. While the specialty residents dozed in their on-call rooms, waiting for her to phone them, Ally was on the front lines. She was run off her feet until after midnight.

At 12:17 a.m. she stood back to watch while the victim of a drunken brawl in a neighborhood bar was trundled away to surgery to have his head cuts stitched. He disappeared through the swinging doors, and Ally plodded back to the nurses' station.

"Who's next, Babs?"

The unit clerk, a cheerful young woman with frizzy red hair and freckles across her nose, grinned. "Nobody."

"No more patients?" Ally asked stupidly. After the steady stream she had seen over the past five hours, that was difficult to believe.

"It's true." Babs dropped her voice to a conspiratorial whisper. "There's nobody else here." There was no one waiting for Ally in the treatment cubicles and there were no new patients in the reception area. She could actually take a break.

"Go back to the lounge and collapse," Babs urged her. "I'll get somebody to bring you a cup of coffee." When Ally hesitated, the girl waved her on. "Go, before somebody sees you and gives you something to do!"

Ally went. The lounge was as Spartan as all the other staff lounges, but it was quiet, and it had a sofa. Nothing else mattered. She staggered in, kicked off her shoes and collapsed on the couch, her head on the armrest and her feet tucked up under her. She'd close her eyes for just a minute, she decided, until she got that cup of coffee.

She was fast asleep when Cruz stopped in the doorway, a paper bag in his hands. She was curled into a ball on the sofa, her cheek pillowed on her hand. She had wisely changed into hospital greens for the night, and her pajama-like pants and loose pullover shirt were covered by her lab coat. The shirt had ridden up as she slept, baring a narrow band of pale midriff. Her skin would be warm, her flesh soft to the touch.

Cruz dragged his gaze to her face. Her breathing was slow and even, her cheeks slightly flushed. The urge to touch her, to hold her, was sudden and powerful, a quick rush of heat through his veins.

He set the paper bag on the lamp table and moved quietly to an armchair in the corner, removing himself from temptation. He'd let her sleep, and she could have her coffee when she woke. The chair, which had seen a lot of better days, creaked loudly beneath his weight. Ally stirred and blinked at him in confusion.

He could tell when she recognized him. Her eyes widened, and she gasped, then shoved herself sharply upright, shaking her hair out of her eyes. She pulled her oversize scrub shirt back into place, and Cruz followed the movement with his eyes, unable to help himself.

"I'm sorry!" She slid her feet into her shoes. "I didn't...I didn't mean to fall asleep." She started to stand, but Cruz stopped her.

"Don't get up." He took her shoulders and pushed her back down onto the sofa. Her bones were delicate beneath his fingers, and her warmth reached his hands through the soft cotton shirt. Hastily he took his hands away.

Ally watched his face as he moved back to the chair, then shook her head, trying to clear away the cobwebs. Her shoulders still tingled from the light pressure of his hands.

"This is so embarrassing." She raked her fingers through her hair, trying to restore it to some kind of order. "I didn't mean to fall asleep."

"Don't apologize. When you're a resident, you sleep whenever you can."

"Granddad warned me about that. He said I'd learn both medicine and the meaning of the word 'fatigue.'" Fully awake, she sat straighter and schooled her sleep-softened features into their usual well-controlled expression. Her mind was clearing, too, and she frowned. "Why are you here? Are you on call, too?"

"No, but I had paperwork to finish. I came down to see how you were doing." He picked up the paper bag he'd brought and dug inside it. "Here." He handed her a cup of coffee and a package of cupcakes.

"Cupcakes?" She looked from the familiar cellophane package to Cruz and back again. "You got me cupcakes?"

"You didn't get to have them for dessert."

"So you . . . ?" She tore the cellophane and peeled it off. "Well, thank you. Would you like one?" Cruz gingerly accepted. Ally chuckled at his expression. "Please tell me you're not one of those desperately sincere health-food freaks who won't eat anything that's not green and organic and covered in alfalfa sprouts!"

She didn't think to wonder at her own temerity in teasing the arrogant ogre; the daylight rules seemed to have been suspended. The hospital was quiet in the small hours of the night, and the starkly furnished lounge seemed almost cozy. The barriers between them were down, and Ally liked it that way. She was even beginning to like Cruz Gallego.

"It's a good idea to eat a healthy diet," he replied with a small smile, "but I've always liked cupcakes." He took a big bite and grinned at her, crumbs and sugary frosting clinging to his lips.

Ally watched him lick the traces away and felt her cheeks warm. It was too easy to imagine kissing them away. She dropped her gaze suddenly and stared into her coffee.

If she kissed those beautifully carved lips he would taste of sweetness and coffee, and if he held her close in his arms, her breasts would flatten against the hard wall of his chest. And why was she thinking this way?

She gulped her coffee and burned her tongue. This was stupid! She refused to moon over a good-looking man like a starry-eyed teenager. She looked at him from beneath her lashes, trying to understand her uncharacteristic behavior. Was it the contrast between this very nice man and the angry ogre who had accused her of scheming and conniving? Or was it simply the man himself?

"Did you have any other problem patients today?"

Ally looked up and blushed, afraid he could read her thoughts. "Problem patients?"

"Besides the boy with the ear infection."

"Jamie. Thank you again for showing me what to do. I'd never have figured it out by myself."

"If I hadn't helped you, somebody else would have. Were there any other problems?"

"Only me."

"You?" He looked at her face. "How's that?"

"It took me twice as long as everybody else. I tried to hurry, but I was afraid if I went too fast I'd miss something important. I was slow, and all those people had to wait for their appointments."

"It was your first day. Nobody expected you to set a speed record."

"All I set was the slow record, Dr. Gallego."

"Cruz. We only get formal when we're with patients."

"And I'm Ally." He nodded, and she felt a little of the tension seep out of her. "All right . . . Cruz." It wasn't hard to say his name. It came easily to her lips, as if she'd always called him that.

"Ask Stacy, in the library . . ." Ally pulled her attention back to what Cruz was saying. " . . . for the folder on doing histories and physicals. She's put together some stuff on how to speed up the process without missing anything.''

''Thank you. I'll do that.''

He drained his coffee and rose, tossing the paper cup into the wastebasket. ''I've got to get going.'' His face altered slightly, the smiling Cruz disappearing back into the arrogant Dr. Gallego. ''I have a warning for you.''

''Warning?'' She was suddenly tense again.

He nodded. ''Be prepared for rounds tomorrow morning, Dr. Schuyler. The staff guys and I will have plenty of questions for you.'' And then he was gone.

Ally watched the door swing closed. She was an idiot! She'd thought he was being so nice, bringing her coffee and cupcakes, but the only reason Cruz Gallego had been there was to check up on her. She wasn't surprised, but she felt a strong sense of letdown. She'd wanted to believe he was changing his opinion of her, but he wasn't being kind, he was just following up on his promise to keep an eye on her.

She swung herself to her feet. He'd warned her to be prepared for rounds in the morning. Since he would be watching her closely, she might as well spend what was left of the night reading charts. Tomorrow was going to be a long day.

The ''long day'' lasted until after six in the evening, and Ally had just enough strength left to crawl home to Sherman Oaks and collapse.

One of eight condos at the end of a quiet cul-de-sac, her home was surrounded by eucalyptus and acacia trees and might have been a million miles from the middle of one of the largest cities in the U.S. City noises were muffled by the trees, and cool evening air flowed through her living room window, carrying the twitter of finches and the buzz of hummingbirds' wings. Ally lay back in a deep armchair by the window, listened to the birds, sipped a glass of iced tea and let herself relax, muscle by muscle.

The phone's shrill ring jerked her out of her reverie, and she reached for the receiver with a weary sigh. It was a man she had known since childhood and occasionally dated, inviting her to a party. No, she told him, she wasn't up for a party tonight. No, really, she was exhausted. Another time, perhaps.

She hung up with a sigh of relief and dropped her head back against the upholstery. She couldn't face a party tonight, especially one of Chip's raucous bashes. He was gregarious and fun, and his work as a publicist suited him perfectly, but he was exhausting to be around.

When the phone promptly rang again, she muttered grumpily as she reached for it. Chip could be hard to convince, but he was going to get this message.

"For the last time, Chip, I'm not going to any party tonight!" she said without preamble. A deep laugh, definitely not Chip's, rumbled through the line, jolting her into silence.

"I'm relieved to hear you're not out partying with people named Chip," he said, heavily sarcastic. "I'd hate to think you were more interested in parties than your internship."

That was so unfair that Ally was bereft of speech for a moment. She gritted her teeth and drew a careful breath before she risked speaking.

"I have no plans for tonight, Dr. Gallego, except a long, hot bath and an early bedtime."

Cruz wanted to laugh at the way she rose to the bait, but his mind was suddenly flooded with an image of Allison in her bath, bubbles clinging to the wet, smooth curve of her breast, the slender line of her thigh. The silence between them stretched into several moments.

"Dr. Gallego?" Ally asked at last. "Why did you call?"

Cruz pulled his wandering thoughts back to the issue at hand. He gave the explanation that he had almost convinced himself was the only one. "I wanted to ask you about the charts you used this afternoon. Did you chart all the medications you signed out?"

"Do you mean on the sheet in the drug closet?"

"Yes. And on the patient's chart, too."

"Yes, I did. I followed the instructions in the procedure manual. Is something wrong?"

"I don't think so. Just keep following the procedure. I'll see you in the morning."

Cruz didn't bother to say goodbye, but replaced the phone quickly, as if it were burning his hand. He scribbled a note on the pad in front of him, but his mind wasn't on the problem of the drug closet.

He knew how she would look in that bath. She'd pile her hair into a golden cloud atop her head, but a few tendrils would escape and cling to her neck in the steamy warmth. Her skin would be pink from the heat, her cheeks flushed. She would use a soap that smelled of roses and wildflowers, and her body would be warm and silky as she relaxed in the water. He shook his head, as if to physically dislodge the image.

He was a fool, indulging in stupid adolescent fantasies. He had problems to deal with, real ones, and no time to waste in stupid imaginings. He bent over his desk, determined to work, but Allison Schuyler's face hovered stubbornly on the edge of his consciousness.

She haunted him all night.

"I've hardly seen him in three weeks."

Stacy smiled at the affronted tone in Ally's voice. "I thought if you never saw him again it would be too soon?"

Ally glowered. The cafeteria echoed and clattered its way through the breakfast rush, while a tray of coffee and pastries sat between them on the small table. Ally broke off a piece of bearclaw and nibbled it without enthusiasm.

"Stacy," she said slowly, "you're my best friend in the world and I love you dearly, but I really hate it when you remind me of what I've said."

"What are friends for?" Stacy shrugged. "I'd have thought you'd be happy Cruz is leaving you alone."

"I guess I am. Dealing with the madhouse of the clinic is easier without all-powerful Gallego looking over my shoulder. He's just another distraction I don't need."

"So why is that suddenly a problem today?"

"Today's my evaluation. How can he evaluate me," Ally asked indignantly, "if he hasn't been watching me work?"

Stacy's coffee went down wrong, and she coughed hard before she could speak. "His spies are everywhere," she said hoarsely. "You can bet he's been keeping up with your progress."

"You think so?"

"Of course!" She shook her head. "You can't have it both ways, Ally. Either he's out of your way, so you can work without distractions, or he's hanging over your shoulder, watching your every move, so he can evaluate your work. Which is it?"

Ally sighed. "I think I'm relieved he's not hanging over my shoulder. I'm nervous when I know he's watching me. I fumble and stammer and drop things. I do fine until I see him, and then everything falls apart."

"You're just nervous because it's all new to you."

"I'm nervous because he told me he'd have me thrown out on my ear if I didn't perform. And I'm scared to death of this evaluation. What if I *haven't* performed?"

"Don't be an idiot," Stacy said, helping herself to a crumb cake.

Ally was glad Stacy had such confidence in her abilities, but that wasn't much comfort as she stood outside Cruz's office door. Her appointment was for two, and she was hovering out here in the hallway five minutes early, unwilling to knock before the appointed hour. She was terrified he'd tell her that she hadn't made the grade.

At precisely 1:59 Ally lifted her hand, took a deep breath and tapped the door with her knuckles.

"Come in."

Cruz came around the desk to greet her, stiffly formal. His hard, handsome face was set into an expressionless mask.

"I've looked over your work," he began when she was seated, his voice cool. "I've reviewed your charts and notes, your case presentations at rounds and the Grand Rounds you presented on food allergies in children. I've watched you work with patients, and I've observed your interactions with the rest of the clinic staff."

He paused and looked down at the notes on his desk. Ally fought the urge to wring her hands in anxiety. She couldn't read his impassive face, and that had to be bad. If the news was good he would smile at her, wouldn't he?

"I've assembled all the information available, and it paints a consistent picture," he said when he looked up. His face was almost grim. Deep lines scored his cheeks, and his eyes were flat and unreadable. "There's only one conclusion I can draw."

Ally's heart began to thud painfully against her ribs. She could barely hear his voice for the blood roaring in her ears.

"I don't quite know how to say this."

Ally wanted to scream at him just to say it and get it over with.

"But the fact is, you have done an excellent job. Your work has been remarkable for someone just beginning her internship."

Ally stared at him, unable to comprehend his words at first. "Excellent?" she breathed at last. "I did well?"

"Yes, you did." Irritation broke through the flat voice. "That's what I said."

A smile slowly lit her face. "I'm sorry I'm not making sense, but I'm so surprised...."

"Surprised that you did well?"

"No, I'm mostly surprised that you'd admit it." Cruz stiffened, and she realized, too late, what she'd said. "I'm sorry!" she gasped. "I shouldn't have said that."

"Probably not." His grim expression softened. "But if you have to apologize, then I do, too."

"For what?"

"For the things I said about your ability as a doctor and about how you gained your position here." He shifted uncomfortably in his chair and raked his fingers through his hair. "I made some unfounded assumptions, and I was wrong. Your work this month has made it clear that you earned your position here on your own merits." He paused and looked into her face. "I apologize."

Ally could feel the pull as their eyes met, even now, when he was being formal and distant. She fought it. After a moment she nodded carefully. "Apology accepted."

"Thank you," he replied gravely. Despite that gravity, his eyes were warmer, brown instead of black, and his lips curved in the beginning of a smile. "Are you ready for the bad news?"

Ally sat back and smiled. Not even the bad news would alter the fact that Cruz Gallego thought she'd done well.

"Fire away."

"All right." He opened a folder. "In going through your write-ups, I've found that you tend to give too much detail about the negative findings and not enough on..."

He talked, and Ally listened and made notes, but only part of her mind was on the criticism and advice he gave her. She would go over it later, and she'd work hard to correct her mistakes, but right now she couldn't stop the one wonderful thought: I did well! I really, truly did well!

"That's it," Cruz concluded. "Anything you don't understand?"

"I don't think so." She tapped her fingertip on the notebook in her lap. "I have it all written down, anyway."

"Good. It's fairly minor stuff, but if you get a handle on your charting and record keeping, it'll speed things up and it'll make your records easier to read."

"All right. Thank you."

He looked at her curiously. "Are you all right?"

"I'm great!" He was still watching her, and she shook her head ruefully. "I'm not making much sense, am I?"

"Not much, but that's okay."

He grinned, and Ally caught her breath at the transformation. He wasn't an ogre at all. In fact, when he turned on the charm that way he was darned near irresistible.

"I'm so relieved I can't seem to be sensible." She laughed. "I was sure you were going to tell me that you were right all along and I wasn't good enough. I'm still having trouble believing the good news."

"It's true. You should know I wouldn't sweeten the pill for you."

Since he was laughing at himself, Ally wasn't afraid to agree. "I didn't expect you to. In fact, I wouldn't have been surprised if you'd thrown me out—and enjoyed it."

Cruz was taken aback by that. He hadn't meant his frankness with her to be taken as personal criticism. "I never meant to make you feel that way," he said quietly. "I didn't *want* to throw you out."

Giddy with relief, Ally didn't notice the change in him. "You made it pretty clear that you didn't want me to stay. I'm so relieved, you know what I want to do?" She twisted in her chair to grin at him.

"What's that?" he asked automatically.

"I want to celebrate. As a matter of fact, I *need* to celebrate. And since you're the one who gave me the good news, why don't you have dinner with me tonight?" She smiled at him. "Will you?"

Cruz looked at her eyes, which were sparkling with happiness, and his lips replied with no prompting from his brain. "Thank you. I'd like that."

"Great!" She jumped up. "Terrific! My address is—"

"I can get it from your file."

"Okay. Take the Van Nuys Boulevard exit off the freeway, and it's a few blocks south of Ventura Boulevard. Is seven okay?"

"It's fine."

"See you then. Bye!"

And she was gone.

Cruz stared at the spot where she'd been standing a moment before. The air still held the impression of her presence, all shimmering excitement and sudden, surprising energy. That energy had blinded him to the foolishness of what he'd done.

He'd committed himself to dinner with her. Alone. The two of them together, away from the neutral ground of the hospital. He was a damned fool! After nearly a month of deliberately avoiding her, of almost dodging around corners when he saw her coming, he had agreed to have dinner with her!

What kind of an idiot are you? He hurled the angry question at himself. She disturbed his sleep, invaded his thoughts, and a month of avoiding her hadn't gotten her out of his system. One flutter of those fabulous lashes and he was having dinner with her, God help him!

He slammed his fist on the desktop. Damn him for being susceptible to her quick wit and her gentleness—and her beauty.

And damn her for being so beautiful!

Chapter 4

Cruz looked around the quiet cul-de-sac, at the carefully kept patches of lawn in front of the two-unit condos, at the trees and flowers and the general air of quiet affluence. So this was where Allison Schuyler lived.

It was a nice neighborhood, so why did he feel so out of place? He wasn't poor anymore. He didn't live in the barrio anymore. He had grown out of that world, away from it. The boy who'd dressed in other people's castoffs and gone hungry or eaten on the nuns' charity so that he could give his lunch money to his younger brothers and sisters didn't exist anymore. So why, Cruz asked himself, did he feel like that boy again, the one on the outside looking in?

Because of Allison Schuyler. She'd been born into this world of grace and privilege. Social skills that Cruz had fought to learn were second nature to her; the life he was striving for was the life she took for granted.

She wasn't from his world; she was as far out of reach as the real leather baseball mitt he had coveted when he was ten. He'd stood with his nose pressed against the toy store window for hours, gazing at that mitt, admiring the rich sheen of the oiled leather, imagining the soft, flexible feel of it on his hand, the satisfying smack as the ball hit the pocket. His enjoyment had all been imaginary. By the time he'd been able to afford that mitt, he had outgrown sandlot baseball.

He hadn't outgrown women, but even so, he felt as if he were ten again, standing with his nose pressed against a window, looking in at her world and wondering if he would ever truly feel a part of it.

He rapped on the door, then turned and scowled out at the street as he waited for her to answer, shifting tensely from one foot to the other. He didn't know who he was so angry with—himself or her.

"Hello!"

He spun around. Ally stood in the doorway, smiling up at him. Her face was flushed, her hair tied with a scarf into a loose ponytail. She wore a blouse of soft, pale green silk and forest-green linen trousers with a frilly yellow apron tied over them. She took his breath away.

"Come in, come in." She drew him into her living room. "Dinner will be ready in half an hour. You can keep me company while I finish up." She walked ahead of him, chattering brightly over her shoulder. "There's a bar of sorts in the chiffonier over there. I'm having mineral water and lime, if you'd pour for me. I've got to get back to the chicken."

With a little wave, she vanished around a corner. After a moment he heard the clanging of pots and pans. Cruz stared after her for a moment, bemused.

Her living room wasn't large, but it was light and airy, with pale peach walls, a sofa and chairs upholstered in pastel chintz and a deep armchair with a footstool in front of it in the corner by the biggest window. He could see several medical journals and an issue of *Vogue* piled on the footstool; that must be her spot to sit and relax.

Cruz had no idea what a "chiffonier" was, but an enormous mahogany cabinet standing against the far wall was the likeliest candidate. He opened the doors and smiled at her idea of a bar. Aside from ginger ale, cola and mineral water, her stock consisted of two bottles, one of peach brandy and one of Irish whiskey. A thimbleful of the brandy was gone, and the whiskey was still sealed. He poured mineral water for them both, added ice and lime, then followed the sounds of cooking.

A round dining table occupied one end of the large, sunny kitchen, while Ally stood at the other, vigorously chopping something on a board. Saucepans simmering on the stove sent out delicious aromas. She smiled at him over her shoulder, her lashes wet with tears.

"Are you all right?" He shoved the glasses on the table and crossed to her in three rapid strides.

"I'm fine." She sniffed and rubbed her nose. "It's just these blasted onions." Picking up the cutting board, she used the back of the knife blade to push the onions into a pan of something tomatoey. "If you'd gotten here five minutes earlier I'd have to put you to work chopping them. Then you'd be the one crying your eyes out."

"Not a chance." He grinned. "I'm way too tough to cry over onions." He plucked a tissue from a box on the counter and caught her hand as she turned toward the sink. "Come here." He swung her around and pulled her close.

"But I've got to wash my hands!"

"In a minute." He lifted her chin and blotted the tears from her cheeks, his fingers sliding over the fragile skin of her throat. She felt like silk, warm and smooth. "You're not too tough, are you? Crying your eyes out over an onion."

"I'm tougher than I look," she protested, but her voice was low and husky. The sound sent a trickle of heat down his spine.

The pulse in her throat raced against his fingertips. Her wet lashes lifted slowly as she looked up at him, her eyes wide and surprised. Her lips were slightly parted, pink and soft and sweet, and he was going to kiss them.

His fingers tightened fractionally on her throat, and her eyelids drooped in instinctive invitation. Though a few inches of air separated them, he could feel the warmth of her body, could feel how it would be if nothing separated them, if her body was pressed pliantly to his, held in his arms.

He knew as surely as if he were already holding her, kissing her, caressing her...loving her. His head lowered toward hers.

Behind them, something spat and sputtered loudly on the stove. Cruz stiffened as the spell shattered and Ally jerked away from him, spinning around to the stove.

She snatched the loudly sizzling chicken and pepper dish off the flame and splashed in a dollop of wine from a bottle that waited nearby. "This isn't supposed to boil, just to simmer. I hope it isn't ruined!"

Cruz cleared his dry throat. "I'm sure it'll be great."

"I hope so." Her back to him, she added more wine and stirred briskly. "I'd hate to ruin it at this stage."

Cruz took a long swallow of mineral water to ease the dryness in his throat. When he moved a few feet away from her, the tension in his body began to ease, as well.

"What can I do to help? And don't say 'nothing,'" he added as she looked up, "because there's always something to do."

"I wasn't going to say 'nothing.' I was going to tell you that napkins and silverware are in the right-hand drawer of the china cabinet, if you'd like to set the table."

"Right." He turned away, looking. "And the dishes?"

"In the hutch on top."

"Got it." He took out cutlery and plates. "This was my chore when I was little," he said after a moment. "I'd set the table while my mother cooked, and we'd talk."

"What did you talk about?" Her voice was soft, wistful.

"The stuff that was important to me when I was nine. School, how my baseball game went. The kind of things you talk to your mother about."

"That sounds so nice." She took a bowl of salad from the refrigerator and brought it to the table.

Cruz looked up from folding napkins and frowned slightly at the sadness he saw in her face. "It was. Didn't you ever talk with your mother like that?"

Her face seemed to close, shutting him out. "Not really." Her tone was light, but it rang false. "Would you hand me the platter for this chicken? It's on the top shelf."

"Sure." She'd closed the subject, and Cruz wondered why.

"That was delicious." He laid his knife and fork across his empty plate after finishing a second serving. "And I'm not just being polite, either. Do you cook like this all the time?"

Ally laughed, thinking of the nights she barely had the strength to lift a fork.

"I cook when I have time," she said. "Some nights cooking is therapeutic, other nights I just put some peanut butter on toast and that's it. When I finally staggered home after that first night on call, I didn't even bother with peanut butter. I was too tired to chew." She rose and picked up the plates. "We can have dessert and coffee in the living room."

There was a smile in Cruz's voice as he followed her to the sink with more dishes. "After that delicious meal, I can't wait to see what's for dessert."

"Brownies." She told him with a grin. "And not just any old brownies. These are the ultimate drop-dead brownies."

In short order the kitchen was neat, the coffee brewed and the dessert tray carried into the living room. Ally settled into a corner of the sofa, sipped her coffee and smiled at Cruz.

"I'm glad you came tonight."

"I am, too," he replied with a note of surprise that made Ally smile.

"You didn't really want to, did you?" His silence spoke for him. "I shouldn't have put you on the spot. I was just so relieved that you weren't going to toss me out on my ear that I didn't stop to think about protocol." She paused, struck by a thought. "Is this against the rules?"

"What? Sitting on a couch having dessert?"

"Not that! Is there a rule against the chief resident having dinner with an intern?"

Cruz shook his head. "Not that I know of. It's just dinner we're having, not a red-hot affair."

"Mm-hmm." Ally laughed, but she bent over her coffee cup, hiding her face. They'd come very close to a kiss in the kitchen. Cruz might joke about a torrid affair, but if he'd kissed her, she would have gone up in flames. She looked across the small space that separated them on the sofa. If he kissed her now, she didn't know what would happen.

It was only the middle of the evening when he looked at his watch and stood. "I know it's rude to eat and run, but we both have an early day tomorrow."

"Since every day is an early day, I think late nights are a thing of the past." Ally didn't know if she was relieved or disappointed. The shared memory of that near-kiss had hung between them all evening. The effort of making light conversation was beginning to tell on her.

Cruz raised one eyebrow. "Used to keep a lot of late nights, did you?"

"All the time!" She rolled her eyes, playing along with the joke. "I was always up in the small hours, hunched over a physiology book or a chemistry book or..."

He grinned. "I shouldn't have asked."

"I don't mind." She followed him to the doorway. "It's kind of nice to know you're concerned about your interns getting their rest."

"It's not my interns I'm concerned about."

She was close behind Cruz, waiting to show him out. He didn't open the door, but turned back to her in the close confines of the narrow entryway.

Ally moved back involuntarily, coming up against a small console table with a Chinese vase on it. She could hear the vase rock and stopped short, separated from Cruz by scant inches. His scent reached out to her with hints of after-shave and hospital and something that was indefinably him.

"I'm not concerned about the rest of the interns," he said softly. "Just about this one."

He slid his fingertips over her cheek, savoring the texture of her skin, then drew them down along the delicate line of her jaw to her throat. Her eyelids drooped as she lifted her face, unable to do otherwise. He was going to kiss her, and she wanted it more than anything in the world. She'd wanted nothing else since that taut, unfinished moment in the kitchen.

A kiss from Cruz wouldn't be something meaningless she could brush off. It would touch her and change her in ways that had nothing to do with his position or hers, but with the man himself and the force that was drawing them together.

When he bent his head, she swayed against him, her body molding to his, welcoming the arms that slid around her and took her weight.

In a remote corner of her mind Ally knew this was insanity, but that didn't seem to matter. The need to feel Cruz's kiss was the greater compulsion, and she reached up to meet his lips.

It was not tentative, not uncertain. It was a lovers' kiss, hot and searching and deep, an explosion, rocking her to the core. He demanded her surrender, and she gave it eagerly, demanding in her turn. Her mouth parted; she nipped and tasted his lips, ran her tongue along the even line of his teeth, abandoning herself to the madness.

Passion grew, beating in their blood, heating the air around them, until they were breathing hard, their skins damp, their hearts racing together. Ally twisted her hands in Cruz's hair, pulling him closer as he lifted her into the curve of his body, his arms steel-hard against her.

He groaned incoherently into her mouth, then turned his face sharply, dragging his lips away.

"No," Ally whispered, trying to pull him back.

He caught her wrists in a painful grip and held her hands away. "Yes." His voice was soft and certain. He held her hands in front of her as he kissed her lips again, quick and hard, almost desperate. "Good night, Allison."

She stood stiffly in the small foyer until the sound of his car had faded into the murmur of the night, her hands clasped together as Cruz had left them. When she moved, unclenching fingers that were bloodless and numb from the pressure of her grip, she walked unsteadily across the living room and dropped bonelessly into a chair. She didn't think, didn't even try, just waited for the strength to climb the stairs to her bedroom.

*   *   *

"Ally, did you want this?" Barbara Clark carried a tray loaded with sample bottles and paper medication cups.

"Not the pain meds. I just need a dose of cough medicine for the little boy in room 4."

"Here." Barbara slipped a two-ounce sample bottle of yellow syrup into Ally's jacket pocket. "Need anything else?"

"Another pair of hands and three more hours in the day."

"Don't we all?" Barbara laughed. "Add a little extra money to that list and I'd be in good shape." Chuckling, she hurried away, while Ally went to give her patient his medicine.

The day had been a killer. The clinic had been pandemonium, hardly what the doctor ordered after a sleepless night. On the other hand, Ally reflected as she waited to get another sample from the drug closet, the frenzied activity had pushed Cruz out of her thoughts, something she hadn't managed to do on her own. Maybe being run off her feet wasn't all bad. She smiled wryly at the thought.

"Here, Ally." Karen Willis handed her the key to the drug closet. "I'll sign the key in to me and out to you."

"Thanks."

Ally understood the need to keep a record of everyone who entered the drug closet. Powerful medications were stored there, including narcotics, tranquilizers and other legally controlled drugs. The constant signing in and out was annoyingly time-consuming, though, and everyone took shortcuts. When she was finished in the closet, Ally would check the log to make sure Karen had signed the key out to her; then she'd sign it back in, and that would be that.

She walked out with two tablets in a paper cup, signed the key over to the next person and turned around just in time to bang into a broad chest.

"I'm sorry, I—" she began, then looked up and saw who she'd knocked into. "Oh! It's you."

"Yes, it is." His face was as blank as her own, and a hint of a Spanish accent colored his voice. She'd heard that slight musical accent when he'd said good-night to her less than twenty-four hours ago. "Excuse me."

Ally felt a chill run down her spine at his stiff tone. This wasn't the passionate man who'd kissed her and set her alight. This was a stranger. When he carefully stepped out of her path, she brushed past him without meeting his eyes. She didn't want to see what might be there.

The clinic scheduled no appointments after 4:30, but it was past six before the last of the patients had been seen. Ally was wrung out and knew that she looked it. She said goodbye to her last patient and plodded back through the clinic, wanting nothing but her home and a hot shower. Before she reached the locker room, Barbara Clark stopped her.

"Ally, Cruz wants to see you before you leave." Barbara's rather worn face was worried.

Ally had tried to stay out of his way all day, but she couldn't refuse a direct order. "Did he say why?"

"No." Barbara shook her head. "But he wants to see everybody on the staff before they go."

"Everybody? Not just me?"

"Everybody. I haven't talked to him yet, but my turn's coming up."

"What's it about?"

Barbara shrugged. "Beats me. It's unusual, though, and it's got everybody nervous. Look at them."

For the first time that day, Ally really looked at the people around her. The staff had separated into small groups, talking in undertones, their faces both nervous and curious. But why?

It took time for Cruz to work his way through the entire staff, technicians and nurses' aides first, then the nursing staff, then the residents. He didn't keep anyone very long, but there were a lot of people to deal with. Ally said as much to Barbara while they waited, sitting on the hard lobby chairs.

Barbara chuckled and leaned back in her chair. "If it seems like a lot now, wait a couple of weeks."

"What happens then?" Ally looked at her watch. It was already 7:15.

"The nursing students come back to school, and there'll be eight or ten of them working here." She didn't sound enthusiastic about the prospect.

Ally glanced at her. "Doesn't it take some of the burden off the nursing staff when there are students here?"

"Eventually it does. But for the first couple of weeks it just raises the chaos level."

"You know what I think?" Ally hid a smile.

"What's that?"

"I think you just like to have something to complain about."

Barbara chuckled. "You're probably right. But with my bills, and my kids who need school clothes, and my car that's gonna roll over dead one of these days, I don't need to go looking for things to complain about."

"I don't suppose anybody does."

"Isn't *that* the tru—"

"Barbara?" A nurse tapped her shoulder. "He wants to see you next."

She stood and gave Ally a thumbs-up. "Wish me luck."

"Of course." Ally watched her go and wondered, along with everyone else, what on earth was going on.

It took another hour for her to find out. When Karen left Cruz's office, she nodded to Ally. "Your turn."

"Okay." Ignoring the butterflies in her stomach, Ally walked down the hall and tapped on the door.

His "Come in" was quick and curt, and he didn't look up when she pushed the door open. "Sit down." She sat and waited, her apprehension growing. When he looked up, his face was grim. He didn't look as if he'd slept any better than she had.

"Cruz, what's the matter?" She was concerned more for him than for the problem, whatever it was.

"That's what I'm trying to find out" was his terse reply.

"But what—"

He held up a hand, silencing her. "I need you to answer some questions for me."

"Well, sure."

"Okay. Did you chart all the medications you took from the drug closet today?"

"I think I did."

"Did you log the drugs on the sheet in the closet?"

"I think so."

"You'd better be more certain than 'I think so'!" he barked. "Did you have the key to the drug closet?"

"Yes, I did." She was relieved to be sure of that.

"How many times?" he pressed.

"I don't know. Four or five."

"You can't pin it down any better than that?"

"Not off the top of my head. It ought to be on the log."

"I have that here." He grimaced in disgust. "For what it's worth. I see your name here—in someone else's handwriting." He pinned Ally to her chair with a cold stare. "How do you suppose that happened?"

Ally looked at her hands, which were knotted together in her lap, and explained in a toneless voice that she had let Karen sign the key log for her.

"I see." Cruz leaned back, watching her with cold eyes. "Were you aware," he asked in softly cutting tones, "that your signature on that log was a legal statement that you took possession of the key?"

"I guess so."

"You guess so. And were you aware that if you allow anyone else to sign your name to a legal document you have no defense if your name is forged?"

"I didn't—" Ally was out of her depth now, floundering. "I didn't know that."

"No kidding," he said with biting sarcasm. "Well, you'd better read up on the legal ramifications of the paperwork you do here or you're going to end up in more trouble than you ever thought possible." He leaned toward her, punching his finger on the desktop for emphasis. "You will not, ever, sign your name to anything unless you know exactly what you're signing!" He paused. "Will you?"

"No," Ally said hastily. "No, I won't!"

"And you will not write anything in a chart or a patient record that you do not personally know to be true."

"No, I won't."

"And you will not ever," he went on, his voice slowly rising, "allow anyone else to sign your name to *anything*. No matter how busy you are!"

"I won't," she promised quickly.

"See that you don't." He held her eyes for a moment longer, then nodded curtly. "That's all."

Ally moved to the door, then hesitated with her hand on the knob. "Cruz?"

"Yeah?"

"What happened today?"

His face was bleak. "That's what I'm trying to find out."

By the next morning the rumors were flying thick and fast. There was an air of suppressed excitement and general nervousness at the clinic, but there was no solid information available until late afternoon. Cruz had canceled the last half hour of appointments and asked the staff to assemble in the meeting room.

Ally went into the meeting feeling worried. She had spent the night agonizing over her record-keeping mistakes. She knew she should never have allowed anyone else to sign her name to anything, but since it seemed to be accepted practice among the residents and nurses, she had gone along with the crowd. If Cruz or the hospital authorities decided to punish her, she would have no defense.

When Cruz began to speak, she found that even in her worst imaginings, she had underestimated the gravity of the situation. Everyone who had any irregularities in their paperwork or in the handling of the key to the drug closet, would have a disciplinary note placed in their employment record. A handout on the hospital's paperwork policies would be distributed.

"You are all advised," he said with a lack of emphasis that was more chilling than shouting would have been, "to read that handout." He looked slowly around the room. "And remember it."

It was a chastened group that filed quietly out of the meeting.

"He didn't say anything about it," said the nurse walking in front of Ally.

"Nothing," agreed her companion. "I wonder if it's true."

"There was a cop here last night. Would a cop come if it wasn't true?"

"I guess not. What if it is?"

They turned and walked out of Ally's hearing. What was "it"? And what had brought a policeman to the clinic? She bit her lip. If it had anything to do with her carelessness, she was going to set it right. She let the others file past her while she waited for Cruz. He was the last to leave the room, deep in conversation with a lean, hawk-faced man Ally didn't know. She didn't want to interrupt, and the two men passed her without seeing her.

There was a message for her at the nurses' station, though. She was summoned to Cruz's office, STAT, which was hospital talk for *immediately*.

He and the hawk-faced man were waiting for her. They both wore the same cool, watchful expression. Cruz introduced her to Detective Sergeant Clay Williams, who was with the sheriff's task force on drug trafficking. Drug trafficking? Ally looked at the sergeant, startled. He had gray eyes, eyes the color of cold steel, eyes that saw a great deal and revealed nothing.

"H-how do you do, Sergeant?" She shook his hand, cursing herself for stammering.

"Dr. Schuyler." His handshake was firm and brief.

"Sit down, Ally." She sat. The two men watched her in silence for several seconds, and she shifted in her chair, wondering what on earth they were thinking. The silence stretched until she had to break it.

"Cruz, what is it? What's going on?"

"Some things turned up missing on the drug count last night."

"Drugs?" She was incredulous, but he nodded. "From the drug closet down here?"

"That's right."

"But that's awful!" She looked from one expressionless face to the other. "What was taken?"

"Narcotics," the sergeant replied. "Tranquilizers and sleeping pills, some painkillers, some stimulants. A real druggie's smorgasbord. The thief took plenty, too. Enough for personal use, or to sell, or pass out to his or her friends."

"Well, who—"

"Who took them, Dr. Schuyler?" He finished the question for her. "We were hoping you could tell us that."

Chapter 5

Ally just stared at the sergeant. He returned her stare without expression, neither hostile nor friendly, simply waiting.

"Cruz?"

She appealed to the cold-eyed stranger on the other side of the desk, but she got no support from him. She could see no trace of the Cruz who had laughed and joked over dinner, who had set the table and talked about his mother. She could see no hint at all of the Cruz who had kissed her and set her aflame. He waited impassively for her answer.

After a moment Ally turned and looked across at the sergeant. "I don't know who stole the drugs." Her voice was level and calm.

"You didn't take them?"

"No. I didn't."

He held her gaze for several seconds longer, then nodded. "Thank you, Dr. Schuyler. There's nothing more."

Dismissed, she rose and turned to go.

"Ally."

She stopped with her hand on the knob and looked over her shoulder at Cruz. "Yes?"

"Would you review your records for the last three days and try to document all your drug transactions?"

"Of course." Her voice was as expressionless as his.

"Can you have that ready tomorrow?"

"All right." She hesitated. "Is there anything else?"

Cruz shook his head. "You can go."

She closed the door carefully and walked a few yards down the hall before her shaking legs forced her to stop. She leaned against the cold tile wall, shaken and nauseated by the knowledge that Cruz suspected her of stealing drugs!

She crushed her fist to her mouth to stifle the anguish she felt. In a strange way, it wasn't the fact that she was under suspicion that bothered her. Drugs had disappeared, and though she hadn't stolen them, she *was* guilty of sloppy record keeping. The police had to conduct their investigation, and as far as Sergeant Williams was concerned, she was as likely a suspect as anyone. She was confident that in time they would find the real thief and she would be cleared. Meanwhile, she didn't blame them for doing their job.

What hurt was that Cruz seemed convinced of her guilt.

She took a deep, steadying breath. She might be a suspect, but she wasn't a thief, and she wouldn't act like one.

Another deep breath and she was ready to go back to the clinic, chin up and head high. But she wasn't prepared for the stares, sidelong looks and whispers that she didn't quite hear. By the time she was halfway across the lobby, she knew she wasn't imagining things. Her color rose, but she kept her smile.

Marsha Mott stood at the nurses' station, and Ally's heart sank. She didn't need a run-in with Marsha right now. On the other hand, what did she have to be afraid of? She set her jaw and marched to the desk.

"Hello, Miss Mott," she said cheerfully, and got a bad-tempered grunt in return. "Could I have my charts for today?"

"Don't see why not," Marsha replied sullenly, and turned her back on Ally. Ally sighed in exasperation. What was this woman's problem, anyway?

"Could you pull them for me, please?"

"Pull 'em yourself."

Ally bit her tongue and counted slowly to five. "I was told not to pull my own charts during clinic hours. And after the chewing-out we just got," she said with all the sweetness she could muster, "I think we'd better stick to the rule book, don't you?"

Marsha turned around slowly, and the sight of her face made Ally catch her breath. She was smiling, but with an open malice that was almost frightening. She knew what was going on. Ally didn't know how or why, but Marsha Mott knew, and she was enjoying Ally's pain.

"Okay, *Dr. Schuyler*." She turned the name into an epithet. "I'll get your charts for you." She paused, and that malevolent smile widened a fraction. "This time." She disappeared into the chart room.

"Got problems, Ally?"

Ally turned and smiled at Barbara Clark. "Nothing I can't handle."

"Marsha's kind of hard to take sometimes. I don't know what caused it, but she's a real bitter lady."

"It's all right." Ally shook her head, dismissing the subject. "I can deal with it." She turned back to the desk as Marsha emerged with several charts in her hands. "Thank you, Miss Mott. I appreciate this."

Marsha just looked at her. "Hope the cops appreciate it." She dumped the charts with a clatter and stalked away.

"What did she mean by that crack?" Barbara demanded.

"Nothing." Ally kept her face tightly controlled as she stacked the charts in a neat pile. "Nothing at all." She walked away, aware that Barbara was still watching her.

It wasn't important, she told herself as she carried the charts into the lounge to start working her way through them. True, Marsha Mott seemed to have a grudge against her for no discernible reason, but, compared to her other problems, that was no more than a minor inconvenience.

She took the summary of her drug withdrawals to Cruz late the next day. He answered her tap at the door with a short "Come in," but kept his eyes on the papers he was studying.

"Cruz?"

He looked up at the sound of her voice. "Yes, Dr. Schuyler. Do you have your report ready?"

There was no welcome in his voice. Ally didn't sit down, but stood stiffly before the desk. "It's right here." She held the paper out to him.

"Were you able to document all the drugs you used?"

"Almost all of them. I forgot to write down a couple of the cough-syrup single doses. I added a note in the chart about those."

"You didn't alter the chart, did you?" he asked sharply, and she hastened to clarify.

"Oh, no. I didn't change anything that was already on it. I added a note with today's date explaining the mistake."

He studied her for a moment with a cold, stranger's eyes, then nodded. "All right. Don't make any more mistakes like that."

"I won't," she promised fervently, and he nodded before bending over his work again. "Cruz?"

"What?"

"I didn't take those drugs."

"That's what you told Clay Williams yesterday."

"It's the truth. I've never stolen anything in my life." She was pleading with him, but she didn't care. She had to make him understand. Surely the man who'd laughed and talked with her, the man who had kissed her, would know she was incapable of this. "I want you to know that."

"I heard what you said," he said without looking up. "The rest is up to the police."

Ally clutched her stethoscope tightly in her hands. "Can you really believe that I would do something like that?" Her voice wobbled in spite of her effort to remain calm.

He tossed his pen onto the desk and sighed in irritation, looking up at her at last. "That isn't my decision to make. It's up to the police."

Ally held herself very stiff and straight. "I see," she said in a tight little voice. "You do believe I stole them." She turned on her heel and walked out, closing the door very softly behind her.

Cruz sat for a moment without moving, then slammed his fist on the desktop in helpless frustration.

Ally paused in the clinic only to sign out for the day and collect her things. She would have given a lot for someone to talk to, but her grandfather was cruising his way through the tropics, and Stacy was teaching her evening class in medical library practice at Pasadena City College.

Hurrying away from the clinic, her eyes brimming with unshed tears, she didn't see the woman standing uncertainly in the hall.

"Ally?" Thea Stevens said as she was about to walk blindly past. "Are you all right?"

Ally stopped and turned, blinking hard. "I'm sorry, Thea. I didn't see you there."

"That's okay. You look like you have a lot on your mind."

Ally gave a short, humorless laugh. "You could say that. You're a long way from the education department. What are you doing at this end of the hospital?"

"I'm trying to find Dr. Gallego," Thea sighed in exasperation. "Do you know where he is?"

"He was in his office ten minutes ago."

"Then I missed him again. I just came from his office, and he was gone."

"If it's an emergency, you can call him at home."

Thea shook her head. "It's not an emergency. It's just that I've been trying all week to track him down."

"It's been kind of a hectic week." Ally's voice broke at the thought, and Thea peered into her face.

"Something *is* wrong, isn't it?" Thea didn't wait for an answer, but took Ally's arm. "Let's go get a cup of coffee."

"It's nothing," Ally said, her eyes brimming again. "Really."

"Right. And 'nothing' makes you cry? Come on." Brooking no argument, Thea led Ally to the coffee shop. When they were seated at a table with coffee cups steaming in front of them, she studied Ally's forlorn face for a moment. "You don't have to tell me about it, Ally, but if you want to, I'll be happy to listen." She grinned, an irresistible, elfin grin. "Otherwise, you can listen to me gripe."

"Do you have a problem with Cruz?"

"Just that I can't find him."

"He's been here every day this week."

"That's what's so frustrating! I leave messages, but he doesn't return my calls. I only need an hour of his time. We're doing the final editing on a tape for the family practice program. Most of the work was done before I started here, but I need his input to finish it."

"I'm sure I'll see him tomorrow. Would you like me to give him a message for you?"

"Could you?"

"Of course."

"I'd be eternally grateful if you could just ask him to call me." Thea sipped her coffee and looked at Ally. "If you'd like to talk about it, I'm a good listener. And if I'm prying, just tell me so."

Ally smiled wearily. "It's been a tough week."

"It's kept your chief resident busy. Has something unusual been going on?"

"Yeah. Drug theft."

"What?" Thea's spoon clattered to the table, splattering coffee.

Ally nodded, her face grim. "Drugs have been stolen from the clinic."

"That's awful! Who did it?"

"The police are investigating, and they have some suspects." Ally looked down. "They seem to think I'm one of them."

"*What?*" Thea's voice was a shocked squeak, and a few people looked around at them. She dropped her voice to a whisper. "I don't believe it!"

"Thank you for the vote of confidence. You seem to be one of the few who don't."

"It doesn't make sense. You're not the type who would—" Thea stopped and shook her head. "I just don't see you as a person who would steal drugs."

"Some people think I would."

"But why?"

"Darned if I know. The reasons don't seem to matter much. And if I was the drug-stealing type, I probably wouldn't be a particularly logical individual, anyway."

"It still doesn't make sense. Don't worry." Thea laid her hand over Ally's. "They'll find the real thief." She squeezed Ally's hand, then looked at her watch. "Oops! I've got to get going. My daughter will be waiting for me, and she gets cranky when I'm late."

"Cranky? How old is she?"

"Eight. Eight going on nine, as she would be sure to tell you." Thea stood. "Don't worry about this business, Ally. It will work out."

"Thanks, Thea."

Warmed by her concern, Ally said goodbye to Thea and walked slowly back toward the clinic wing, smiling. She wouldn't have thought she'd smile today, but just being with Thea Stevens was cheering. She had to pass Cruz's office on her way to the parking lot. The door was open, and she glanced in as she hurried past, meeting Cruz's startled gaze. She looked quickly away and walked on.

"Dr. Schuyler!" She was two steps past the door when he called to her. She stopped in the hall, staring at her feet.

"Yes?"

"Would you come in here, please?"

She closed her eyes and took a deep breath, then went back. She stood in the doorway and looked at him, her face blank.

"Come in and close the door, would you?"

She did so, then waited stiffly before the desk, ready to leave as soon as she could.

Cruz frowned. "Sit down," he told her. "Please."

She shook her head. "I'd rather stand. What did you want?"

He studied her face for a moment, then shrugged. "What are you doing here? I thought you'd gone home."

Ally thought she heard a note of accusation in his voice, and she bristled. "You were wrong. And I could ask you the same thing. *I* thought *you* were gone."

"I'm not."

"Neither am I, and I don't see what right you have to pry into what I do with my time!" Her anger boiled over. "Damn you, Cruz! You can accuse me of stealing drugs, but you can't expect me to account to you for my spare time!"

She turned on her heel, but before she touched the doorknob Cruz was out of his chair and around the desk.

"You're not going anywhere!" He caught her elbow and spun her around. "Not yet. I may not have the right, but I'm going to ask anyway. What have you been doing for the last hour?"

Ally clenched her teeth, fighting the urge to struggle against his hands. It would be useless; he needed only a fraction of his strength to hold her. She stood rigid, her eyes glittering with impotent fury.

"I was working. And then I had a cup of coffee with Thea Stevens," she ground out between clenched teeth. "Can I go?"

"Who the hell is that?"

"She's the new media coordinator, and she's been trying to get in touch with you all week." Ally smiled, saccharine-sweet. "If you paid any attention to your messages, you'd know that."

Cruz glared down at her for a moment, his face as grimly angry as hers. He muttered something succinct in Spanish. "Who are you to tell me how to do my job?"

"Maybe it's time somebody told you!" she snapped, too angry to be cowed. "Since you can't seem to do it yourself!"

"I do fine, and I damn well don't need advice from you!"

Ally jerked against his grip on her arms, furious that she couldn't make him let her go. She flung her head back, goading him with her angry eyes and sharp tongue. "What *do* you need, then?"

There was a taut pause. Cruz's fingers tightened on the soft flesh of her arms before he jerked her into a hard embrace. "This." His voice was a low rasp. "This is what I need." He crushed his mouth onto hers.

Off balance, Ally fell against him. The kiss was angry, demanding, but all that mattered was that she was in Cruz's arms, that Cruz was kissing her, hot and searing, angry and passionate.

This was what she'd wanted, what she'd forced him to give her, and it rocked her to her core. Her mind wasn't her own; her body was out of her control. She locked her arms around his neck, molded her body to his, her movements instinctive, inflaming. She was filled with a heady sense of feminine power. She couldn't fight his greater strength, she couldn't force him to let her go, but she had made him kiss her. She had pushed Cruz past the edge of his control.

His lips were hot and hard, forcing hers apart to tease and taste. Ally matched his hunger and passion with her own, nipping at his lips, tracing their outline with her tongue.

His arms tightened, and he lifted her onto her toes, sliding a hand beneath the hem of her cotton sweater. He shaped her slender waist, his palm slipping over her silk chemise, warm and strong and slightly rough. Ally caressed his hair, twisting her fingers into the crisp curls to hold him close as he brushed his lips across her cheek to press kisses on her jaw, her eyelids, the slender curve of her throat.

She shuddered when his hand left her waist to slip upward over her ribs, moving with teasing slowness until his thumb brushed the soft undercurve of her breast. The thin silk slid over her flesh, the heat of his hand warmed her skin, and her breast swelled to fill his palm as he cupped and caressed her. Her nipple tightened to aching hardness, and her back arched in instinctive offering.

Cruz brushed his fingertips over the lace at the top of her breast, then dipped beneath it, seeking the softness and warmth that waited for him. He murmured something low in his throat as he took the soft weight in his hand. Ally felt a thrill of something that was half fear, half primitive excitement. He pushed the folds of her sweater up, baring her to his gaze, and was bending his head to take her breast with his mouth when the office door rattled under a fusillade of sharp knocks.

They froze. Sick dismay washed over Ally as rational thought returned. A bucket of cold water thrown over her would have been less of a shock. She stared in frozen horror at the door and was only dimly aware of Cruz shielding her with his body as he pulled her sweater into place, covering her modestly again. If she hadn't been suffocating with humiliation, she might have been touched by his consideration.

"Cruz?" a man called. "Are you in there?"

"Yeah!" Cruz's voice was low and rough with desire. "I'm with someone. Can you give me a few minutes?"

"Sure. I'll be in the lounge."

Ally stood in the circle of Cruz's arms, her head bent, listening to the retreating footsteps.

"Are you all right?" Cruz loosened his arms and looked at her downbent head.

Ally nodded silently.

"Are you sure?" He took her chin in his fingers and forced her face up. She stared at him with eyes that were wide and dark with hurt and anger. His face tightened into a mask.

"I'm fine," she whispered. "Can I go, now? *Please?*"

"Of course you can." Cruz released her and stepped back, his hands spread wide. "You're always free to go."

"Am I?" she wondered in a tight little voice. She stared into his eyes for a moment, then jerked at the hem of her sweater, pulling it more firmly into place. "Am I really?"

She picked up her purse with shaking hands and walked out, her spine very straight, her head high, praying that her trembling legs would carry her to her car.

She must be crazy. She must be losing her mind—what little was left of it after working in this madhouse. Cruz thought she was a drug thief. He had grilled her about her movements as if she were a convicted felon. And then he kissed her.

That wasn't the whole story, though. She had pushed him into kissing her. She had taunted him, goaded him into losing his temper. It wasn't a pretty thing she had done, and she wasn't proud of herself. She had pushed Cruz over the edge, then followed him into madness. She was very much afraid that if he had wanted to make love to her, there in his office, she would have gone to him like a moth to a flame.

And how was she ever going to face him again?

Facing him turned out to be the least of her problems. When they passed in the hall the next morning, she nodded, he said hello, and that was that. It was more difficult to ignore the gossip about herself.

This scandal, new and riveting, had erupted just as the initial gossip about Ally had been dying down. Though nearly everyone was a suspect in the drug theft, the general consensus held her the prime candidate. Maybe it was because she was the new girl in the clinic, maybe because she'd been in the wrong place at the wrong time, and maybe just because someone wanted to see the rich girl brought down.

Whatever the reason, gossip identified Ally as the prime suspect, and she found herself the center of another uproar. She kept her head high and her thoughts to herself, but as the days slid into a week, she felt as if she were walking through an enemy camp rather than hospital halls.

By the following Monday she was feeling the strain, and when Thea Stevens brought a box of pamphlets to the clinic late in the afternoon, Ally was too tired to dissemble.

"What on earth is wrong?" Thea asked in an urgent whisper. "You look awful!"

"Thanks!" Ally smiled wanly to take the sting from her tone. "I'm just getting a little tired of being talked about."

"Or being suspected of drug theft?" Thea supplied. "I've been hearing the things they're saying. It's so unfair! Anybody could have stolen that stuff, but they're picking on you!" She took a deep breath, her teeth clenched. "I've been telling people that it's all garbage."

"Thanks, Thea. I appreciate the vote of confidence."

"Keep telling yourself that it'll pass." Ally nodded halfheartedly, and Thea began to smile, satisfied. "Would you like to hear some minor good news?"

"You bet. Any good news is worth hearing."

"I finally saw your chief resident."

"Cruz?"

"Mm-hmm. We went over the tape today and got the problems ironed out, and I'll have the final print done this week!" Thea's pride was palpable, and Ally smiled with her.

"That's great, Thea. I'm glad you got hold of him."

"It wouldn't have happened without you."

"What did I do?"

"He said you told him I needed to see him, so he cleared a couple of hours for me. I came down mainly to thank you for giving him the message." Thea looked past Ally's shoulder at someone behind her. "Thank you again, Dr. Gallego."

"No problem," Cruz replied from a few feet away. "I'm just sorry I didn't get together with you sooner."

Ally fought the urge to turn around. She'd been aware that he'd been watching her for several days now. She wondered bitterly if he was waiting to catch her stealing.

"That's all right. Thank you again. And thank you, too, Ally," she said, smiling. "I've got to get going. Bye."

"Bye." Ally watched Thea go, then turned slowly to Cruz. "I'm glad you met with her."

"You brought it to my attention."

Ally flushed and bit her lip, remembering what "bringing it to his attention" had led to. "Yes," she said after a pause. "I've got work to do."

She brushed past him, toward the examining rooms.

Cruz's face was impassive as he watched her, but his thoughts were troubled. He'd seen the signs of strain, the shadows beneath her eyes, the tightness around her mouth. The thought that he was responsible for some of that strain nagged at him.

He knew that gossip about her had flared up again, and he'd stifled the urge to defend her. It was his responsibility to remain impartial. He could show no favoritism. He could not speak out in her defense.

Yet she was hurting. He could see it in her face, and he would have given everything he had to comfort her. But he couldn't do that. Like her, he had to wait and see.

"Did you want to see me?" Ally had gotten the message to go to Cruz's office as soon as she arrived at the hospital. He was waiting for her, grim-faced.

"Yes. Do you have any idea why?"

She shook her head, thinking. "Not really. Unless it's Mrs. Brown with the eclampsia. I checked to make sure I ordered the correct tests."

"It's not Mrs. Brown," Cruz said heavily. "It's three bottles of pills that were taken from the drug closet some time yesterday. Tranquilizers and painkillers. Sergeant Williams will be here later this morning. You'll have to give him a statement about your movements."

Ally could feel the blood drain from her face. Cruz half rose as she swayed on her feet, reaching across the desk for her, but she shrank away from his hand. He saw her flinch, and his face tightened.

"Are you all right?"

She swallowed hard. "I'm fine. Why shouldn't I be?" She steadied herself with a hand on the back of the chair, her voice light and bitter. "I'm a suspect in an ugly, sick, disgusting crime. Why shouldn't I feel just great?"

Chapter 6

Sergeant Williams recorded Ally's statement, which was given in a quiet, toneless voice. She had been holding herself together by the narrowest margin since she had hurled those furious words at Cruz and fled from his office three days earlier.

Several other Clinic staffers also had to give statements, but that was little comfort to Ally. Except for Barbara Clark, they weren't people she knew well, and as the suspicion grew, they avoided each other, as if the taint were catching.

Ally gave her statement, and then she concentrated on not falling apart before she got home. She might have managed it if she hadn't rounded the wrong corner at the wrong time.

She didn't see Marsha Mott until it was too late. It wasn't a headlong crash, but they bumped shoulders hard as they tried to sidestep each other. Miss Mott's tray of medications went flying and landed with a tremendous clatter, spilling pills and syringes and sticky syrups across the floor.

They stared at the mess for a moment; then Marsha looked at Ally, her face a mask of venomous anger.

"Clumsy bitch! Can't you watch where you're going?"

"I'm sorry about this." Ally stooped to help clean up the mess. "I didn't see you coming—"

"I know you didn't," snapped the nurse. "You're probably too high from all those drugs you've been stealing!"

That was too much. Ally dropped three syringes on the tray and straightened, her face cold. "I've never stolen anything in my life," she said, then walked away.

She hurried through the halls, deaf and blind to the people around her, ducked into an empty examining room and burst into tears. Her face in her hands, she huddled against the tiled wall, shaking with the sobs she'd been suppressing for so long. She didn't hear the door open behind her.

"Ally?" It was Cruz's voice, deep and mellow.

She hunched her shoulders and ducked her head, keeping her back to him as she dug in her jacket pocket for a tissue.

"Ally, are you all right?"

"I'm fine." She scrubbed her cheeks and sniffed hard. "What are you doing in here?"

"Barbara Clark told me you were here." He closed the door and moved over to her. "What's wrong?"

"Nothing!" She sniffed again. "And Barbara shouldn't have said anything to you."

"She saw you run in here." He took her shoulders and gently turned her around. "She thought you needed someone. Now that I see you," he said, bending to peer into her face, "I think so, too."

"Well, I don't!" Ally averted her face and sniffed again. "I don't need anybody."

Cruz drew her a little closer, close enough that she could feel the warmth of his body. She stiffened, resisting the light pressure on her shoulders.

"I think you do." He could see the strain in her face, and from the feel of her beneath his hands, she'd been losing weight she couldn't spare. "Everybody needs help sometimes. You've been tough as nails ever since you came to this hospital. It hasn't been easy for you, it's been damned hard, but you've held your head up in the face of gossip and prejudgment. You've been strong long enough, Allison. You need somebody.'' His voice dropped to a caressing murmur. ''You need me.''

Ally shook her head, defeated. ''Everything is such a mess. How can you help?''

''Like this.''

When he pulled her into his arms, she didn't resist. He kissed her tenderly, gentle and sweet and healing. There was no punishing passion, only warm, firm lips moving over her mouth, caring, soothing, coaxing her. Ally melted inside, mindless as she gave herself up to his care. She was exhausted, mentally and emotionally, with no strength of her own. He was her strength now, and she was safe with him.

She slid her arms around his waist beneath the white coat, pressing her palms to his back. Hard muscles shifted beneath smooth cotton as he moved his feet to take more of her weight against him. He lifted his lips from her mouth to brush them softly across her face, pressing small kisses to her jaw, her cheekbone, her hair, as she turned her face into his shoulder.

She could hear his heartbeat, strong and steady beneath her cheek, and she was comforted. Whether or not he suspected her, he was here now, holding her, and she murmured a soft protest when he released her.

''You've got to get out of this place,'' he told her. ''Come on.'' Before she knew what was happening, she had signed out for the day and been deposited in the passenger seat of his car, and was riding through the crowded evening streets.

''Where are we going?'' she asked after several miles.

''To have dinner.'' He glanced over at her, frowning at what he saw. ''You don't look like you've been eating.''

''I haven't been hungry.'' She let her head fall back against the seat. ''Nothing seems to taste good.''

Cruz's lips thinned, but he kept his voice light, teasing. ''I guarantee that this will be so good you'll have to eat.''

''I'm not promising anything,'' she replied with a faint hint of her normal spark. ''What kind of place are we going to?''

''The best Sonoran-style restaurant in the Los Angeles metropolitan area.''

"That's a pretty sweeping statement. There are a lot of Mexican restaurants in L.A."

"Not like this one." He threw her a grin. It was working; she was beginning to smile. "An old friend of mine, Victor Nieves, owns it, and there's no question—this is the best."

Ally considered for a moment. "How are his *chiles rellenos*?"

"Can't beat 'em."

"Flautas?"

"Unequaled."

"What if you're wrong, and the food is crummy?"

"Then you can pick the restaurant next time. Deal?" He stuck out his hand.

"Deal." They shook on it, and he held her hand for a moment before releasing it to shift gears and pull up to the *porte cochere* in front of "Victor's". Ally studied the elegant restaurant for a few moments, then turned to Cruz with a half smile on her lips.

"This is not your average taco stand."

"Only the best." A valet opened Ally's door, while Cruz got out and gave another young man the keys. Cruz took her arm to lead her into the graceful stucco building. "I told you."

"So you did." The lobby was decorated in shades of cream and rose and gray. "You didn't tell me it was beautiful, too."

"I wanted to surprise you."

He spoke softly to the maître d', who greeted him with a delighted smile and a burst of Spanish too rapid for Ally to follow. They were seated immediately, side by side on a quiet corner banquette, with white wine for Ally, Mexican beer for Cruz and menus to peruse.

Ally sipped her wine, which was light and dry and smooth, looked around the rose-and-cream-and-brass dining room and sighed comfortably. "This is delightful."

"I'm glad you like it." He turned toward her, his arm resting along the back of the brocade seat, his hand near her shoulder. His face grave, he said, "I want you to relax and enjoy your meal, which will be at least as good as I promised, and forget everything else.''

''That won't be easy.''

''You can do it.'' He squeezed her shoulder briefly. ''If you can work, with all that's been going on, I know you can put things out of your mind for an hour or so.'' He lowered his arm and picked up his menu. ''Do you like fish?''

Ally could still feel the pressure of his fingers on her shoulder, warm and comforting. It took her a moment to follow the change of subject. ''Fish? Yes, I like it. Why?''

''Because Victor's Sole Veracruz is the best.''

''All right.'' She closed her menu. ''I'll have that. What about you?''

''Steak Picado, I think. Will you trust me on the appetizer?''

''Of course.'' She smiled and leaned back into the soft comfort of the banquette. ''You know, for the first time in days, I'm actually hungry. I put myself in your hands.''

An hour later she sat back again, replete. ''I made the right decision.''

''What decision was that?''

''To put myself in your hands. That meal was exquisite.''

Cruz sat back and slid his arm behind her shoulders. ''I wanted you to enjoy yourself.'' He looked into her face. ''Do you feel better?''

She dropped her head back against his arm and smiled up at the ceiling. ''About a million percent.'' She rolled her head to the side to turn her smile on him. ''You were right when you said I could put it out of my mind for a while. It helped.''

''I'm glad.''

''There's something I don't understand, though.'' Her smile faded, and she studied the hard planes of his face. It was a difficult face to read. He was smiling, but Ally could see something else behind that smile.

''What's that?''

''Why did you do this?''

He glanced away for a moment, uneasily, Ally thought. ''I wanted you to have a good meal and relax.''

"But that's not all of it. What's the real reason for this dinner?"

He straightened, taking his arm from behind her to lean his elbows on the table, hands together. "I need to talk to you."

Ally's heart sank. She had an idea what he wanted to talk about, and it wasn't a pleasant prospect. "Yes?"

He looked at her, then down at his hands again. "This isn't easy for me to say."

"Are you going to fire me?" she whispered.

He jerked his head around to stare at her. "Fire you? What on earth would give you that idea?"

"Well, what else? You think I've been stealing drugs!" Her voice trembled on the edge of control. "So you bring the condemned woman here for a last meal—"

"That is *not* what this is about!" He kept his voice low, but his words were as forceful as a shout. He caught her shoulders, shaking her slightly. "I'm not going to fire you!"

Ally's eyes opened wide. "You're not?"

"Of course not."

"Then what?"

When he hesitated, she hurried on. "Before you start, there's something I want to say."

"There's no need..." His fingers tightened on her shoulders.

"There's every need! Just let me say it, okay?" She waited until he nodded. "Thank you. I know what you think of me." He opened his mouth, and she raised a hand. "I know you think I'm a spoiled little rich girl who got into this program on my grandfather's coattails, but, Cruz, you have to realize that I wouldn't steal drugs!"

For several agonizing seconds he stared at the tablecloth. "I know," he said heavily. Ally held her breath, not certain she'd heard him right. "This isn't easy for me to say, but I owe you an apology. I probably owe you several of them." Ally stared at him, and he nodded. "I've been watching you work."

"I know you have. You've been watching to see if I'm stealing drugs."

"I've been watching you *work*," he repeated, "ever since you started at Memorial, and I realize that you earned your admission to the program. You're a good intern, and you're going to be a good doctor. I was wrong to allow anything but your work to influence my opinion."

Their gazes locked and held, and after a moment Ally dipped her head in a nod of acceptance. "Thank you."

"I also know you're not a drug thief. I'm sorry I led you to believe otherwise. I was trying to be impartial. Because of the way I feel about you, that was difficult, and I tried a little too hard, went a little too far. I'm sorry."

Ally looked down at her hands. She had no idea what to say. This was too much to absorb all at once. As she watched, his hands came into her frame of vision and covered hers. She lifted her head slowly and looked into his eyes. They were dark and shadowed in the dim light, but she could see a message there, a message meant for her alone.

Her breath caught in her throat. She could feel a pull, like a physical force, drawing her toward him. She didn't understand that pull; it both tempted and frightened her. It was terrifying and enticing and quite, quite mad. But it was irresistible. She wanted to be close to him, to be held in his arms again, to be kissed by him again, to make love....

"Will you accept my apology?"

She blinked, and the spell was broken. "Yes," she said, her voice breathless and soft. "I accept your apology."

"Thank you. That means a lot to me." A waiter approached, and Cruz turned away to order coffee.

In that moment of respite Ally took a deep breath and tried to get a grip on herself. When he turned back to her, that secret message was gone from his eyes. He was concerned and caring, but he was no longer seducing her with a look.

"We have another problem to deal with."

"What's that?" She tried to match the matter-of-fact tone.

"We have to clear your name and rebuild your reputation."

"Oh, of course we do," she said, heavily sarcastic. "And how are we supposed to do that? A construction crew can build a house, but it can't do a thing about my being a suspect."

Cruz laughed. "I wasn't suggesting a hammer and nails."

"Then what?"

"We have to find the real thief."

Ally laughed aloud. "Right. What else? We find the real thief. No problem."

"Sarcasm doesn't become you."

"Well, insanity doesn't look too good on you," she retorted. "It's nuts. Anybody could have stolen that stuff. The police can't figure it out, and neither can the sheriff's department, so we're supposed to?" She folded her arms and scowled at him. "Sure."

"I know it sounds like a bad joke, but think about it. Yes, there are lots of people who work in the clinic, but the list has already been narrowed down to the people who were there at the times of both thefts."

"Really?" Ally leaned forward, interested in spite of herself. Then she shook her head. "No, no, no. This is silly. I'm not a detective, and neither are you. It's ridiculous."

Cruz sipped his coffee. "I don't think so." He put his cup down and took her hands, looking into her eyes as he spoke. "I'm not suggesting we play Dick Tracy, Ally. I'm suggesting we go to Sergeant Williams and see if there's any way we can help."

Ally shook her head slowly. He was persuasive in spite of her reservations. "Why should he want our help? What can we do that the police can't?"

"We're on the inside. We may see things the police don't see. What can it hurt to ask?"

Ally didn't have a ready answer to that, and in less than thirty minutes she was at the sheriff's station, waiting in a tiny office to meet Clay Williams. The office was a windowless cubicle furnished with an ancient metal desk and file cabinets, the walls covered with memos and lists thumbtacked to the crumbling plaster. Ally perched uneasily on a battered folding chair, already regretting the decision that had brought her here.

"We shouldn't be here," she whispered to Cruz, who was sitting at ease beside her.

"Why not? What do we have to lose?"

"He's going to think we're both idiots!"

Cruz took her hand, and she could feel warmth flowing into her from his touch. "It can't hurt to try, Ally. The worst he can say is no. Remember that."

"The worst he can say is 'You're under ar—'"

She bit the word off as the door squeaked open and Clay Williams walked in. He sat behind the messy desk, leaned back, folded his arms across his wide chest and regarded them impassively.

"Dr. Schuyler, Dr. Gallego." He nodded to them. "You wanted to see me?"

"Yes, we did." Cruz glanced at Ally. "Shall I explain?"

"It's your story. Feel free." Her uneasiness was clear, and Clay Williams tossed her a quick, amused glance before he turned to Cruz.

"Well, Dr. Gallego?"

"We have a suggestion to make," Cruz began, and quickly explained his idea. When he'd finished, Sergeant Williams looked down at his desk for a moment.

"I don't like to involve amateurs in an investigation," he began, and Ally threw an "I knew it" look at Cruz. "But," Clay went on, and Ally looked at him in surprise, "in this case, I may make an exception. You're right," he told Cruz, "when you point out that the police officers in the hospital have too high a profile. It's easy to identify them as outsiders and avoid them. An insider might see things those officers don't."

"Then we can work with you?" Cruz asked, and Clay nodded.

"As observers *only*. You are not police officers, and I don't want you acting like television cops. Just watch and listen and tell me if you notice anything unusual."

They agreed; then Ally looked at Clay. "Sergeant Williams?"

"Yes?"

"Why are you willing to let me do this? I'm a suspect myself, aren't I?"

He shook his head. "You're no longer a suspect."

For a moment the surge of relief blotted out everything else. Then she began to think. "Why was I a suspect in the first place? I've never understood why anyone would think I would steal drugs."

"At first, everyone in the clinic was a suspect. About half of them still are, because they haven't been able to establish alibis for the time when the thefts occurred. The fact that you and a lot of other people kept sloppy records just complicated the issue for us."

"But what reason could *I* have for stealing drugs?" Ally demanded. "Why would I do that?"

"Any number of reasons. You could have been stealing them to support a drug habit of your own." She made a protesting noise, and he went on. "It's not that unusual. You must have seen 'respectable' drug addicts in the hospital. If you were a user and you couldn't get prescriptions to maintain your habit, stealing would be the easy way. Or you might be in debt, living beyond your means and selling drugs to support your life-style. The stuff that's been taken would generate quite a bit of money on the street. Or you might have taken them to support the habit of a friend or a family member."

"But I could write a prescription for a friend."

He shook his head. "Prescriptions leave a paper trail. Pharmacies send records to the state, and a doctor who writes too many, especially for controlled drugs, eventually gets caught. It would be safer in the long run to steal them." He leaned forward to make his point. "You weren't an unlikely suspect, you know. I've seen far too many affluent, educated people who got involved in drugs and turned to criminal behavior. It's quite common, actually."

"Maybe I'm naive, even after four years of medical school, but I still find it hard to believe." She smiled suddenly. "But I'm glad you don't suspect me anymore. How did you realize I wasn't the type?"

He watched her, cynically amused. "You were investigated."

"What?" She was outraged.

"You were very thoroughly checked out. Your background, friends, financial status—which is quite solid, by the way."

"Thanks a lot!" she snapped, and he grinned.

"You're welcome. You came up squeaky clean, but you're no longer a suspect because you were in a residents' meeting during the second theft. Through our interviews, we narrowed the time down to a two-hour period. You weren't in the clinic then."

"Oh." There was ice in her voice as she asked, "Did you have to pry into my life that way?"

"We did." He made no apology. "This is serious business, Dr. Schuyler, and we can't do the job halfway. We intend to catch the thief. It might make you feel better about working with us if you consider the fact that if it weren't for the real thief, you would never have been investigated."

"So let's catch him right away?" she said, finishing the thought.

"Or her."

"Or her," she agreed grimly. "By all means, let's do it."

Clay came around to lean against the front of his desk. Perched on her squeaky chair, with the tall policeman looking down at her, Ally felt like a schoolgirl about to be chastised. Cruz sat beside her, still utterly relaxed.

Clay looked from one to the other. "Let's do it," he repeated. "I want both of you to understand something, though. I'll accept your help, but only up to a point." He leaned forward, stabbing his fingertip against his leg for emphasis. "You can watch and listen—and if you see or hear anything unusual, you tell me right away. You do *nothing else.* No amateur heroics. *None.* If you can't agree to that now, then the whole thing is off." He studied their faces. "Well?"

"No problem," Cruz agreed.

Clay turned to Ally, and she nodded. "I'll do what you say. I won't deny that I'd like to do more than watch and listen, but you're right. I don't have the training for that."

"That's right. You don't. Hey—" His voice softened, and he touched her shoulder lightly. For the first time, Ally felt that Clay Williams might be more a friend than an enemy. "I know how frustrating it is. Keep in mind that even though you can't go in there with guns blazing and arrest the bad guy, you may see or hear something that's the key to clearing this thing up."

"I'll cling to the hope," Ally told Cruz as they walked out of the station. The night was cool, the air clear now that the afternoon's smog had dissipated. "And I'll feel a lot better when this nightmare ends!"

"Remember what Clay said. Act normal. Don't do *anything* unusual." Cruz took her arm as they crossed the street to his car. She waited while he opened the door for her.

"He said the same to you."

"I know." Cruz closed her door and walked around. He slid behind the steering wheel, put the key in the ignition and paused, hands on the wheel. "But you know," he said in a voice filled with suppressed violence, "I would really love to get my hands on this guy!"

The violence in his voice would have been shocking if she hadn't been feeling the same way. "At least you know that if you found him, you *could* punch him out!" she cried. "I can't even say that!" She looked at her hands. They were capable enough, but they'd never be as strong as a man's. "No matter what I do, I can never have the satisfaction of doing that." She punched her small fist into her palm, echoing the violence of his wish, then caught herself. "I shouldn't have said that."

"Why not?" Cruz turned in his seat and took her hands. "It's true." He turned them over in his, stroking her soft palms, sensing the fragile bones beneath. "We forget, don't we?"

"Who forgets what?" She was breathless, and her heart thumped against her ribs as he stroked her sensitive skin.

"We men. We forget that women live with limits we never have to consider."

His voice held concern and a touch of anger. It was there in his face, too.

"It's the way things are," she said after a moment. "You can't change it."

"But that doesn't make it fair."

Ally suddenly felt old. Older than Cruz, older than time, with the knowledge that all women are born with. Her mouth curved into a sad little smile. "Life isn't fair, Cruz."

"I used to think it could be," he said sadly. "I always thought that things evened out, that life was fair in the end."

"Men," she said with a smile in her voice. "Men are so idealistic. Women are the pragmatists. I think we're born knowing that life won't be fair."

"Maybe so. And maybe nature planned it that way." He lifted her hands to his lips and kissed her palms, one after the other. "But it isn't fair." His fingers tightened for a moment, and she automatically returned the pressure before he released her. "I've got to get you home."

He started the engine with an angry roar and drove to her house in silence. Ally watched his face in the flickering lights of the passing city and wondered what had made him so angry.

On her doorstep, he held out his hand for her keys. "I'm coming in with you."

"Do you want some coffee or—"

"I want to check the house. I'm sure everything's fine, but just in case, a burglar would have more trouble with me than with you," he said grimly.

Ally handed over the keys and followed him inside. He walked quickly through the rooms, turning on lights and peering into closets until he was satisfied there was no one there.

"It's all right," he said when he returned to Ally, who was waiting in the living room. "Here are your keys."

She returned the key ring to her purse. "Would you like a cup of coffee?"

"Yes. Thanks," he said curtly.

When she returned from the kitchen he was still standing in the middle of the room, staring at the carpet. "Cruz?"

"Yeah?" He didn't look around.

"Would you please tell me what's wrong? Are you mad at me?"

"What?" He turned to face her. "Why should I be mad at you?"

"That's what I've been wondering all the way home."

"I'm not angry at you. If I'm angry at anyone, I'm angry at myself."

"But why?" She stepped closer, peering into his face.

"Because of what I put you through. Because I treated you like a criminal."

"You were trying to be evenhanded. You can't blame yourself for that."

"Yes, I can!" He stroked her shoulders, her upper arms, holding her a few inches away. "I was trying to be fair, but I ended up coming down hardest on you. I was kidding myself, trying to pretend—"

He broke off, and she frowned. "I don't get it. What were you trying to pretend?"

Cruz looked past her for a moment at the blackness outside the window. She couldn't see what was in his eyes, but his lips were pressed together in a thin, hard line.

"Cruz, what is it?" she asked.

He looked at her then, a muscle jumping in his jaw. "Don't you know?" he asked in a husky rumble. "Don't you know?"

His fingers tightened on her shoulders. Ally could feel the tension in him, as well as the effort it cost him to control it. And then, with a muttered oath, he abandoned the effort, pulled her into his embrace and took her mouth in a hard, hungry kiss.

Chapter 7

He overwhelmed her, driving everything from her mind but warmth and wanting and need. She melted into him, winding her arms around his neck, answering his kiss with a hungry demand of her own, wanting him so badly that there was room for no other need. His hands roved restlessly over her back, and the thin fabric of her blouse became an annoying barrier. He touched her throat, but she wanted him to touch her breasts, to caress her body, to make love to her until the night was gone.

Cruz struggled to keep from going over the edge, struggled against the passion she aroused in him, against the demands of her mouth and hands, of her body moving softly against him. She was so tempting. He could take what she offered, strip the thin summer clothing off her body and touch and taste every inch of her, make love to her until she was his alone. But not now.

It would happen—he would make it happen—but not now. Not yet. It was still too soon.

"No," he breathed into her mouth, fighting to bring his clamoring body under control. It hurt to push her away when all he wanted was to bring her as close as it was possible to be. She clung to him, murmuring little protests low in her throat, twining her arms around him like the tendrils of a vine, clinging and sweet. His brow beaded with sweat, his breathing heavy, he took her shoulders and put a slight distance between them.

"Yes," she murmured, her body swaying toward his. He held her off and unwound her arms from around his neck.

"Not now," he whispered hoarsely. "Not yet." He touched her face, tracing the lines of her brows with his fingertip. He kissed her forehead, and then he was gone.

She stood there long afterward. They would make love; that was what he'd meant. Sometime in the future he would be her lover. She shivered as her heated body cooled and rubbed her palms over her arms to warm herself. The shiver was not from chill alone, but from excitement, as well.

"This is the list of people who've been cleared?"

Ally took the typed sheet Cruz handed her and scanned the short column of names. It was 6:30 in the morning, and she squinted against the brilliant sunlight slanting through his office window. They'd met early to avoid being seen working together. They planned to give the impression that Ally was still a suspect so that the thief wouldn't realize she was working to catch him.

Cruz had telephoned her at 5:15, waking her, his tone brisk as he asked her to meet him in his office two hours before the clinic opened. Their conversation had been brief and businesslike. Neither was pretending last night's shattering embrace hadn't happened, but, by silent consent, they had agreed to postpone discussing it.

"And these are the people who can't be ruled out yet." He handed her the second list, which was three sheets long, closely typed and stapled together.

"This is progress?" Ally looked from one list to the other. "They've only ruled out about two percent of the possibilities."

"You take what you can get." He scanned a copy of the longer list. "We should split this up. Why don't you check off the people you see regularly, and will be able to keep an eye on, and I'll do the same?''

"Sergeant Williams said we shouldn't do amateur detective work.''

When Cruz looked up, his expression was bland. "Nobody said we couldn't try to make some sense out of this, did they?''

Ally studied him for a moment, then bent over her list. "No,'' she said, smiling to herself as she penciled a small check mark by a name. "No one said that.''

So they were going to take some action after all. That was just fine with her. Of course, any way to speed the process of catching the thief was fine with her. When they divided the list, Ally had about a third of it and Cruz, who had worked at the hospital for three years, had the remainder.

"It doesn't seem fair that you should have so many.''

"No problem.'' He took her list and locked it in a lower drawer of his desk. "I know most of these people by sight. The ones who aren't clinic personnel are in and out of here, but not every day. I think Clay's right, the thief is probably a clinic staffer, since nothing's been stolen from any other department.''

"I hate to think that it's someone from down here,'' Ally said, distressed. "I like those people. Most of them are friendly and they work hard, and they've helped me when I've had trouble.''

She walked to the window behind his desk. A gardener was watering the flowers and shrubs, the spray from his hose making diamonds in the air, while a ground squirrel searched for edibles beneath a salmon-colored hibiscus. She watched the squirrel dart up the trunk of a fan palm, then turned back to Cruz.

"I don't want to spy on people I like and respect, Cruz. There's something . . . dirty about it.''

"There's something dirty about one of those people stealing drugs, Ally. And there's something damned dirty about a liar and a thief letting honest, hardworking professionals take the rap. Everyone in the clinic has been stained by this thing, and it's not fair.''

He rose and stood beside her, reaching out to brush a lock of hair off her forehead. Instinctively she turned her face into his palm. It was warm and slightly rough, and she laid her cheek against it before he took it away. She missed the warmth, and she didn't see him ball his hand into a fist and jam it into his pocket.

He was right, but Ally wasn't happy about what she had to do when she walked into the clinic later to start work. A liar and a thief, Cruz had said. She was looking for a liar and a thief. At the nurses' station, she studied her appointments for the day and let herself listen to the conversations around her.

"So then he tells me that it's all right. He believes in the equality of the sexes, and I can pay for my own dinner!" Karen Willis, who seemed to have a date with a new man every evening, grinned wryly at her own anecdote.

Ally didn't know where Karen got the energy for a social life like that; personally, she was too knocked out at the end of the day to even contemplate dinner and dancing. The thief? She glanced sideways. Not Karen, who could coax a smile out of the most frightened child. It was impossible.

Karen picked up a chart and moved away, laughing with the nurse. "Some Mr. Cool! He's nothing but a polite cheapskate!"

Ally looked down again, scribbling appointments in her notebook.

"How's my favorite intern?" An arm dropped around her shoulders, and Charlie Parsons kissed her cheek with a loud smack. "You missed a great party last night, sweet lips."

Ally laughed at his nonsense. "Another sacrifice for my career. One of your parties and I'd be exhausted for a week!" She fixed him with a severe stare. "And my lips, sweet or not, are none of your concern, *Dr.* Parsons."

"Oooh!" He touched a fingertip to the top of her head and recoiled sharply. "Hot temper!" He backed away, hands up in surrender.

"Don't mess with me!" Ally cautioned, laughing.

She watched him bop down the hall to some tune playing in his head. The smile faded slowly from her lips. Were Charlie's parties as wild as they sounded?

"... and now the fuel pump!" Voices were approaching. "Do you know what a fuel pump costs?" There was a murmur of sympathy. "I really wish somebody would steal that heap. Then I could spend the insurance on something that runs. Hi, Ally."

She turned to Barbara Clark and hoped her smile didn't look as sickly as it felt. Barbara was warm and cheerful and always ready to help out where it was needed. She was a wonderful nurse, and Ally had come to think of her as a friend. Spying on her left a sour taste in Ally's mouth.

"Hi, Barbara. How are things this morning?"

"Well enough, except for the rolling disaster area," Barbara replied with a comical grimace.

"Your car?" Ally asked innocently, hating herself.

"My car, which is going to disintegrate into its component parts any day now." Barbara shook her head as she reached across the counter for a pencil. "I can't figure it out. The component parts are costing me more than the car did!"

"That's the way it always goes."

"Ain't it the truth?" Barbara grinned, made a note and dropped the pencil back on the counter. "I just hope my budget lasts as long as the car repairs do. See you!"

Ally scrawled the last appointment in her notebook and walked away rapidly, biting her lip. A need for money was one of the reasons Clay Williams had listed for stealing drugs. Barbara made no secret of the fact that she barely scraped along on her nurse's salary. But she wouldn't steal drugs to ease her financial situation. Would she?

Ally shook her head hard, her hair bouncing around her face. She couldn't answer that question. All she could do was look and listen and wait for something out of the ordinary to happen. Nothing that she'd heard was unusual. Barbara had complained about her finances, Karen had joked about her dates, and Charlie had teased her about his wild parties. Everything was normal.

The rest of the day was just as normal: busy, harried, confused. Ally kept on schedule until she was called to the nurses' station as she was charting a patient's diagnosis.

"Dr. Schuyler?" Ray Walcott, the nursing assistant at the desk, covered the mouthpiece with his hand and looked up at her.

"What is it, Ray?"

"They need you in the ER, STAT." He turned to the phone again, spoke softly, then hung up and began searching through the huge revolving file for a chart.

"Me? Why?"

"One of your patients just came in with an anaphylactic reaction. A little girl named Jennie Coates."

"Oh, Lord!" Ally remembered the little girl she'd evaluated for severe allergies the week before. "What did she eat?"

"Coates, Coates...here it is!" Ray pulled the chart and passed it to Ally. "They think it's strawberries!" he called after her as she set off on the run.

"Thanks, Ray!" Ally sprinted around the corner.

The emergency room was in the next building, and Ally ran down the dingy back hallway, less used than the cleaner, brighter main hall. She didn't expect to meet anyone there, so when she raced around a corner and found someone coming toward her, she had to jump awkwardly aside, then look up at her nemesis.

"I'm sorry," she began, only to be rudely interrupted.

"Why don't you look where you're going?" Marsha Mott snapped. "Running through here like some stupid—you could have killed somebody!"

Since she hadn't even touched Marsha and the only thing hurt was her own twisted ankle, Ally didn't see the need for such hostility. She pushed herself back to her feet, rubbing the spot where her shoulder had bumped the wall.

"I wasn't expecting anybody to be here."

"So that means you can run people down?" Marsha wasn't going to give an inch.

Ally gave up. She didn't have the time or the inclination to mollify Ms. Mott. "No, it means I have to get to the ER. Excuse me."

Only slightly hampered by her sore ankle, she shot into the emergency department, running full tilt. She narrowly missed a technician with a tray of lab samples.

"Pardon me!" she gasped breathlessly. "Can you tell me which cubicle Jennie Coates is in?"

"Sorry." He shrugged. "They'll know at the desk."

"Thanks!" She took off for the desk. "I'm Ally Schuyler," she told the unit clerk. "You called me for Jennie Coates."

"Oh, yes, Dr. Schuyler." The clerk hurried out from behind the desk. "I'll take you."

Ally jerked to a halt when she saw Jennie. This was not the happy child she'd played silly word games with last week. The little girl's face was blotchy with hives, and her throat was swelling so badly that she had to struggle for each breath. Several people were working around her. Ally stood back, out of the way, until someone had a moment to speak to her.

A nurse caught sight of her. "Dr. Schuyler?"

"Yes."

"Dr. Thomas, Dr. Schuyler's here."

"Great." A tall, heavyset man of about fifty turned to glance at her, then bent over his patient again, checking her blood pressure. "I need some information from you. You saw Jennie last week?"

"Yes. She had a regular allergy appointment. She's had patch tests, and she's been on an elimination diet."

"What foods did you get reactions to?"

"Strong ones to some of the common things—eggs, wheat, citrus, strawberries and chocolate. She's mildly reactive to spinach, and clear for the rest."

"No problem with milk?"

"No. She's okay on milk and milk products."

"Any drug allergies?"

"None that we know of."

"Then it must be the strawberries." He turned to a nurse. "Epinephrine," he said softly, and she passed him a pre-filled syringe.

"Do you know what happened?" Ally asked after he'd given the injection.

"Apparently she was playing with the neighbor kids. Their grandmother didn't know about her allergies. She gave all the kids big bowls of ice cream with strawberries. Jennie loved it."

"Oh, Lord," Ally groaned. "I'll bet she did!" She looked past him to the little girl. "How is she?"

"She's doing better."

When epinephrine was effective for an allergic reaction it worked with magical speed. Jennie was responding already.

"You're feeling a lot better, aren't you, Jennie?"

Dr. Thomas stepped back, motioning Ally forward. The little girl was blinking at all the faces around her. She focused on Ally's face, the only one she recognized. "Dr. Ally?" she whispered.

"Yes, Jennie, I'm here." She took one of the little hands that reached up for her. The girl's fingers were ice-cold, and Ally clasped them warmly. "Are you feeling better now?"

"Yeah." She looked at Ally a moment longer, then closed her eyes. "I'm tired."

"You've had a pretty tough day, sweetheart. It's all right to be tired."

"That's right," agreed Dr. Thomas. "And now we're going to take you up to a room where you can rest for a while. Your mom can read you a story, okay?"

"Okay," she whispered, and he picked her up in his arms to carry her to her room.

"Dr. Schuyler?" He paused beside Ally.

"Yes?"

"Come by my office later, would you? I want to update our records on her."

Ally agreed, waved goodbye to Jennie, then headed for the clinic with a smile on her face. She walked sedately back through the main hall, past Cruz's office. She was three steps beyond the door when it opened.

"Ally?"

"Yes?" She looked back and saw Cruz standing in the doorway, his face grim.

"Could you come in here, please?"

She walked into the office, and Cruz closed the door behind her. "What's the matter, Cruz?"

"There's been another theft."

She dropped into the side chair. "Oh, no. When?"

"It was discovered at two this afternoon. Sometime before then."

"What was taken?"

"Seconal. Five hundred tablets."

They looked at each other, aware of the implications. Five hundred Seconal could generate a lot of money on the street.

"Have you called Sergeant Williams?"

"Yeah. He'll be here by six. Can you stick around this evening? He'll talk to the others first, and then we'll see if the three of us can put anything together."

Staying late was no problem. What she found difficult was spending the rest of the afternoon spying on the people she worked with. She talked and laughed, all the while knowing that one of them was deceiving her, deceiving all of them, in a particularly nasty way.

It was after seven when she finally joined Cruz and Clay in the office. Clay was leaning on one of Cruz's war-surplus file cabinets, which listed alarmingly under his weight. Cruz was sitting behind his desk, frowning.

"I can't make any sense out of it," she told them tiredly.

"That's why we're here." Cruz reached for her hand. Ally started when he touched her, but he closed his hand around hers, the palm slightly rough and oddly gentle. She let her hand relax, feeling warm and comforted, no longer alone. "To try to make some sense out of it."

"That's part of the problem. When we do make sense out of it and learn the truth, it may be something I really don't want to know."

"That's what's so ugly about this situation," Clay said. "The betrayal. Someone on the staff is betraying all of you, using your trust, damaging your reputations and your credibility in order to steal drugs from the hospital." He watched Ally's face while that sank in, then shifted his position against the file cabinet, which groaned in protest. "Who did you talk to today?"

"Practically everybody in the department, at one time or another," she replied dryly. "Do you want me to tell you everything that happened?"

"I'll read through the list of names," Cruz offered. He squeezed her hand, then released it so he could pick up his copy of the staff list. Ally could feel his warmth lingering on her skin, and she curled her fingers over the spot he'd touched. "Tell us who you remember dealing with and what went on."

"Okay."

Her reply to most of the names he read was a shake of her head or a brief comment that a particular person had said hello, or helped her with a patient, or nodded in passing.

"Barbara Clark," Cruz read.

"I talked to Barbara this morning." Ally looked down, studying her hands as if she'd never seen them before. "She was talking about her car. It needs work, and she says there's never enough money. She needs a new fuel pump."

Clay nodded. "Anything else?"

Ally shook her head. "She was friendly, like always."

The next name Cruz read that got more than a nod was Marsha Mott's. "I almost ran her over," Ally said, "in the back hall."

"Which hall is that?" Clay asked.

"There's another hall between the clinic and the ER," she explained. "Hardly anybody ever uses it, but when I got a STAT page to the ER, I went through there. It's faster."

"Why doesn't anybody use it?" Clay asked.

"It's dark and creepy, and somebody was mugged there."

"But you took it today because it's the fastest route to the emergency room?"

"That's right."

"So what was Ms. Mott doing down there?"

"Beats me." Ally looked at Cruz, who shrugged.

"Except for the fact that it's quicker, I don't know why she'd use that hall rather than the main one."

"So you were surprised to see her there," Clay said.

"I was surprised to see *anyone* there. I was running, and I nearly knocked her down."

"Was she surprised to see you?"

"Probably. She was angry. Maybe because I scared her."

"Maybe," Clay repeated.

"Or maybe," Ally added, "because she can't stand me."

"What do you mean?" Cruz asked.

"She doesn't like me." Ally shrugged. "A lot of people were hostile to me when I started here, but most of them have relaxed. She hasn't."

"Has she done anything to you?" he demanded. "I'll see that—"

"She hasn't done anything overt." Ally broke in before his righteous anger could get out of hand. "She's just rude and unpleasant."

"I'll speak to her."

"Please don't." Ally shook her head. "That would just make things worse. I can handle it."

Cruz held her gaze for a long minute, but when he was satisfied that she meant it, he nodded and returned to his list.

She told them about Charlie Parsons and his parties, about Karen Willis and her many dates and about Ray Walcott.

"He's a quiet guy, kind of nerdy, but he's always very courteous and helpful. He pulls charts for me, goes for supplies without being asked, that kind of thing."

"Is he friendly?" Clay wanted to know. "Or familiar?"

"Neither. He's extra-polite, kind of like those old movies where people call each other 'Dr. Jones' and 'Nurse Smith.' But he's very nice," she added quickly.

Clay smiled at her. "I know you don't want to carry tales about your co-workers, Ally. You've found something nice to say about everyone except the one nurse who's rude."

"Marsha Mott," Ally supplied. "She is a good nurse, you know. And she's civil to everyone else."

"You're the only one she's rude to?"

She grinned wryly. "Maybe she just doesn't like my face."

Clay grinned back. "It's a lovely face. I can't imagine anyone disliking it."

She blushed and laughed. Watching, Cruz felt a surge of primitive jealousy, shocking in its intensity. He wanted to punch Clay Williams's face, hard, just for noticing she was beautiful, for smiling at her and sharing a joke.

Was he going crazy? He hid his feelings, but that didn't make them go away. He knew damned well what was wrong with him, but knowledge didn't make it any easier to tolerate. She was a fever in his blood, a tempting specter haunting his dreams. He wanted her for his own, his woman, but that was impossible. Her laughter, light and silvery, slid over his skin, and he very deliberately unclenched his fist.

"I don't want anyone treating other members of the staff with discourtesy," he said abruptly.

Ally turned to him, her face still bright with laughter. "Don't worry about Marsha, Cruz. I can handle her." The smile slid away, leaving her eyes shadowed with sadness. "She may not like me, but at least she's honest about her feelings."

Cruz understood. It was the thief, the one who was lying to them, that they had to worry about. "Is there anything else?" he asked Clay.

"Not right now. Of the people Ally spoke to, one throws wild parties, one has a social life that should be running her ragged, and one is chronically short of money. There's also a medical student on the clinic rotation who has been in treatment for drug use. He's supposed to be clean now, but the relapse rate for drug users is too high to ignore. We'll keep a close eye on him."

He smiled, and it was the cynical smile of a man who has seen too much of life's seamy underbelly. "They could all be pure as the driven snow, but at first glance we seem to have too many motives and not enough criminals."

His words echoed in Ally's ears as she made her way home, tired and depressed. Far from clearing any of her colleagues, she had cast suspicion on everyone she'd talked to.

It didn't help her mood to walk out of Cruz's office and find Marsha Mott standing in the hall. The other woman's shift had been over since 4:30 but Ally didn't bother asking why she was there. She nodded as she passed, and Ms. Mott smirked knowingly and watched her walk away.

It was past dinnertime when she walked into her house. She should have been hungry, but she wasn't. She flopped into an armchair and opened a magazine, turned a few pages, then tossed it aside. A quick scan of the channels revealed nothing on television except several versions of the evening news, filled with crime and politics, reruns of tired sitcoms and old movies, and a soap opera on the Korean channel. She watched that for a few minutes, but even with subtitles it didn't make much sense. She punched the power button again, silencing the set.

It wasn't supposed to be like this!

She swung to her feet in sudden anger. She'd come to Memorial to work and learn and become a good doctor. She hadn't bargained on crime and suspicion. She didn't want to face Barbara tomorrow, or Charlie, or Karen, or even Marsha Mott, knowing that the things she'd said about them were going to end up in a police file somewhere.

"I wish this whole rotten thing had never happened!" she whispered to the silent room. "I just wish—"

The doorbell pealed, startling her into silence. She stared at the door for a moment, trying to remember if she was expecting someone. No, she hadn't invited anyone over, hadn't called any repairmen. If it was a salesman or a pollster, she'd send him packing in a big hurry. The bell pealed again.

She opened the door on its safety chain and stared through the four-inch gap in astonishment at the man standing there.

Chapter 8

Cruz looked down at her and wondered what he was doing there.

He'd come on impulse and was irritated with himself for giving in to it. It had been a subtle form of torture to sit at his desk that afternoon, listening to her low, musical voice, breathing the fragrance of her scent over the mixture of dust and antiseptic that usually perfumed his office. He was a fool to come to her home and subject himself to more.

He'd wanted to punch Clay Williams for laughing with her—and Cruz prided himself on not being that kind of man. This woman brought out the idiot in him, just as she brought out a *machismo* that he hadn't thought he'd inherited from his father.

He'd never acted *macho* like his younger brother Carlos, strutting like a rooster before the hens, posturing and fighting with the other roosters. But now, with this woman, he was feeling things that shook his very concept of himself.

In his small apartment he'd changed into jeans and a sweatshirt, then opened the refrigerator and stared at its meager contents for several minutes, pretending he was going to fix a meal. He'd been kidding himself. He had to see her.

He'd called himself every kind of fool on the drive to Ally's house, but the moment she opened the door, he knew he'd never had a choice. She was impossibly beautiful, even with her hair mussed and her face pale from fatigue. Her perfume reached out to him, warm and soft. Cruz cleared his throat.

"May I come in?" he asked when it appeared that she was simply going to stand there staring at him.

"Oh, yes! Yes, of course!" Cruz waited while she pushed the door closed to unhook the chain, then swung it wide to admit him. "I'm sorry I was rude," she said as she followed him into the living room, "but I wasn't expecting you."

Cruz stopped uncertainly in the center of the room. "I didn't expect to come," he muttered.

Ally tried to convince herself that she didn't notice how the faded red sweatshirt stretched across his wide shoulders as he shrugged. His head was bent, and his hair waved down onto his neck, where a few small curls strayed from the rest. She longed to reach out and touch those curls, to thread her fingers through his hair and stroke the tanned skin of his neck. She moved a few jerky steps away, out of reach of temptation.

"Why did you come?" she asked. There was a moment of silence in answer. "I'll—I'll make coffee," she said to fill that silence. She moved toward the kitchen, but he caught her elbow and stopped her.

"I don't need any coffee, thank you."

"But why...?"

"Why did I come?" He grimaced. "You were upset when you left the hospital. I wanted to make sure you were all right."

"How should I feel after what happened today?" She pulled herself out of his grasp and folded her arms tightly across her chest. "I cast aspersions on the character of the people I work with. It leaves a bad taste in my mouth. I don't like suspecting people, Cruz. I don't like having to. I just want to do my job, but it's all gotten so complicated!''

"I know.'' Cruz pulled her into his arms, holding her lightly. "Life is complicated, Allison. It's never simple.''

"I know,'' she said in a shaky voice. "But I came to Memorial to work and learn. I didn't ask for all this.'' She tipped her head back to look up at him, her eyes bright with tears that she blinked angrily away. "I meant it when I said that Marsha Mott is refreshing to be around. *She* doesn't talk behind my back. She's nasty to my face!'' She laughed softly. "Did you know she was outside your office when I left today?''

"She was?'' he asked sharply. "Why?''

"I don't know. She didn't say anything, just smirked when I walked out. I guess she thought you'd been interrogating me about that bottle of pills.'' Ally shook her head. "I don't know why, but she really doesn't like me.''

Cruz smiled. "Maybe she's jealous.''

"Of what?'' she asked blankly, and his smile widened.

"You're young, beautiful, intelligent. What could she possibly be jealous of?''

Ally leaned back against his arms and laughed up at him. "If you keep up that line, I'll get a swelled head.''

"It's not a line,'' he said quietly, the laughter gone. "It's the truth.''

In the silence that followed Ally was acutely aware of Cruz's strong arms around her, of his body so close to hers. Their gazes locked, and her eyes widened as she swayed helplessly closer.

Cruz lowered his head for an instant, then dropped his arms and stepped back. "Have you eaten dinner?'' His voice was husky.

She shook her head, coming back to reality. "What did you say?''

"Have you had dinner?''

"No. I'm not hungry.''

"You've got to eat.'' He gave her a gentle shove toward the stairs. "Go put some jeans on. We'll go get hamburgers.''

"But . . ." She hesitated, and he nudged her again.

"Go on. Jeans and a sweater."

She wasn't sure why she was falling in with his plans so readily, but she changed quickly into jeans and an oversize purple sweater. He approved and insisted she bring along a jacket. A few minutes later she settled comfortably in the passenger seat of his elderly car. It didn't matter where he was taking her; she was content for the first time all day.

The radio played softly as he drove through the coastal mountains to the Pacific Coast Highway. In Malibu he stopped at a hamburger stand, a relic from the fifties with a giant fry cook on the roof holding a giant hamburger. With their dinner carefully balanced on Ally's lap, he drove a little farther up the coast to an access road and the beach.

There were houses a hundred yards away and huge boulders strewn along the sand, but this stretch of beach was deserted. The sun was sliding below the horizon, but the sand held the day's warmth, and the sky was a rosy pink shot with gold and purple. In the distance to the southeast they could see the dim outline of the Palos Verdes peninsula. Gulls wheeled and screeched overhead, and a pair of pelicans skimmed low over the water, searching for unwary fish.

There was a blanket in the trunk, which they spread at the base of a cluster of ten-foot-high boulders. The aroma of beef and onions wafting up from the hamburger bags had awakened Ally's dormant appetite, and she plopped cross-legged onto the blanket and began setting out the meal.

"Yours has mustard and what else?" she asked as she rummaged in the bag.

"Salsa and peppers," Cruz replied. "And yours is lettuce, tomato and mayonnaise." He peeked inside a paper wrapper and passed her the burger. "This one's yours."

"And this is yours." Ally traded with him, peeled open the wrapping and took a big, messy bite. "Mmm, great!" She wiped a dab of mayonnaise off her chin. "How did you find that place?"

"Charlie Parsons told me about it." He grinned, his teeth a flash of white in the gathering dusk. "He knows every hamburger stand from San Diego to Santa Barbara."

Ally lifted her burger, then lowered it without taking a bite. Her face fell. "I like him, you know."

"Charlie?"

"Yeah. He's a good doctor, too. I hate what I did today."

"You did what you had to do. And if something you remembered helps to catch the thief you'll have done us all a favor." Cruz lifted her face with a finger beneath her chin. "Remember that you're working to solve this mess. You're not making it worse, you're helping to end it."

She gazed into his eyes, and after a moment she nodded. "I'll remember."

"Good." He leaned over to place a swift kiss on her lips, then straightened before she could respond. "Now eat your dinner. You won't get a meal like this very often, you know."

"Yes, sir." Ally saluted snappily, smiled and dispatched the rest of her burger. When she'd finished, she lay back on the blanket, feeling the sand crunch and shift beneath her.

"Whew!" She patted her flat stomach. "I can't believe I ate all that."

"Neither can I." Cruz eyed her pile of empty wrappers. He wrapped the scraps of his meal and put them in the sack with the rest of the trash. "I thought you weren't hungry."

"So did I. It was smelling them that did it." Something sharp dug into her hip, and she pushed at the sand beneath the blanket. "There's a shell or something under here."

"Come over here." Cruz pulled Ally closer, into the curve of his arm. He rolled his jacket into a pillow, pushed it beneath their heads and lay back with her. "Comfortable?"

"Mmm." The monosyllable covered a myriad of feelings, with "comfortable" well down the list. She was snug, safe. The sand beneath her was warm, the boulders sheltered them from the wind, and seabirds wheeled and called overhead in their last flight of the day. The rosy glow was fading from the western sky, and a few stars began to prick the deep blue overhead.

Cruz shifted, settling himself, and tucked her more closely against his side. She breathed the scent of him, a faint woodsy after-shave, hospital antiseptic and male skin, mingling with the salt air and wood smoke from someone's fireplace. There was something seductively dangerous about feeling so safe in Cruz's arms; it led to other feelings.

His chest rose and fell with his breathing, lifting her face in a gentle rhythm. His sweatshirt, soft beneath her cheek, smelled faintly of bleach. It had ridden up, exposing a strip of tanned skin above his waistband. Ally tried not to notice that, or the narrow line of dark hair that disappeared into his jeans, just as she tried not to notice how the worn denim strained over the muscles of his thighs, or the way the sweatshirt sculpted his chest, or...

She shifted uneasily, turning her head to stare up at the darkening sky, and drew a deep, shaky breath.

"I know how you feel about spying on your co-workers." He'd misinterpreted her sigh, but Ally was willing to let him think it was because of the events of the day. "In a hospital," he went on quietly, "you have to feel that the people working with you are competent and reliable. What's happening in the clinic is a strain on all of us. It's an ugly situation, and I'll be glad when it's over."

"Oh, so will I!" She sighed heavily. "It's all so sad."

"It won't last forever." He rolled onto his side, bracing himself with his free arm so he could look down into her face. "It'll end." His breath feathered over her cheek, and she turned toward him.

He was so close that she could see the shadows of his lashes on his cheek. Her gaze dropped to his mouth, and her heart jerked, then settled into a heavy pounding beat. Helpless with wanting, she watched his lips. The arm beneath her head tightened, muscles flexing, bringing her closer as he moved his body half over hers. He stroked a fingertip along the side of her face, savoring the feel of her skin.

Something began to melt inside her, warm and flowing, spreading through her from the point of his touch. He traced his fingertip across her mouth, tugging lightly at her lower lip. Her chin tipped up, inviting more, and pleasure flowed along her veins, loosening her muscles, leaving her heavy-limbed and lax.

His lips brushed across hers, only a touch, but the gentle river of pleasure was suddenly a hot torrent, inviting surrender, demanding passion. She hadn't expected this. She hadn't known she'd react this way to a kiss that was still tentative, still exploratory. Her neck arched, offering, asking, and Cruz replied slowly. He brushed his lips over hers again, feeling them part beneath his mouth, but he forced himself to be patient.

He kept his passion under tight control. He had to be gentle with her. He had to make it perfect for her. Her skin was satin where he touched her, her mouth soft and sweet, heating his blood. His body was tense with the strain of control; his hands trembled slightly with the effort gentleness cost him. He wanted to go slowly, but her lips parted, and then he had no will to resist.

He slid his mouth onto hers, savoring the heat, the sweetness, the taste of her chocolate milk shake. He traced his tongue along her soft inner lip, prolonging the torture until she moaned something soft and incoherent into his mouth and pushed him over the edge. He took her mouth then, hard and demanding, and met an answering passion that surprised and inflamed him.

Ally had expected pleasure, and she could have dealt with that, but she hadn't known that a kiss could explode inside her this way. It deprived her of thought and reason, and she could do nothing but cling to him and let the storm rage around her.

He drove her with him on the tide of need, rolling his body over hers as the kiss deepened, surrounding her with sensations. His body was big and hard and curiously gentle, fitting against her softer contours as if made for that purpose. She shifted beneath him, her unconsciously seductive movements fanning the flame as she sought to get as close as she possibly could.

His leg slid over hers, his knee nudging between hers as he moved his body more fully above her. His hands touched only her face and throat, but the pressure of his body was a caress from breast to knee.

She wound her arms around his waist, finding bare skin when she pressed her palms to his back. She stroked the line of warm flesh between his sweatshirt and his jeans, delicately exploring him. Her fingertips slipped inside his waistband, and he shuddered at her touch.

Ally spun dizzily into a world she'd never dreamed existed. She had read romantic novels, had watched love scenes in the movies. She thought she knew what to expect, but this was outside her experience, a need as fundamental as the need for air, and it was terrifying. It frightened her because she couldn't fight it, because when she was drunk on these new feelings and sensations she didn't want to fight it.

He slid one hand down her side, over her ribs and past her waist to the gentle curve of her hip and the hem of her sweater. He slipped his hand back up, under her sweater, and caressed her stomach. Her muscles tightened in anticipation as he stroked slowly upward over her ribs to reach the soft undercurve of her breast.

He lingered there for a moment, his fingertips resting just below her breast, where her heart beat hard beneath the skin. The heartbeat under his fingers came faster; her breathing was fast, too, and shallow, and as her back arched he accepted the invitation. Her bra was a ribbon of nylon and lace, no barrier at all to his caress. He covered her breast with his palm and felt it swell beneath his hand, her nipple tightening in pleasure as he stroked across it.

Each touch sent new and greater waves of pleasure through Ally, building into a rhythm. He kissed and nibbled his way from her lips to her throat and then to her collarbone. She arched her body against his, her head falling back to give him free access, only to have him frustrated by the barrier of her sweater.

He stretched the sweater down to kiss her collarbone, then eased himself away long enough to strip it off and toss it aside. He gazed down at her skin, silvered by the rising moonlight. Though her bra was a transparent wisp, she made no move to cover herself. She watched his face in feminine triumph as he drank in the sight of her, his eyes hooded and dark with desire. She was so beautiful it hurt to look at her.

Cruz stroked his fingertips over the sheer fabric, watching the dusky shadow that was her nipple tighten at his touch. He slowly traced the edge of the lace to a single clip between her breasts. It snapped open, and he pushed the fragile fabric off her small, high breasts. He covered her with his hands, holding the slight, warm weight, savoring the teasing, inflaming them both until she moaned a wordless plea and tangled her fingers in his hair, guiding him.

No man had ever seen her body. No man had ever touched or kissed her like this, yet she felt no shyness of Cruz, no fear, only a kind of fierce pride that she could put that look in his eyes. He gazed at her, then bent his head to her breast, and the world spun away in a blur of warmth and light and feeling. He took the small, tight bud of her nipple between his lips, teasing with tongue and teeth, and she clung to him, shuddering. His hands and lips wove their spell, and with a little sigh she gave herself up to the magic.

He loved her breasts with his mouth, stroked her arms, shoulders and breasts with his hands, then caressed the velvety skin of her stomach and found the little depression of her navel, just beneath the snap that closed her jeans. She sucked her stomach in, and there was room for his fingers to open the snap. It popped, and he slid the zipper down halfway and covered her soft belly with his hand. She held her breath, waiting for his hand to move again.

Cruz simply savored her. He had known it would be like this, that she would take him past passion to madness. That was why he'd struggled against this dangerous attraction, and why he had known all along there could be no escape. She was satin-skinned and soft in his arms, pliant and sweet and surprisingly strong, exciting beyond imagining. When he kissed her, he had to touch her, and when he touched her, he knew he had to make love to her.

"Hey, guys! There's a fire ring over here!"

The voice that penetrated the haze of passion in his brain was loud and inebriated, though still some distance away. It was answered by other voices, equally beery, equally loud.

With a killing effort he pulled his lips away from the sweet temptation of Ally's breast. He used his body to cover her while he buried his face in her hair, which was spread across the blanket, fighting a bitter struggle to regain control. Ally didn't make things any easier, murmuring wordless protests, clinging to him with hands that promised ecstasy.

The voices were rapidly approaching, talking loudly about camp fires and "radical partying."

Cruz muttered a strangled curse and levered himself a few inches away from Ally. With hands that shook he carefully zipped her jeans, then pulled her bra back into place and fastened it. He bent and pressed a quick kiss into the scented valley between her breasts, then sat up, his breathing ragged.

"Cruz?" Ally propped herself on her elbow, shivering a little in the night air.

The beach partyers were quite near. Cruz pulled her into the shadow of the biggest boulder, positioning himself to shield her from prying eyes. He grabbed her sweater and pulled it over her head.

"Are you all right?" He brushed her tumbled hair out of her face and studied her.

"Yes." She took a breath to strengthen her thready voice. "I'm okay."

"Good." He kissed her hard, sending a jolt of heat down her spine. He stood and pulled her to her feet. "It's about to get too crowded around here."

As he spoke, a dozen or so college students walked into view. All they saw was a man and a woman, neatly dressed, shaking the sand from a blanket and folding it up.

"Hey, man!" one of the students called cheerfully. "Don't leave on account of us!"

"No problem!" Cruz called back. "It's time for us to go."

And that, Ally thought as she followed him across the deep sand on legs that felt like jelly, was the understatement of the year. Another five minutes and they'd have been making love on a public beach.

The final few yards up to the road were a steep scramble. Ally slipped and slid on the loose gravel.

"Here." Cruz reached back to take her hand and haul her briskly up the slope.

As soon as her feet were safely on the pavement she pulled her hand away, because that brief, businesslike touch had made her pulse race. The night air was cooling more than her skin, and with a cooler head came second thoughts.

He parked in front of her house and followed her inside without comment. She switched on a couple of lamps and stopped in the center of the room, her face pale and expressionless.

"Would you like coffee?" she offered in a husky voice she scarcely recognized as her own.

"Yes," Cruz replied with grave politeness. "Thank you."

He waited in the living room while she brewed it and poured two cups. When he took his cup from her, their hands brushed, and Ally's jerked, slopping coffee into the saucer. She couldn't look at his hands without thinking of how they'd touched her, how they'd made her feel. She burned her mouth on a sip of scalding coffee and set her cup aside, looking at the floor, at the wall, at anything but Cruz.

"Ally." His voice was quiet.

"Yes?"

"Would you look at me, please?"

Reluctantly, she lifted her head. She didn't know what she'd expected to see in his face, male triumph perhaps, or the passionate hunger that had been in his eyes when he'd looked at her body. Instead, his face was inscrutable, his eyes dark and shadowed.

"You've had second thoughts."

It wasn't a question, and she nodded silently in reply. He set his untasted coffee aside and rose. Ally walked with him to the door, where he stopped and turned back to her, cupping his hand around the nape of her neck.

"I could change your mind," he murmured, frustrated desire roughening his voice. "But that wouldn't be fair."

Ally looked up without flinching, her eyes apprehensive. She knew all too well how easily he could prove the truth of his words.

He shook his head. "It's too soon."

His fingers tightened on her nape, pulling her close for a kiss that was hard and hot, almost angry. It went through Ally like a bolt of lightning, melting her bones and igniting her skin. When he lifted his head he examined her face, and this time she could see the male triumph there.

"It *will* happen," he whispered. *"Pronto. Cuanto antes mejor."*

And then he was gone, leaving Ally leaning limply against the doorframe and staring after him. It wasn't until his taillights had disappeared around the corner at the bottom of the hill that she went back inside.

She automatically fastened locks, turned out lights and checked windows before she went upstairs, but her mind was far away. She didn't know much Spanish, but she knew what he'd said. She shivered. His words might have been a promise, but they had sounded more like a threat. "Soon. As soon as possible."

She was almost glad to be on call Saturday, because it kept her thoughts off Cruz. Sunday was her day off. She woke early from force of habit, though she would have preferred to sleep in. Too wide awake to snuggle down for a few more minutes of slumber, she scowled at the sunlight swimming on the ceiling, then threw the covers back with a sigh of resignation. Showered and dressed in shorts and a light shirt, she carried the newspaper and her breakfast out to the patio.

Her "yard" was little more than a large patio with a three-foot-wide strip of earth around its perimeter. Ally had planted the strip with herbs and roses, and large terra-cotta pots of marguerites stood around the patio. Her fence was tall on the sides of the yard for privacy and low across the back, where the hillside fell away. The hill had been landscaped with trees and shrubs, but through a gap in the plantings Ally could see the San Fernando Valley spread out below her.

Distance muffled the city noises, but finches twittered in the trees, and the raucous yawp of a scrub jay punctuated the quiet. Ally set her coffee and toast on the patio table and settled herself comfortably with her feet propped on a chair, the unopened newspaper in her lap. The morning air was cool, but the sun was warm, and she could feel the tension draining out of her.

She broke off a bit of toast and tossed it onto the pavement a few feet away, then waited, motionless. Within a minute two finches were making a cautious approach, eyeing Ally warily as they hopped and fluttered nearer. When they'd decided she was harmless, there was a brief tussle over possession of the bread, a few loud chirps and then a flurry of wings as they flew back into the trees.

Ally chuckled into her coffee. The finches were cautious, but a jay would have flapped down to the toast, squawked at her to keep her distance and eaten at his leisure. She closed her eyes and tipped her face up to the sun. In a way, she was like those small birds, edging warily, timidly, toward what she wanted. She wanted to be held in Cruz's arms, wanted his kisses and caresses, and yes, if she was honest with herself, she wanted his lovemaking. But she was afraid.

It was more than a virgin's natural fear, though that was undeniably a part of it. She was frightened by the emotions and sensations Cruz aroused in her, by the ease with which he could make her lose control. She'd always thought, naively perhaps, that she would only feel these things for the man she fell in love with. Did that mean she was in love with Cruz Gallego?

Ally shook her head at the idea. It didn't make sense for her to fall in love with Cruz Gallego. She could list at least a dozen reasons why it was impossible for her to be in love with him. She'd only known him for a few weeks. Besides, he was her boss, and one did not fall in love with one's boss. And . . .

She tried to come up with more reasons and failed. She frowned at the trees. Oh, come now, she chided herself, there must be more. She thought about it, but instead of negatives, her treacherous brain kept coming up with positives.

Cruz was brilliant, of course. He was a good doctor, a wonderful doctor. He was an excellent teacher and a good administrator, and he took his duties as chief resident seriously.

He was kind to little children, and probably to small animals, too. He worked well under stress and seemed to know intuitively what to say in a tense situation.

And he was gorgeous. Just the right height, with a body that was nothing short of beautiful, wide shoulders, narrow hips, muscles in all the right places.

And his face. There ought to be a law against that face. It wasn't exactly handsome, she decided after some serious consideration, but it was fabulously attractive all the same. Utterly male, with hard angles and good bones and eyes a woman could drown in, deep and dark and fathomless, and those lips—

She remembered what those lips could do.

Ally jerked upright in her chair. She was being an idiot, sitting here doing an inventory of Cruz's good points as if he were a horse she was going to buy. She was behaving like a fool, and it was going to stop!

She needed to occupy herself with something constructive. She needed to *do* something. She looked around her. Something like pulling up the weeds that were trying to invade her herb garden. She swung to her feet and went to get her gardening tools.

Chapter 9

Cruz rang the doorbell a third time, leaning on the button for several seconds, listening to the distant chime. Again there was no answer. He'd seen her car in the garage, so where could she be at 10:30 on a Sunday morning? He gave up on the bell. If she was home, she wasn't answering it. Or maybe she couldn't, said a worrisome little voice in his head. She might be sick or hurt and unable to come to the door.

With the seed of worry planted, Cruz had to know she was all right. He rattled the door, but it was securely locked. A gate in the fence led to the side yard, where people usually kept their garden tools and garbage cans. He picked his way past those predictable items and paused at the corner of the house.

She wasn't hurt. She hadn't heard the doorbell because she was outside, gardening. A strip around the edge of her patio brimmed with roses and green plants. Ally knelt at the edge, singing to herself as she pulled weeds. Cruz leaned a shoulder against the corner of the house, smiling at the sight of her. For the moment he was content just to watch and enjoy.

She was sweaty and grubby and beautiful, and she was clearly enjoying the simple chore. She was singing an old rock and roll song under her breath and tossing the up-rooted weeds over her shoulder with a flourish. Her hips, in brief pink shorts, kept time to the beat. The thin fabric strained over her bottom as she tugged at a recalcitrant weed.

"You've lost that lovin'..." She interrupted her song to yank at the weed with both hands. "Come on, you!" It came up, scattering dirt over her arms, and she tossed it away. It landed in the vicinity of the pile of debris she was accumulating, and she reached for the next one. "...lovin' feeling..."

"Now it's gone, gone, gone..." Cruz walked onto the patio, singing along in a rich baritone.

Ally had been concentrating on her weeds, so she was startled half out of her wits. She whirled around, scraping her knee on the patio and dropping her trowel with a clang. When she saw Cruz, she plumped down on her seat, one hand at her throat where the pulse hammered.

"You scared me to death!" she gasped. "Do you always sneak up on people that way?"

"I didn't sneak." Cruz swung a wire chair around to face her and sat down. "You didn't answer the doorbell, so I came around here."

"You rang the bell? I didn't hear a thing."

"I know." He grinned. "I wondered if there was something wrong, so I came to check. I'm glad to see you're fine."

"What would be wrong?" She pulled off her gardening gloves and wiped her forehead, then frowned. "Unless something's wrong at the hospital. Is that why you came?"

"No, nothing's wrong." He looked her up and down, grinning, and Ally felt the heat rise in her cheeks.

She fought the urge to turn away when his gaze lingered on her breasts and then her legs, long and smooth and lightly tanned. She didn't know whether to be flattered or embarrassed, but she was acutely aware that her T-shirt was stuck to her back, her face was sweaty, and there was dirt on her knees and hands.

"Are you finished gardening for this morning?"

She looked at the neat bed of roses and the substantial pile of weeds. "I haven't done the herbs yet, but they're not as bad as the roses were. They can wait."

"Good." He smiled, and Ally wondered why he looked so satisfied. "Will you come with me today?"

"Come where?"

"Nowhere, anywhere. How do you feel about just taking a Sunday drive?"

"Okay," Ally heard herself say. There were alarms ringing in her brain, but she ignored them—easily.

"Cruz?"

He sat relaxed in the driver's seat, one hand on the steering wheel, the other resting lightly on the gearshift. His window was partly open, and the rush of air ruffled his hair. The hand on the gearshift was square and tanned, the back lightly sprinkled with dark hair. He wore no jewelry save a watch, but Ally thought a heavy gold ring would look very much in place on that elegant hand. He watched the freeway ahead, but there was a half smile on his lips.

"Hmm?" He kept his eyes on the road.

"Why are you doing this?"

"Taking this road? Because it's here."

"That's not what I mean, and you know it." Ally turned sideways in her seat so she could watch his face. "Why did you come to my house today? Why did you want to take me out?"

He shrugged. "I thought I ought to get to know the residents better."

"I see." Ally kept her voice neutral. "Is that why you took me to the beach?" And nearly made love to me, she added silently.

She could see a muscle tighten in his jaw. "I took you to the beach because you were unhappy. I hoped it would take your mind off the hospital."

"It worked." Ally hadn't meant that to sound as sarcastic as it did, but she was getting angry. He might not want to talk about what had happened on the beach, but she refused to push the subject under the rug.

He glanced at her, his face grim. "All right," he said tightly. "You want to talk, we'll talk."

He gunned the engine and swung the car across three lanes of the freeway traffic to the next exit. He shot down the off-ramp into a busy Hispanic neighborhood, its sidewalks filled with Sunday promenaders. Fathers and sons wore their best suits, mothers were elegant in high heels and hats, small girls were resplendent in ruffles and hair ribbons. Cruz swung into the first parking space available, directly in front of a theater, and set the parking brake with a jerk.

A queue was forming for the Spanish-language double feature, but Cruz ignored the curious glances they received. He sat staring at his hands on the steering wheel.

"If you want the truth," he said after a moment, his voice harsh, "I don't know why I came. Maybe because I couldn't stay away. You're the wrong woman for me, and you probably know I'm the wrong man for you, too. But I'm damned if I know why I can't seem to stay away from you!"

For a moment Ally stared at him, fury warring with hurt. How could he dismiss what was between them with a few cruel, casual words? In the face of the magic they shared, surface differences paled into nothingness. How could he pretend that had no meaning? As disbelief faded, fury won out.

"I see." Her voice was utterly polite and edged with finishing school ice. "I would like to go home, Cruz."

Cruz's anger had been self-directed, but he'd vented it on her. The ice in her voice couldn't disguise the pain in her eyes, and it struck him like a blow to the heart.

"Ally, that's not what I meant—"

"Your meaning was quite clear. I want to go home."

"Not until we've talked about this. I want to—"

"I don't *care* what you want!" Her taut control began to crumble. "Just take me home!"

"Hey, Cruz! Amigo!" The shout from the sidewalk on the far side of the street interrupted whatever he was going to say. A slender young man of about twenty trotted across the street, grinning widely at them.

"Oh, God, just what I need!" Cruz groaned, and then the young man stopped beside them.

He rested his folded arms on the door as he spoke to Cruz in an exchange of Spanish too rapid and colloquial for Ally to follow, though she heard her own name and the name "Geraldo."

She looked away long enough to swipe at her eyes with a tissue, then turned back to find the young man regarding her with frank admiration. She forced herself to smile.

Cruz was clearly uncomfortable with the young man's inquiries, and after a moment Ally realized that he was stone-walling questions about her. It took several minutes, but finally the young man abandoned his interrogation. He stuck his head into the car and grinned at her.

"Good afternoon, *señorita*. I'm Paco Ramirez. Happy to meet you."

"Buenos dias, Señor Ramirez," she replied in the best accent she could muster, and was rewarded with a brilliant smile and another burst of Spanish that had something to do with being enchanted. Cruz cut that short by starting the engine.

Paco backed off reluctantly as the car began to move. *"¡Adiós!"*

Ally looked back as they turned the corner at the end of the block and saw Paco standing in the middle of the street, staring after them.

Cruz glanced in the mirror and swore. "If the networks had Paco, we wouldn't need newscasts!"

"Who is he?"

"A friend of my brother's. He and Geraldo went to school together. He's a gossip, worse than any old lady."

He signaled and turned at the next corner, but the turn took them away from the freeway.

"I thought you were taking me home," she said.

"There's somewhere I need to take you first." He stopped at a traffic light and turned to her. "If you would please accept my apology. The things I said were unforgivable. I was angry at myself, and it was wrong to take it out on you." He stared straight ahead. "I do know that I want to be with you today. Will you forgive me?"

Ally spread her hands helplessly, unable to hang on to her anger. "Yes, I will. Anyway, what you said was true."

He glanced at her as the light changed, his expression unreadable. "Maybe," he said as he drove through the intersection. "And maybe not. Will you come with me now?"

"I'm in your car. Do I have a choice?"

It was a weak attempt at a joke, and he didn't smile. "You always have a choice."

She looked at him for several seconds, and then, because it was what she wanted, too, she nodded. "Yes, I'll come with you."

They drove for fifteen minutes before she asked, "Where are you taking me?"

"You'll see." He half-smiled, and that emboldened Ally. "Is this some big secret?"

"It's not so big, but I'll let it be a surprise."

"What if I don't like surprises?"

"Tough tuna."

Ally gaped for a moment, then sputtered with laughter. "Tough tuna?" she gasped through her giggles. "Our chief resident says *tough tuna*? I'm going to put that up on the bulletin board in the clinic!"

"No, you won't."

"Why not?"

Cruz gave her a smug glance. "Because I'm your boss."

"That's a low blow." She folded her arms and scowled at him. "Throwing your weight around."

"What good is clout if you don't use it?" He grinned, and she stared out the window, pretending to pout.

He turned off the wide thoroughfare they'd been traveling on into a quiet upper-middle-class residential neighborhood. Ally glanced at him. "Where are we going, Cruz?"

"About three blocks from here."

"That's no answer."

"You'll see in a minute," was all he would say.

Ally sat in silence until he turned into the driveway of a big two-story stucco home. The yard was immaculate, a swath of vivid green bordered by carefully pruned roses and hibiscus. There was a cabbage palm in the center of the yard with a neat circle of orange-and-gold marigolds around its base.

"Cruz, whose house is this?"

He killed the engine. "My mother's. She lives here with my brothers and sisters. All except Ofelia. She's married and lives in the Valley." He checked his watch. "They all go to church on Sunday morning, but they should be home by now."

Ally swallowed, and the lump in her throat settled in her stomach, cold and heavy. "You brought me to meet your family?"

"That's right." He reached for the door handle.

Ally grabbed his arm. "No!" She pulled his hand away from the door. "Cruz, I can't go in there!"

"It's just Sunday dinner, Ally, nothing special."

"I can't!" There was a thread of panic in her voice, and she could see Cruz's surprise in his face.

He took her hand in both of his. "Yes, you can. They're harmless."

She forced a wan smile. "I know they won't bite."

"Then what's the problem?"

"This—" She waved helplessly at the house. "Family, Sunday dinners. I don't know what to do."

"It's simple." He gave her hand an encouraging squeeze. "You say hello to everybody, laugh at their jokes, eat a lot and let my mom give you a doggie bag."

"I don't know...."

"There's nothing to know. You'll be all right, Ally. I'll be with you all the time."

"Promise?" she demanded quickly, her grip on his hand tightening.

"I promise. Now can we go in?" He glanced at the house and grinned. "My sisters are watching us from behind the curtains."

Ally jerked around to look up at the second-story windows. She could see a ruffled curtain move. "Why—"

"Because Paco's already called and told them about you. That's why we're here. Let's go in now, okay?"

She nodded, then let Cruz walk her up to the porch.

The knob rattled as someone unlocked the door, and Cruz bent to whisper, "Smile!" in her ear. Ally ignored the sinking feeling in the pit of her stomach and smiled as charmingly as she could at Cruz's mother.

Two hours later she wondered what on earth she'd been afraid of. Graciela Gallego was a youthful forty-nine, slim and elegant, with thick black hair dramatically streaked with white at the temples. She had invited Ally into her home as if she were a lifelong friend of the family, showing no hint of curiosity about her son's new friend. Her children were less restrained.

Cruz's brothers, Carlos, twenty-five, and Geraldo, twenty, clearly approved of her looks, if nothing else. Fifteen-year-old Martin and seventeen-year-old Alfonso agreed. His sister Luz, twenty-two, and Alfonso's twin, Lydia, were more reserved, treating Ally courteously but with less warmth. They were reserving judgment.

But she had one wholehearted champion. Margarita, at ten the youngest, shyly asked if Ally wanted to see her dolls before dinner. When Ally said yes, Rita led her to the pretty bedroom she shared with Lydia and introduced her to a large collection of dolls and stuffed animals. Ally enjoyed learning their names, and by the time she and Rita rejoined the rest of the family, she had made a friend.

Rita stayed close by her the rest of the afternoon. Eventually married sister Ofelia arrived for a visit with her small son Luis and they ate a delicious midafternoon dinner. Ally knew that she was being checked out, but she couldn't resent it. It was obvious that they loved their brother and that they wanted the best for him.

Love. The love they shared was a tangible thing, but it was something she'd never really believed in. They shared family jokes, teased their mother about her glamorous image and her business, an elegant dress shop she had bought after her husband had died suddenly of a stroke. They teased each other about boyfriends, girlfriends, school and grades, and they teased Cruz mercilessly, about anything and everything—except Ally herself.

How would it feel, Ally wondered, to be inside that circle of love, to be part of a family? It was utterly unfamiliar to her, and she found it a little overwhelming. They were noisy, happy, boisterous, delighted to be in each other's company.

The contrast with her own childhood was painfully sharp. She tried to keep the sadness out of her face, but she could feel Cruz watching her, and she knew when he decided she'd had as much family togetherness as she could take.

At five, he made their excuses. No, thank you, they wouldn't stay to supper, they were still full from that enormous dinner. No, thank you, they didn't need to take any of the leftovers with them. It took several minutes, but they finally made their escape, parrying invitations to other dinners.

Ally waved goodbye until they turned the corner, then sat back and closed her eyes, suddenly inexpressibly weary.

"Was it that bad?" Cruz wondered teasingly.

She made herself smile. "No, of course not. They're all charming, and Rita is adorable."

"She didn't bore you to death with those dolls?"

"Not at all! I loved hearing about them."

"She must have been thrilled. She can't get the rest of the family to listen anymore."

The rest of the family. As if she were a part of it. Ally turned her head toward the window, biting her lip. The city streamed past, houses, stores, streets, but she saw nothing.

"Ally?" Cruz said quietly. "I know something's wrong. Did one of them say something that upset you? If they did, I'll—"

"That's not it!" She shook her averted head. "They were all charming."

"Then what's wrong?" She said nothing, and Cruz swore under his breath as he changed lanes and turned onto a side street. He parked in the first available space and killed the engine. "What is it?" He took her arm, pulling her around in her seat. "Ally, tell me what's wrong."

"All right!" Ally faced him. "All right, I'll tell you!"

"Is it my family? Did they—"

"No!" she interrupted. "I told you, it's not them." She glanced at him, then looked down at her hands in her lap. "It's not *your* family, it's *mine*."

"Your family? Do you miss them or something?"

"Or something." She laughed shortly, without humor. "No, I don't miss my family. I've never missed them that way." She paused. "I was wondering what it would be like to have the kind of family you have."

"All families are different, I guess."

"Different," she agreed in a bitter little voice. She looked up at him, and the concern in his eyes almost shattered her control. "My family wasn't like yours."

"I thought you lived with your grandfather."

Ally nodded. "I went to live with him when I was eleven."

"And before that?"

"Before that, I lived with my father."

"Not your mother?"

"She died when I was two. She committed suicide."

Cruz took her hand. "I'm sorry. I didn't mean to bring up painful memories. If you'd rather not talk about it—"

"It's all right. It was a long time ago." She drew a deep, steadying breath. "I don't remember my mother. I know what she looked like, from pictures, but that's all."

"And your father?"

"I think he must have loved her. Maybe he even loved her a lot. I never felt he loved me." Cruz made a sympathetic sound and she shook her head. "I'm not looking for pity. It's a fact, that's all. I've always felt that he blamed me for her suicide. And I can't help but wonder if it was having a baby, having me, that pushed her over the edge."

Look what we've got for you:

. . . A FREE compact umbrella
. . . plus a sampler set of 4 terrific
Silhouette Intimate Moments® novels,
specially selected by our editors.

. . . PLUS a surprise mystery gift
that will delight you.

All this just for trying our preview service!

With your trial, you'll get SNEAK PREVIEWS
to 4 new Silhouette Intimate Moments® novels a
month—before they're available in stores—with
9% off retail on any books you keep (just $2.49
each)—and FREE home delivery besides.

Get 4 FREE full-length Silhouette Intimate Moments® novels.

Plus
a handy
compact
umbrella

Plus
a surprise
free gift

▼ PLUS LOTS MORE! MAIL THIS CARD TODAY ▼

Silhouette's Best-Ever "Get Acquainted" Offer

Yes, I'll try the Silhouette preview service under the terms outlined on the opposite page. Send me 4 free Silhouette Intimate Moments® novels, a free compact umbrella and a free mystery gift.

240 CIL YABG

PLACE STICKER
FOR 6 FREE GIFTS
HERE

NAME _____

ADDRESS _____ APT. _____

CITY _____

STATE _____ ZIP CODE _____

Gift offer limited to new subscribers, one per household. Terms and prices subject to change.

PRINTED IN U.S.A.

Don't forget...

...Return this card today to receive your 4 free books, free compact umbrella and free mystery gift.

...You will receive books before they're available in stores and at a discount off retail prices.

...No obligation. Keep only the books you want and cancel anytime.

If offer card is missing, write to: Silhouette Books, 901 Fuhrmann Blvd.,
P.O. Box 1867, Buffalo, NY 14269-1867

No Postage
Necessary
If Mailed
In The
United States

BUSINESS REPLY·CARD

First Class   Permit No. 717   Buffalo, NY

Postage will be paid by addressee

Silhouette® Books
901 Fuhrmann Blvd.
P.O. Box 1867
Buffalo, NY 14240-9952

"That's ridiculous!" he burst out.

Ally gave him a level look. "Maybe so. Or maybe she had a severe postpartum depression, or maybe she was clinically depressed. You know how often depressed people commit suicide."

"I know, but you can't blame yourself," he said. "You were a baby. What about your father? Is he a doctor?"

"He's a businessman. Granddad wanted his son to be a doctor, but he was never interested in medicine. He did go to med school for a while, but then he dropped out. I guess they fought about it, because they don't get along. They never have, not since I can remember. My father has an import business. It's headquartered in New York, but he travels most of the time. I lived in the New York apartment."

"He left you there alone?"

"Not alone. There was always a housekeeper or a nanny, and I spent most of the year at school, anyway."

"Boarding school?" Cruz's voice was empty of expression.

"Yes. One of the housekeepers, Mrs. Hodges, even came to school for parents' days and things like that, since my father was away." She smiled at the memory, but Cruz's face was grim.

"What did your father do, when he wasn't traveling?"

Ally shrugged. "When he was in New York, he had business meetings and entertained people."

"But he didn't spend time with you?"

"I didn't see much of him, but that was all right. He's never been comfortable around me, and I've never been able to relax with him. When I was eleven Granddad came to visit, and he brought me back to California with him."

"Were you glad to leave New York?"

"At first?" She grinned wryly, remembering. "Not a bit! I'd been put on a plane and dragged across the country by a grandfather I'd never even met before, and I was livid. I did my very best to hate him, and I tried to drive him crazy so he'd send me back to New York. I might not have been very happy there, but at least it was familiar."

"So what happened?"

"My grandfather didn't try to make me love him *or* California. He just kept me from burning the house down or stealing the car, and eventually I ran out of anger. Once I got to know him, I couldn't help but love him." She smiled easily at Cruz. "I was happy living with him."

"And your father?"

Her smile faded, and her gaze slid away. "I've seen him a couple of times since I came to California."

"Recently?"

She shook her head.

"When was the last time you saw him?" Cruz pressed.

"It's been a while." Her face was tight. "I sent him invitations to graduations and things, but he always had business somewhere else. The last time I saw him was seven years ago, by accident. He came through L.A. on his way back from Hong Kong to sign some papers for my grandfather. I was in college, living in the dorm. I just happened to drop by the house when he was there. He said hello, how was I? I said I was fine, and that was that."

She looked at him, deep pain in her eyes. "He probably doesn't even remember I'm a doctor," she finished in a whisper that shook with suppressed tears.

"Come here." Cruz reached out to pull her close and pressed her cheek against his chest. She could feel his face resting lightly on her hair. "I'm sorry. I didn't mean to hurt you. I didn't know what I was going to dredge up."

Ally sniffed hard and scrubbed the tears off her cheeks before lifting her head to look at him. "That's okay."

"It's not okay. I hurt you."

"No, you didn't hurt me. It's just—it's just that I never knew a family like yours. Granddad and I are close, but it's not the same as having brothers and sisters. I suppose every only child says this, but I think it would be wonderful to have brothers and sisters to share things with."

"It can be wonderful, but it has its drawbacks, too." He smiled. "Like when your little sisters spy on your dates or your little brothers steal your shirts. I wouldn't change anything, though. I love them."

"It shows," she said softly. "It's nice."

"Yeah, it is nice. It can be a lifesaver, too. It was when my father died."

"What happened?" When he didn't answer for a moment she said quickly, "I'm sorry, I shouldn't have asked."

"Why not?" He smiled and settled her more comfortably, and Ally nestled in the safe circle of his arms. "*I* asked *you* a lot of questions." He laid his cheek against her hair again, and when he spoke, his voice was soft with memories.

"I loved my father. I admired him, too. He was a citizen, born on a farm outside San Diego, but he didn't learn English until he was in his twenties. He worked hard, then studied at night to learn the language that would be his ticket into the mainstream.

"He worked his way out of the vegetable fields. He loved us and wanted us to go to college, to learn the things he never had a chance to learn, to have the kind of success he never did. He had a fatal stroke when I was a freshman in college. Rita wasn't even born yet."

"Oh, Cruz, how awful for you."

"It wasn't a good time." The simple words glossed over a deep well of pain and grief. "Not for any of us. I was going to quit school and get a job to help my mother, but she wouldn't hear of it."

"What did you do?"

"I stayed in school. She used the insurance money and the savings to buy her shop. I got some school loans and a part-time job, and we got by, together."

"She's doing a lot more than getting by," Ally pointed out. "Her shop sounds really special."

"It is. She amazes me. She never wanted to be anything but a wife and mother, but when she had to go out in the world and earn a living, she did. She found that she has a real talent for retailing, too. She's thinking about opening another shop, one that Ofelia would manage."

"Ofelia would be good at it, wouldn't she?"

"She sure would. She's worked with Mom for several years, and she knows the business inside out. They talked shop over dinner every night when I lived at home. Sometimes I miss that.''

''Where do you live now?''

''I have an apartment. Not much, but it's close to the hospital.''

''I never really thought about where you live.'' Ally smiled and turned to face him. ''You know what I'd like?'' she asked eagerly, then stopped herself.

''Go on. What would you like?''

She shook her head. ''No. I'm being presumptuous.''

''Let me be the judge of that. What is it?''

''Well...'' She looked up into his face. ''Would you think I was terribly pushy if I asked you to take me to your apartment and make me a cup of coffee?''

She smiled, but her smile faded as the seconds slipped by and Cruz said nothing.

Chapter 10

The silence stretched past awkwardness into embarrassment.

Ally's heart sank. Of course Cruz didn't want to take her to his apartment, and she was a fool to have invited herself.

"I'm sorry," she said in a tight, jerky voice. "I shouldn't have asked. You don't want to—"

"No, no, that's not it," Cruz reassured her hastily. "It's just that my apartment . . . well, it's not much."

"Is that all?" Limp with relief, Ally sighed. "I don't care if you don't live in the Hearst castle, for heaven's sake. *That's* not important."

"Are you sure you don't mind?" He loosened his arms and leaned back to look into her face.

She laughed at his worry. "It's just an apartment. How bad can it be?"

"I don't think I'll answer that." He let her slide back into her seat and started the car. "It's not as nice as your place, though. Are you sure you want to go over there?"

"Now that you've made me curious, I *have* to." She was teasing, but it was the truth. He'd piqued her curiosity, and she was determined to see where Cruz Gallego chose to live.

The sun was setting when he parked the car a few blocks from the hospital by a small stucco apartment building. The top story was at street level, but the hillside fell steeply away from the street and the building extended five stories down the hill. Cruz had the apartment on the top floor at the rear. The hallway that led to his door was narrow, but clean and well lit.

"It's kind of small," he warned her; then he opened the door and ushered her inside.

His living room was indeed small, with a big window at one end and a tiny kitchenette at the other. The room was immaculate, but sparsely furnished, with a short sofa upholstered in a soft shade of gray-blue against the long wall, at an angle to an armchair in faded floral chintz. The end tables and lamps looked a lot like the ones that had furnished her college dormitory room. The effect was Spartan, but not unpleasant.

Cruz stood by the door, waiting tensely for the verdict.

Ally smiled. "It's comfortable. I like that."

He laughed aloud and walked to the kitchenette, switching on lights. "Don't try to be tactful. It's pretty awful."

"No, it's not." She followed him. "It's not black leather and chrome or something. It's homey and comfortable."

He looked around the small room as if he'd never seen it before, then at Ally. She was surprised by the uncertainty in his face. "I just wish I had a nicer place for you to visit."

"Cruz," she said, laying her hand on his sleeve, "I feel at home here. Please don't treat me like a freak because my grandfather is wealthy."

His face relaxed into a smile, and he touched her cheek with his fingertips in a feathery caress. "Do I do that?"

"Sometimes." Ally gazed soberly into his eyes, searching for the words to make him understand. "I'm *me*, Cruz, not some abstract 'rich person.' I'm just a woman, no more, no less."

Just a woman. Cruz's fingers trembled against her cheek, and he dropped his hand, jamming it into his pocket. She was a great deal more than just a woman; she was everything a woman should be. She was all the woman he could ever want.

He turned abruptly to the three-burner cooktop. "Are you still interested in that cup of coffee?"

"Of course." There was a teasing smile in her voice. "After all, that's why I invited myself over, isn't it?"

"Coffee coming up. How about something to go with it?"

"You're actually hungry after that enormous dinner?"

"I wouldn't mind a little snack. There's a pizza place near here, and I can order in. How does that sound?"

Ally laughed. "I've never turned down pizza in my life."

"I'll remember that. Pepperoni, green pepper and sausage?"

"Sure. Shall I make the coffee while you order?"

"We can have wine with the pizza, and coffee afterward."

"That sounds good."

It was. The pizza was hot and savory, and they ate it at the minuscule dinette table, washing it down with a half bottle of inexpensive but good red wine. Cruz took the coffee, a strong, cinnamon-scented Mexican brew that he claimed was a secret family recipe, to the coffee table. Dusk was fading into night, and the lamps filled the room with a warm glow.

"Mmm, this is delicious!" Ally told him after her first sip. "How do you make it?"

"Uh-uh-uh. I told you—that's a family secret."

"I bet if I asked your mother she'd tell me." Ally smiled smugly into her cup.

"That's cheating." He settled himself comfortably, his arm lying along the back of the sofa behind her shoulders. "But it'd work. She'd tell you anything you wanted to know."

"I like her a lot. She made me feel welcome."

"I could tell that she liked you."

"I'm glad."

There was a moment of comfortable silence. "There is one thing that's special about this apartment," Cruz said.

"What's that?"

"This." He switched off the lamp beside him, then reached past her to turn off the other one. "Come here."

He led her to the window, and Ally gasped as she saw what he meant. From their hillside vantage point they looked out across the city, a breathtaking panorama of miles of glittering lights.

She gasped, eyes wide and glowing with wonder. "It's beautiful, Cruz. Just beautiful."

She leaned her shoulder against the windowframe, gazing out, and Cruz moved to stand behind her. She tensed when he slid his arms around her and clasped his hands in front of her waist, but then she relaxed, letting him pull her back to lean against his chest. She felt him kiss her hair softly, and let her head fall back to his shoulder so she could smile up at him.

She was too shy to consciously invite him to kiss her, but subconsciously...? Later, Ally would be unable to answer that question, and at that moment, looking out at the city lights and the rising moon, she wasn't thinking at all. And when she smiled up at him, Cruz slowly bent his head to touch his lips to hers.

It was a breath of a touch, sending a shock of desire rushing through them both. She breathed something, maybe his name, and turned in his arms so he could pull her close. He cupped the back of her head with his hand and lifted his lips for a moment to gaze at her face with dark, heavy-lidded eyes. When he moved closer again, Ally let her lids fall closed.

He kissed her mouth tenderly, wonderingly, as if he'd never kissed her before. Their lips touched, brushed to and fro, and then slowly, so slowly, he covered her mouth with his and took what she offered. Ally thought she knew what to expect, but the power of it took her by surprise. There had been both passion and tenderness when he'd held her and kissed her on the beach, but this time the tenderness was quickly overwhelmed until there was only passion. It was not a yielding and a giving, but a demand met by a demand and by a heat that flared quickly into flame.

She was soft and slim, warm and strong and dizzyingly beautiful, and when she twined her arms around him, clinging and sweet, the flame became madness, a madness he embraced willingly. He gave himself up to the desire that had gnawed at him since the first time he'd seen her. Slowly, with exquisite care, he let his hands drift down her flanks, loving the size and shape of her, the softness and strength he sensed beneath cotton and silk. He fought his body's demands, forcing himself to wait and to savor.

Her thin cotton blouse slid smoothly over her skin, and she swayed against him, molding her supple body to the harder, more angular contours of his. She fitted him perfectly, as if she'd been made just for him. Her mouth was hot and eager as she tasted his lips, then nibbled her way along his jawline to a spot beneath his ear that sent a shaft of heat to his belly.

Ally shivered when Cruz caught her hair and pulled her mouth back to his with a tightly restrained power that surprised and elated her. She could feel the taut strength in him, the need and the barely controlled passion. There was an answering need in her, a passion she had never imagined until Cruz had taken her in his arms that first time. He sparked something dark and elemental in her, overwhelming in its strength, impossibly exciting in its pleasure.

She had to have more of him, had to have all of him, and she ran her hands over his body, savoring the strength of his bone and muscle and wanting more. She struggled clumsily with his buttons, so he took his arms away long enough to whip the shirt off. A button snapped off and clicked softly against the floor, and then she was in his arms again, stroking his back and shoulders, flooded with new and exciting sensations as she learned the feel of him.

Solid muscles flexed beneath warm skin that was smoother than she'd expected. His arms were powerful, his shoulders wide and heavily muscled, his waist narrow. She traced the line of his spine, then ran her fingertips lightly along his waistband. His muscles tightened under her touch as her hands stroked around to meet in front, just below his navel, and when she slid her palms slowly upward, spreading her fingers across his chest, brushing over the mat of dark hair, tracing his flat nipples, he gasped into her mouth.

His hands were moving with the same restlessness, sweeping from the fragile bones of her shoulders to the curve of her bottom. He shaped the softness there, then cupped his hands beneath her to lift her onto her toes, into him. Ally murmured wordlessly when he tugged her blouse free of her slacks and ran his hands beneath it, warm and slightly rough on the thin skin of her waist.

He brushed his thumbs over the undercurves of her breasts, lightly teasing, then covered them with his hands, circling his palms over the fragile lace covering her nipples. Ally was lost. She was boneless under his hands, wanting nothing more than him, not water to drink nor air to breathe.

When he lifted his lips and slid his hands down from her breasts to hold her waist lightly, she murmured a protest and swayed against him. "Allison," he whispered, her name a caress.

She blinked dazedly, struggling to bring his face into focus. It was a strong face, handsome, the face of the man she loved, his eyes dark and dilated with the emotion they shared.

"Allison?" he murmured again.

"Yes?" Her voice was a breathless whisper.

"Will you come with me?" He inclined his head toward the door that led to his bedroom.

Ally was touched almost to tears. He wouldn't attempt to sweep her off her feet or overwhelm her with passion, though they both knew he could easily do so. This decision would be hers alone.

She traced her fingertip across his lips, and his tongue flicked out in a quick caress. "Yes," she whispered, almost formally, the words almost a vow. "I will come with you."

He nodded, then startled her by sweeping her into his arms to carry her through the doorway and lay her across his bed. A beautiful mahogany antique, it had been brought from Mexico nearly a hundred years earlier. It was huge and heavy and ornately carved, high and wide and soft, and it filled the small bedroom.

Cruz undressed her slowly, first the blouse, then the bra, then the rest. With a patience she was unable to match, he took each piece of clothing, dropped it on the floor and savored each newly revealed bit of her with his lips and hands. He kissed her breasts, caressed her body until she twisted beneath him, deaf and blind to the world outside that room. She moved beyond thought to pure feeling. Sensations flowed through her until she was drowning in them. He made slow, sweet love to her, kissing and caressing sensitive places she hadn't known she had, creating needs she'd never dreamed of.

She wanted to kiss and caress in return, to give him the same pleasure, but instead she could only cling to him, following where he led, faster and farther, spiraling higher and wilder. Her heart hammered in her chest; the blood thundered in her ears like the coming of a storm.

Her head rolled from side to side on the pillow, and her fingers tangled in his hair as he drew his mouth from her throat to her breast, then to the soft swell of her belly. She gasped, then pleaded wordlessly, asking for things she didn't even understand. When he answered her, he moved back up to cover her body, kissing her deeply, nudging her knees apart and wrapping her in his arms before he made them one. She clutched at him, her fingers digging into his shoulders, but there was no pain, only a brief resistance.

He froze. "Allison?" he whispered.

She wound her arms around his neck and kissed him deeply. "Love me, Cruz. Please, love me." Her hips moved instinctively, and he moved in response, unable to help himself, in a rhythm that began slowly, then quickened. A building, twisting, tightening spiral formed inside her. Tighter and tighter it wound until she thought she would burst with need. And then she splintered into a thousand pieces as pleasure swept through her.

Cruz struggled to hold on to his sanity, but the scent of her skin, the satin warmth of her body against him and around him, created a passion, a desire, that dwarfed any-

thing he had ever felt. When her body suddenly tensed and
she gasped his name, his desperate control shattered, the
world spun madly, and he buried his face in her hair and let
the whirlwind take him, too.

An eternity later, Ally floated back to reality. It was a
warm, soft reality, where she lay cocooned in blankets, secure in Cruz's arms. Her face was pressed into the hollow of
his shoulder, and she breathed in rhythm with him. Her
body was lax and sated, yet utterly alive, aching and glowing, her skin tingling. She was exhausted and exhilarated,
and she was afraid.

She'd made love with Cruz. She'd given her body to the
man she loved, and that was wonderful. But she had also
made love with the chief resident, and that was *not* wonderful.

She wasn't afraid of the lovemaking, for it wasn't lovemaking that made you vulnerable, it was loving. She hadn't
wanted to fall in love with Cruz, but she knew it had been
inevitable from the first time they had faced each other.

The spark had always been there between them. That was
why his suspicion had hurt her, though she had shrugged off
the suspicions of others. She loved him, loved his arro-
gance as much as his kindness, loved his gentle strength, his
anger against the injustices of life. But where you loved you
could be hurt.

She'd guarded herself against that kind of pain for so long
that it was second nature to hold her emotions in check and
keep her distance from people. Only her grandfather and
Stacy Alexander had been allowed past her emotional walls.

So where had that reserve gone when she really needed it?
She'd known Cruz Gallego was dangerous the moment she'd
met him, but she hadn't been able to resist playing with fire,
and now it was too late.

Cruz stirred lazily, sliding one long leg over hers. He
moved his hand in small circles on her hip, then slid it up her
back to cradle her nape. She shivered from a mixture of
pleasure and fear. Exhausted as she was, she wanted him
again. It frightened her.

Cruz felt the same renewed desire. He kneaded her nape with his fingertips, then let them drift around to her throat. The pulse there skipped in a hasty rhythm, and the skin under his hands warmed to his touch. She was everything he had imagined and more, sweet and strong and utterly female. And she'd been a virgin. If he'd known...

Cruz clenched his stomach muscles against desire. If he'd known, he wouldn't have been able to do a damned thing differently. Her passion and her eagerness had caught him by surprise; her inexperienced lips and hands had driven him to the edge of madness.

He should let her rest. His hand moved over skin that was like warm, fragrant satin. He should leave her alone. He rolled his body half over hers, savoring her softness. He should let her sleep. He dropped his face into her hair, inhaling her fragrance of wildflowers and woman.

The desire growing in him, hot, insistent, made a mockery of all those "shoulds." She pressed her lips to his shoulder, and desire became demand. He shouldn't...

He lifted her face to his, seeking her mouth again. He knew that when he kissed her he would be lost, and he was.

"Time to get up."

Ally mumbled a protest and burrowed deeper into the pillow. Warm and comfortable, she didn't want to wake up.

"Ally!" A firm hand shook her shoulder. "It's time to get up."

"Don' wanna," she mumbled, and squirmed away.

Cruz stood smiling down at her. She was adorable, her cheeks flushed pink, her hair tousled from sleep and lovemaking. He wanted nothing more than to crawl back into bed and make love with her again.

"Well, you'd better get up," he said, his voice roughened by desire. "It's Monday morning, and you have a clinic full of patients waiting for you."

She lay very still as that penetrated. Then she rolled onto her back, clutching the sheet to her breasts, and looked at him with stricken eyes.

"Monday?" she whispered.

"Monday morning." Cruz smiled.

"What time is it?"

"6:15."

"Eeep." She slid down, pulling the sheet above her head. "I've got to get ready."

"I know." He lifted the sheet off her pink face. "So get up and get dressed. Your clothes and your purse are over there," he said, indicating a chair, "and there's a new toothbrush in the bathroom. Need anything else?" She shook her head, her cheeks scorching. "Okay." He bent and kissed her mouth hard, then walked to the door. "And you'd better get moving if you want breakfast!" The door closed behind him.

Her lips still tingling from his kiss, Ally flung herself out of bed and ran for the bathroom.

They had no time to talk, and perhaps that was just as well. Ally didn't know what on earth she would have said, beyond asking for sugar for her coffee. They ate in shifts, Cruz packing his briefcase while Ally bolted the eggs he'd scrambled.

"Do you want to go home first?"

She looked up, her mouth full of toast. "Yeah." She washed the toast down with the last of her coffee. "I need to change and get my car and some papers."

"There's time. When you're finished, I'll drive you."

"I'm done." She carried her dishes to the sink.

"Leave those," he said when she turned the water on to wash them. "I'll do them tonight."

"But if you let them sit—"

"Let 'em sit! We don't have time to fool with them now." He was already walking out the door when she grabbed her purse and hurried after him. They talked about the clinic during the drive to her home. The other things, the important things, were too near the surface to be talked about just yet.

Cruz parked in front of her house. "Will you be all right?"

"Yes." Her answer was just a bit too quick. "I'm fine. I'll see you at the clinic."

She was halfway out of the car when he clamped his hand around her wrist and pulled her back. "Don't be sorry," he ordered roughly. "Don't be sorry about anything."

Ally met his eyes for a moment, then nodded slowly.

"Good." He pulled her close to kiss her, deep and hard. "I'll see you there."

He drove away as she was unlocking her front door, and she didn't see him again until midmorning. They passed in a crowded hallway; she nodded, he nodded, and that was that. They might have been casual acquaintances, except for the long look they exchanged.

She was summoned to his office shortly before noon. She tried to act as if nothing was amiss and didn't notice Marsha Mott following her into the hallway. Cruz glanced up from his paperwork when she opened the office door.

"Would you close the door, please, Ally?" His voice was cool, but when the door clicked shut, he rose to his feet and smiled. It was a lazy, seductive smile that brought quick heat to Ally's cheeks. He pinched his fingers together and made a twisting gesture to pantomime turning the lock.

She locked the door, then walked around the desk and into his waiting arms, knowing she had come home. It was that simple. Their mouths met, and long seconds flowed past before anything else was allowed to matter.

When the kiss ended, Cruz tucked Ally's head against his shoulder and rested his cheek on her hair. He could hardly bear to let her out of his arms. He wanted to drown himself in her every time she was near, and the craving was growing rather than lessening. If he'd thought one night of lovemaking would satisfy him, he'd been a fool.

"How are you?" he whispered.

She was wonderful, now that she was safely in his arms. She told him so.

"You're cute when you sleep."

She hid her face in his chest. "Liar! I know how I look in the morning."

"You look beautiful." His voice was low and caressing. "You're pink and soft and warm, and your hair's all messed up. You're beautiful." He smiled against her hair. "Were you comfortable last night?"

"Mm-hmm. Except you hogged all the covers."

He could feel her smile, and laughed softly. "There's a method in my madness."

"There is?"

"If I do that, you have to snuggle up to me to keep warm."

"Cruz!" Cheeks flaming, she burrowed her head farther into his chest.

"I shouldn't tease you, should I?" he asked softly. "You aren't used to it." He loosened his arms and lifted her face from his white coat. "It was your first time."

Ally closed her eyes before she nodded her reply.

"You should have told me."

She looked up, searching his face for some clue to his feelings. "Maybe."

"No maybes. I needed to know."

She pulled out of his arms and moved to the window, head bent, to trace patterns in the film of dust on the windowsill.

"But how was I supposed to tell you? 'By the way, Cruz, I'm a virgin'?" She gripped the windowsill, and her knuckles whitened.

"That's not what I meant, Allison."

"Then what did you mean? That you wouldn't have wanted me if you'd known?" She bit her lip, and Cruz moved closer. She stepped away, and he let his hands drop.

"I meant that I would have been more gentle. I would have been careful not to hurt you."

"Oh." It was a very small syllable.

She looked at him shyly then, and when he reached out to her, she went into his arms. "I would have wanted you. I can't imagine not wanting you. If I'd known—" He kissed her brow tenderly. "I would have made things special...for your first time."

Ally lifted her head and smiled shyly at him. "It couldn't have been more special."

"Oh, yeah?" he chuckled. "I promise, I'll show you that it can be." He kissed her again, long and deep, and the familiar melting began, but he broke the kiss before she dissolved completely. His arm around her shoulders, he steered her to the chair. "I'm afraid this is going to cause some problems."

Ally closed her eyes. Oh, yes, it would certainly do that. She took a deep breath. "I realize that."

"I'll have to assign you to another supervisor," he said, surprising her.

That seemed so trivial compared to the things that worried her. She didn't know how to tell Cruz that this simply couldn't work.

"We're in this together, Ally." He reached for her hand. "Remember that. We can handle the problems together."

The thought should have filled her with warmth, but instead it chilled her. She looked at their linked hands resting on the desk and blinked back the tears that welled in her eyes. She couldn't allow herself to become accustomed to this. The problems Cruz was talking about were surface problems. The true problems were far more fundamental.

She and Cruz were very different people. After meeting Cruz's family, Ally knew they were too different. The love they shared was a wonderful thing, and utterly foreign to her. What did she know about families, about being part of a family?

She loved Cruz, but it was a love with no future. Cruz had a right to expect a family life with the woman he chose to love. Ally didn't delude herself that she was the woman who could give him those things. She forced herself to smile at him.

He smiled back. "Don't worry, Ally. It'll be all right."

"You don't need to worry about me."

"I can't help worrying about you, so you might as well get used to it."

She bit her lip and drew her hand from his. "I'd better get back to work." She kept the smile pinned on her face until she had closed the door behind her.

She turned around and stopped short. Marsha Mott was standing a few steps down the hall. Ally schooled her face into an expression of polite indifference. "If you want to see Dr. Gallego, he's free now."

Marsha grinned slyly at her. "I don't need to see him."

Puzzled and more than a little uneasy, Ally watched the woman turn and saunter away. For someone who didn't want to see Cruz, Marsha Mott seemed to spend a lot of her time standing outside his office.

Chapter 11

Spying?'' His skepticism came clearly through the telephone lines. ''On us?''

''It's not *that* farfetched. There are only two offices on that hallway, and the other one was empty. If Marsha Mott wasn't waiting to see you, what was she doing there?''

Cruz had phoned about an hour after Ally had gotten home. The more she thought about finding Marsha Mott in the hall, the odder it seemed, and she'd told him so. She could imagine only one reason for Ms. Mott to have been standing in that hall.

''It's not paranoia, Cruz. What else was she doing there? She's made it clear she can't stand me, and if she heard us—''

''I don't know.'' Cruz sighed heavily. ''Maybe she just likes to listen at doors. She couldn't have heard anything incriminating this afternoon, though. I don't mean to minimize your concern, but I don't think there's anything to worry about.''

''I hope you're right.'' Maybe he was. And if Marsha Mott wanted to listen at doors, it might be strange, but it was probably harmless. ''I don't want any gossip about us.''

"That's the least of my worries," he said tiredly. "I have a problem here, I'm afraid. I called because I can't see you this evening."

The tension in his tone gave him away. "Was there another theft?"

"Yeah."

"And I worked in the clinic today. Is someone still trying to frame me?"

"You, or someone who works the same schedule. I don't want to talk about this on the phone. I'll fill you in tomorrow." There was fatigue in his voice, and disappointment. The nightmare wasn't over. Someone on the clinic staff was still stealing. Drugs were still being used in a way they had never been intended for.

Ally said goodbye and hung up the phone gently.

Who was it? Who was this thief who stole with impunity while the police, the hospital and even Ally and Cruz tried to catch him. The situation was eating away at Cruz. Ally would have given anything to take the burden from him, but she was helpless, as they all were.

The next day was a bad one. She was better able to deal with hectic days than she'd been at the start, but that didn't mean she had to like them. Murphy's Law was in full force, too, so when the third patient of the day arrived to have stitches removed, she had no suture-removal pack.

"This is healing very nicely, Mr. Herman," she told the fortyish man sitting on the table as she examined the row of stitches in his beefy arm. "I'll take those out right now."

"Will it take long?" He glanced at the stitches and then looked quickly away. Ally hid a smile. For all his macho posturing, he didn't like the looks of his injury.

"Not long at all. Then all you'll have is a little gauze dressing." She wet a towel with sterile saline solution and laid it over the sutures. "If you would hold this on for a moment—like that—I'll go and get the equipment I need."

She left him holding the towel on his arm and hurried out to the desk. Marsha Mott was alone there, standing behind the desk with a magazine and a cup of coffee.

"Excuse me, Miss Mott." Marsha didn't look around. "Miss Mott," Ally repeated, a little louder, and after a moment Marsha turned to her.

"Yeah?" She spared Ally a glance.

"I need a forceps pack. Could you bring me one, please?"

Marsha smiled the spiteful smile that Ally was coming to detest and turned her back. "I'm on my break." She picked up her cup and sauntered away.

Ally bit her tongue as Marsha ambled into the lounge. She was an intern and couldn't call a nurse on the carpet for unprofessional behavior. She wouldn't make a scene in front of the patients, either, something that Marsha was probably counting on. One of these days, she promised herself, she would have it out with Marsha Mott. One of these days.

"Is something wrong, Dr. Schuyler?"

Ray Walcott was walking toward her. His jerky gait, combined with his thin build and unattractive face, reminded Ally irresistibly of Ichabod Crane. She couldn't quite make herself like Ray, and she felt guilty, because he was always polite and helpful to her. There was just something about him that she had trouble warming up to.

He shook his lank hair out of his eyes. "Can I do anything for you, Dr. Schuyler?"

"Yes, if you don't mind." She made her voice warm. "I've got some stitches to remove, and I need a forceps pack."

"Sure, Dr. Schuyler" He brought the pack promptly. Ally thanked him and went back to work, but when she left the exam room with Mr. Herman, Ray was waiting for her.

"Anything else you need, Dr. Schuyler?" He fell in step with her as she headed for the nurses' station.

"No, Ray, but thank you anyway."

"That's okay." He looked furtively around him and dropped his voice. "Did you hear?"

"Hear what?" Ally asked absently. She flipped open Mr. Herman's chart.

Ray propped his elbows on the counter. "Some more drugs were stolen yesterday," he told her in a conspiratorial whisper.

Ally's hand jerked, and the tail of a *Y* crossed two lines. Deliberately she finished the loop and resumed writing. "I'd heard that." Her voice was level and showed no particular interest.

"It happened sometime in the afternoon."

"Yeah?" Thinking hard, she signed the chart and closed the metal folder. Was Ray's curiosity just vicarious interest, or was there more to it? "I didn't know what time it was."

"They called me to the office this morning," Ray confided. When Ally looked at him, his eyes were bright and avid.

"Who did?" She put more friendly interest in her voice than she really felt.

"Dr. Gallego and that cop. You know him."

"Sergeant Williams?"

"Yeah. They gave me the third degree again. Where did I go, what did I do all afternoon, stuff like that."

"I guess they ask us the same questions every time."

"I guess so." He glanced at her, his eyes shadowed by half-closed lids, and grinned, showing uneven teeth. "They usually make you wait till last, don't they?"

"Do they?" She shrugged. "I hadn't thought about it."

"I think it stinks!" His sudden anger surprised her. His face twisted into ugly lines, and he slammed his hand on the counter. "They call you in there at the end of the day and keep you there for hours! They're picking on you!"

Touched that he was concerned about her, Ally patted his hand lightly. It was clenched into a fist.

"Don't worry about me, Ray. I don't know why they call me last," she lied, "but it's no big deal."

"It's like they suspect you."

"But they don't." She saw the surprise flash across his face. "At least, I don't think so. At first they did, and they questioned me a lot, but I had an alibi for the second theft."

After a moment he nodded. "That's good, Dr. Schuyler. I wouldn't want anyone to hurt you."

As he walked away, Ally stared after him wonderingly. Why was Ray so concerned about her?

What if he had a crush on her? As a medical student she'd been the unwilling object of a teenage patient's fervent adoration. His attitude had resembled Ray's, sometimes puppylike admiration, sometimes anger at the other people around her. Ally relaxed a little. If it was a crush, she would deal with it. It was discomfiting to be the object of such feelings, but at least it meant she had an ally.

She was pleased with herself as she went to the locker room that evening, because she'd finished her appointments on time. Karen Willis was there, changing into tights and a leotard for a workout in the employee fitness center.

"You're done early." She grinned as Ally opened her locker. "It doesn't take long to do your histories now, does it?"

Ally grinned back, shaking her head. "Everybody told me I'd get better at it, but I had to see it to believe it. I may even get out of here early someday!"

Laughing, Karen shook her head. "Didn't you know? There's an unwritten rule against residents leaving early. Interns add on another half hour just because they're interns!"

While they were chuckling, Karen draped a towel around her neck and waved goodbye. "See you tomorrow!"

Ally turned to her locker, smiling. Her lab coat went on a hook, and a pink linen blazer went over her silver-gray dress to make a stylish ensemble she wore as casually as jeans and a sweatshirt. Her black snakeskin clutch bag should have been propped on the small shelf at the back of the locker, but it had fallen into the clutter at the bottom.

Grumbling under her breath, she pushed the white coat aside and groped in the depths of the locker for her purse. She could feel it at the back, behind her spare shoes and her umbrella. She managed to grasp it with her fingertips and eased it out. The umbrella fell out, too, and opened in her face when the automatic-open button hit the edge of the locker. It wasn't until she had collapsed the umbrella again that she saw the envelope. An ordinary business-size envelope, it had fallen out, landing on the toe of one black pump.

"What in the world . . . ?"

She stuffed her umbrella in the locker and picked the envelope up. It was hospital stationery, slightly crumpled, with a misspelled version of her name printed unevenly on the front. "Dr. Alisen Skyler," it said. The flap was sealed, then taped, as sloppily as her name was printed. It almost looked like a child's handiwork—one of her young clinic patients, perhaps?

She slit the envelope and pulled out a single sheet of Dodd Memorial letterhead. She unfolded it and quickly scanned the few lines of crude block printing. Her hands began to shake, and the note slipped from her nerveless fingers. She forced herself to pick it up, to read the obscene and threatening words again.

Her mind shied away from the scrawled hate and filth, translating it into other words. She was the drug thief, it said, and she was other, less appealing things as well. She'd stolen those drugs, the poison-pen writer said, and the police would catch her, and then she'd get what she deserved. When Ally started to read what she "deserved," her hands shook so violently that the vile words blurred before her eyes.

"My God!"

Shaking and nauseated, she leaned against her locker, her thoughts scrambling madly, seeking reason where there was none. Who had done this? How had they gotten it into her locker? Who hated her so much? The vicious words echoed again and again in her skull, and she fought for control. She couldn't let her fear show. She repeated that like a mantra as she hurried down the hall as fast as her shaking legs could carry her. *I can't let it show.*

She knocked softly on Cruz's door, then couldn't turn the knob with her icy fingers.

"You coming in or not?" Charlie Parsons asked as he swung the door open for her. He had been laughing at something Cruz had said, but when he looked at her, his face changed. "Ally . . . ?"

He started toward her, but Cruz was faster, coming out of his chair and around the desk before she or Charlie realized he'd moved. He caught her hands, watching her chalk-white face. "What is it, Ally?"

"It's—" Her voice cracked. "In my locker—" Tears welled up in her eyes and spilled over, and Cruz pulled her into his arms.

"Close the door on your way out," he said softly over her head, and Charlie murmured a quiet reply. The door clicked closed behind him.

Ally bit her lip, sniffed hard and lifted her head from Cruz's shoulder. She dashed the tears from her eyes and blinked rapidly. She would not cry. She never cried, and she wouldn't let some sick, pathetic piece of hate mail make her cry.

As a child, she had cried her tears alone, in her beautifully decorated bedroom, after the housekeeper had said good-night. As she had grown older, she hadn't cried at all. She took a deep, shaky breath and brushed her hair off her face.

"I'm sorry." Her voice was only slightly thin. "I didn't mean to do that." She pulled away from Cruz, folding her arms tightly across her chest.

"So why did you?" He watched her carefully, more worried than he cared to admit. She wasn't easily upset, but something had sent her running into his office white-faced and terrified. "What happened?"

She took a deep breath, then blew it out as she collapsed into the side chair. "I went to my locker, a-and—" Her voice wobbled.

"Do you need a drink?" Cruz stepped closer.

She gave a little spurt of laughter, nearer to hysteria than she knew. "You have booze in your office?"

"Brandy. For medicinal purposes only."

She chuckled again when she realized he meant it. This time the laughter came easier. "No, thanks. I don't like brandy."

"How about coffee, then?" He was already pouring a cup from his small office coffee maker.

"Thank you." She took the mug and wrapped her icy fingers around it. "Mmm. Thank you."

"De nada." He leaned against the desk, looking down at her. "Can you tell me what happened now? Did someone hurt you?" The urgency broke through his carefully calm tone.

"No. It was the letter."

"What letter?"

Ally looked at her hands, mildly surprised to find them empty. "I was bringing it to you. I must have dropped it."

"What does it look like?"

"Just a sheet of white paper. Hospital letterhead."

"Like this?" He crossed the room and picked up a crumpled sheet from the floor near the door. "Is this the letter?"

Ally looked at it, and her lips tightened. "That's it."

Cruz smoothed the paper out and began to read. As he read, he swore. Ally didn't know the Spanish he was using, but she knew swearing when she heard it.

"Where was this?"

"In my locker."

He dropped the letter on his desk. "I'll call Clay." Ally stayed in the chair, sipping her coffee while he telephoned. Cruz cradled the phone. "He'll be here in fifteen minutes."

"Good. I hate to admit this—" she looked down, hiding her face from him "—but it scared me to find that."

"It's just a note, Ally." Cruz took her hands and lifted her out of the chair and into his arms. "Notes can't hurt you."

"The person who wrote that really hates me!"

"The person who wrote that is sick and cowardly." He hid his own fury. "Too cowardly to face you and say those things."

"Who could say those things out loud?" Ally wanted to know. "I don't even like to think about it."

"They're only words, Ally. Remember that." Cruz glanced at the note again, and his fingers tightened on her shoulders. "It makes me angry," he admitted. It was a massive understatement. "But it's probably nothing."

"Who would send me something so awful?"

He shrugged. "Someone who dislikes you."

"Dislikes?" Ally shook her head. "That's hatred."

"No sane person could hate you." He stroked her cheek, and she turned her face into the caress. "You're a very lovable person, Allison Schuyler."

"I agree."

They jerked apart as Clay walked into the office, a smile on his lips that didn't reach his eyes. He closed the door and turned the lock, then folded himself into the creaking metal chair by the file cabinets and looked at Ally.

"So what happened?" he asked.

"She got this," Cruz answered for her.

He kept Ally close to his side, an arm around her waist. Clay noted the possessive stance, filed the observation away and concentrated on the business at hand. Holding the note by the edges, he took it from Cruz.

He looked at them and smiled. "I don't suppose either of you thought to try and preserve the fingerprints, did you?" They shook their heads guiltily. "We'll get fingerprints from you both, then, and let the lab deal with it." He read the note, then laid it on Cruz's desk again. "Somebody has a colorful vocabulary," he commented. "And they don't much like you, Ally."

"No kidding," she said. Cruz tried to pull her closer, but she drew away. She was not going to let this reduce her to crying and clinging. "'Hate' is the word you're looking for, Clay."

"I think it's a crank note," Cruz said. He clenched his fists to keep from reaching for Ally again. "Some nut is too *cobarde* to say anything to her face, so they wrote a note."

"Could be." Clay's cool, dry voice was noncommittal. "Where did you find this, Ally?"

"It was in my locker. It fell out when I got my purse."

"It was on your purse?"

"No, my purse had fallen off the shelf. It was on the bottom of the locker. The note was down there, too." She thought a moment. "It could have been dropped through the vents in the door."

"That would be easier than breaking the lock. Who has access to that locker room?"

"Any female employee in the hospital," Cruz replied.

"Men?"

"They aren't supposed to be there, but it wouldn't be hard for a man to slip in and out without being seen."

Clay nodded. "Then we can't say that a woman did this."

"So it could be anybody?" Ally asked grimly. "Somebody who seriously wants to hurt me?"

"We can't assume anything," Clay said.

Simultaneously Cruz said, "You don't know that, Ally."

Clay's voice was as dry and placid as ever, while Cruz spoke placatingly, as if he were calming an upset child. That bothered Ally. She was scared and angry, and she wanted the men to be angry on her behalf. Their calming words had the opposite effect.

"No, I don't!" she snapped. "That's the problem! I don't know whether this note-writing nut is harmless, or if he's a maniac who means to kill me!"

"Ally, you don't need to be melodramatic—" Cruz began.

She cut him off. "Don't you patronize me!"

"You can't assume the worst from one note, Ally," Clay told her. "The odds are that it's no more dangerous than a crank call. The thief probably wrote it."

"The thief?" She turned to him. "But why?"

He nodded. "That's one person who has a reason for trying to frighten you. You may have said or done something that made the thief nervous. If this is an attempt to scare you off, it means we're getting close enough to make our guy take a risk. You mustn't blow it out of proportion. This kind of threat is almost always an empty one."

"Almost?" Ally repeated with a tinge of sarcasm. "You'll understand if that doesn't make me feel a whole lot better."

"You have to calm down," Cruz said, and Clay murmured agreement. They presented a united front.

Ally looked from one to the other and sighed in frustration. "I know that's what you think, and I pray to God you're right, but I don't know...." She shifted her shoulders, as if she'd felt a chill. "Something is wrong. I can feel it. Something is really wrong. I wish you understood."

"Ally..." Cruz took her shoulders and looked down into her face. "Listen to Clay. I know that note is ugly and frightening, but you can't let it get to you. Think about what he said. This means we're getting closer to the thief. If you look at it that way, it's a positive sign."

"I wish I could see it that way," she said as she rose, "but I can't. You're right about one thing, though."

"What's that?" Cruz watched her set her delicate jaw at a surprisingly pugnacious angle.

"I'm not going to let this stupid, trashy note get to me. It won't scare me, because I'm too mad to be scared!"

Chapter 12

She managed to stay that way all the way home. Slamming doors and banging things helped, and eventually the anger dissipated. Then she realized that she was alone, and she was scared.

Suddenly she wanted the drapes drawn over the windows, the doors securely locked. When she checked the back door for the third time, she caught herself. "This is stupid!"

She marched into the living room, plopped into an armchair and folded her terry-cloth robe around her. The beginning of a headache was nagging at her temples, and though it was late, she knew she wasn't ready for sleep. If the intent had been to scare her, it had worked. Whenever she closed her eyes she saw the note, those vicious words dancing across the paper.

She finally settled herself in bed with the driest, dullest medical journals she had in the house and a cup of cocoa topped with melting marshmallows that stuck to her lips. She read until exhaustion took over in the small hours and she dropped into an uneasy slumber.

The telephone's shrill ring jerked her rudely from deep sleep. She bolted up in bed, heart pounding, and fumbled for the receiver. She dragged it to her ear on the fourth ring.

"Hello?" Silence was her answer. "Hello?" Nothing but silence. The heavy thud of her heartbeat echoed in her ears. "If nobody's there, I'm going to hang up," she announced.

"No, you won't, bitch."

The voice was so heavily muffled that she couldn't tell if it was male or female, but the hatred and contempt came through clearly. "You won't get away with it, you stupid slut. The police are gonna get you, and if they don't, someone else will."

"Who is this?" Ally tried to make the question an arrogant demand, but it didn't come out as forcefully as she wanted.

"Wouldn't you like to know, slut?" Her tormentor laughed, chillingly. The laughter was followed by a stream of obscene filth, of the kind that had been in the letter. Ally listened, frozen, for several seconds, then slammed the phone down, breaking the connection.

She sat stiffly in her bed, her shaking hands clenched together, fighting panic. She wouldn't give in to it. She *wouldn't* let that sick animal make her panic. Though her heart raced and the blood thundered in her ears, she forced herself to breathe slowly and regularly. She groped for the bedside lamp with fingers that trembled and breathed easier when the soft glow of the bulb pushed back the darkness.

He might call back.

As the thought took shape, she snatched the handset off the cradle and sat among her tumbled bedclothes, the buzzing receiver in her hands.

"Think," she muttered to herself. "Think!"

Cruz. Her mind formed the thought, and she knew it was right. The dial tone had changed to a noisy beeping designed to warn that the phone had been off the hook too long. Ally pressed the button to restore the open line and rapidly punched out his number.

The ringing phone roused Cruz from a sound sleep. It wasn't unusual for the hospital to call him at night, and he reached for the phone before he was fully awake.

"H'lo?"

"Cruz?" said a thin voice he didn't immediately recognize.

"Yeah. Who's this?" He pushed himself up on one elbow and raked his fingers through his hair.

"It's me. It's Ally." He frowned and swung around to sit on the side of the bed.

"Ally?" The tightly strung voice didn't sound like her. "Is something wrong? Are you all right?"

"I—" He heard her draw a deep breath. "I'm okay. I'm sorry to wake you, but I just got an obscene call."

Cruz forced himself to speak calmly. "Those don't mean anything, Ally."

"This wasn't just a crank call," she corrected him. "This was from the person who wrote the note."

There was a moment of silence. "*Dios!* Are you sure?"

"He—he said the same things that were in the note. He said—"

Cruz broke in quickly. "You don't have to say it, Ally. I know what you mean." He raked his hand through his hair again, trying to think clearly. "He called you at home?"

"Yes. I was in bed."

Cruz pushed away the image that brought to mind. She'd be soft and warm from sleep, wearing some kind of bedroom confection in silk and lace. And that pervert had called her.... "Are all your doors and windows locked?"

"I checked them before I came to bed."

"Good. Keep 'em that way. And stay put. I'll be there as soon as I can."

"All right," she whispered.

"Take the phone off the hook, and don't open the door for any reason until I get there!" He banged the phone down and ran for his closet, swearing steadily under his breath.

Ally waited in the living room with the light on, pretending to read a magazine. The peal of the doorbell brought her out of the chair with a bound, but she didn't rush to open it. The bell rang again; then a fist hammered on the panels.

"Ally?" Cruz called. "Ally, come and open this door!"

She blew out her breath in relief. "I'm coming!" She fumbled with the locks, her hands unaccountably clumsy, and when she finally unfastened them all, Cruz flung the door open. He dragged her into his arms to kiss her with all the fear and fury and passion that burned in him. The door crashed against the wall and rebounded to slam closed again, but neither of them noticed.

Ally clung tightly to Cruz, her hands moving over his back, his shoulders, through his hair, as her mouth clung to his with a desperate hunger. She'd held herself together as long as she was alone, but now she could let down her guard. She could kiss him with all her suppressed emotion. Cruz was there and holding her, and she was safe.

As fear faded, passion grew, overwhelming everything else. Cruz moved his mouth from her lips to kiss her cheek, her jaw, the soft skin below her ear, and when he muttered something against her throat, the vibration from his voice ran over her skin like rough velvet. She shivered and pressed more closely against him, uninterested in his words, concerned only with his presence.

"Ally?" He lifted his lips. "Did you hear me?"

"Hmm?" She lifted her head and stared fuzzily at him.

"Did you hear what I said?"

"What you said?"

Her eyes were wide and confused, dilated with passion, her lips soft and moist from his kisses. Desire slid through him to coil in a tight knot low in his belly. When he spoke, his voice was strained.

"I said you'd better tell me about this call you got." He smiled a little as he pulled the loose neckline of her robe closed. "Before I forget all about asking."

Ally blushed and ducked her head. "Okay."

"Can we make a cup of coffee? Instant, maybe?"

"Sure." She led the way into the kitchen. "But I'll never get back to sleep if I drink coffee at this time of night."

"Would you get to sleep anyway?" Cruz took out a jar of instant and two mugs while she put water on to boil.

"Probably not."

"I'll make decaf." He spooned granules into the cups. "Now tell me about this call."

It took a few minutes, but she told him everything she could remember. When she'd finished, the water was boiling. Cruz poured some into the cups and stirred his, considering.

"I think you're right."

"That the threats are serious?" she asked quickly.

"I think it's the letter writer who called."

"But you still don't think I have anything to worry about?"

"I don't think those threats are serious," he replied carefully. "Clay and I talked about it after you left today. We both believe the thief is behind the note and probably this call, too. It looks like he, or she, is trying to scare you."

"Well, he or she is doing a good job!" she snapped. She shoved her mug onto the counter, and coffee slopped on the tile. "I keep telling myself I won't be scared, I *won't* let this creep scare me—but I'm scared. When I heard that voice on the phone, I was scared to death! And it makes me furious! If I let him scare me, I'm letting him win!"

"Ally, sweetheart, I understand how you feel." He pulled her into his arms and held her lightly, stroking her back soothingly. "I'm mad, too." He murmured that bit of heroic understatement into her hair. "But we're going to get this guy. We're *going to*. You and me and Clay Williams and all his cops are going to get this guy and send him to jail."

She let out a long, shaky breath. "If it was just the obscene stuff, I don't think I'd feel this way. But being threatened, even if Clay doesn't think it's serious—"

"I know it's scary, but nothing is going to happen to you, Allison. I promise you that." The brave words were meant to reassure her—and himself. "I won't let it happen."

She touched his face lightly. His lips were set in a firm line, and her mouth curved in a small, indulgent smile. "Is that a promise?"

He blinked, startled, and then he smiled, too. "Promise." He looked into her face and leaned closer. Ally tipped her head back, inviting his kiss, but he pulled back, stiffening his shoulders and dropping his arms. He turned away to refill his cup. "Do you want more coffee?"

"No, thank you." She picked up her cup again. "I've still got some." She glanced at the wall clock and whistled under her breath.

"What is it?" Cruz turned around, stirring his second cup.

"The time. I didn't realize how late it was."

"You ought to go back to bed. You can get a couple more hours' sleep."

She laughed under her breath. "As if I could get to sleep!"

"You can." He took her cup from her hand, set it beside his in the sink and took her arm. "Come on."

"Come where?" she asked as he pulled her through the living room and started up the stairs. "Cruz, what are you doing?"

"Taking you to bed."

"What?" She stopped short on the third step.

He stopped a step above her and turned around, smiling. "That's not what I mean." He looked her up and down very slowly. "Not that I don't like the idea."

"Cruz!" Ally dropped her head, blushing.

"Come on." He started upstairs again, pulling her along in his wake. "You're so easy to tease, it's ridiculous."

"If you were a gentleman," she said starchily, "you wouldn't bring it up."

"I'm not." In her bedroom he switched on a lamp, then pushed her into the adjoining bath. "My mother tried to make a gentleman out of me, but it didn't work. Brush your teeth."

"Yes, Your Highness." She stuck out her tongue at him, then closed the bathroom door before he could retaliate.

Smiling, Cruz turned from the closed door and looked around him. Her room was like her, graceful and pretty and utterly feminine. It was decorated in floral prints in shades of mauve and soft green, from the delicately patterned wallpaper to the quilt on the graceful cherrywood bed. The matching armoire and nightstands stood on a thick cream carpet. The room was as different from his Spartan apartment as night from day.

The only chair in the room was a woman's piece, a fragile chaise longue by the window upholstered in silky pink. He brushed his fingertips over the fabric and felt the slight roughness that meant it was real silk. He could picture Ally lying back on this dainty chaise, her hair fanned across the silk, reading a novel and eating bonbons like an eighteenth-century aristocrat waiting for her lover.

Waiting for him. Cruz felt a little out of place in this room, but in her romantic novel he'd be the lover, a pirate perhaps, climbing a trellis to the balcony window for an assignation with the lonely and beautiful lady of the manor.

He moved around the room, lifting a porcelain perfume flask, then replacing it carefully amid the feminine clutter atop her vanity table. He knew without being told that no other man had entered this boudoir.

He knew he was the only man ever to make love to her. Cruz wasn't a monk, but he had been too busy working and studying to pursue a career as a Don Juan. He had never made love to a virgin before Allison, and he was surprised to find that it made a difference to his feelings. He was the only man she had ever known; he had made her his in that act of love and passion.

His. On the deepest, most fundamental level, she was his. He was responsible for her; he had to protect her and care for her. Despite her determination to remain independent, she needed someone now. She needed him. He had deliberately minimized his fears for her safety and his rage at her unseen tormentor. She needed his calm reassurance, and though he was sick with fear for her safety, he would not let her see it.

His chance would come. The vermin who'd done this to her would be captured soon. All Cruz wanted was a few moments alone with him. Just a few minutes. Then the police were welcome to what was left. It was a satisfying thought.

Ally walked out of the bath and stopped short at the sight of Cruz's face. He was standing by her vanity table, looking at her perfume bottles and smiling a thin-lipped smile that sent a chill down her spine.

"Cruz?" He blinked, and the grim menace left his face. "Are you all right?"

He turned to her with an easy grin. "Isn't that supposed to be my line?"

Ally shrugged. "You had a strange expression on your face. I thought something was wrong."

"A stray thought, that's all." He looked her over. "Are you ready to sleep?"

"Yes, I am, and don't you dare try to tuck me in. I have to let you out and lock up after you, anyway."

He half smiled. "I'm not leaving."

She froze in the act of tying her robe. Her mouth opened, then closed. "Oh."

His smile widened a fraction. "It's practically morning, anyway. By the time I drove home it'd be time to get up, so I might as well stay here. You won't be so scared, I won't worry about you, and if we're lucky, we both might get a little sleep."

Too relieved to be shy, she watched him turn down the comforter and pull back the sheet.

"Come on, get in."

Her shyness returned. She bent her head as she untied her warm terry-cloth robe and slipped it off. She wore a sleeveless summer nightgown, cotton batiste with cutwork across the bodice and around the scooped neckline. It was almost prim, but knowing Cruz was watching her and remembering, she felt as if it were transparent.

He held the sheet for her as she got into bed, and since she wouldn't look at his face, she looked at his hands. They were tanned and strong, very male hands, holding floral sprigged sheets. There was something exciting about that contrast, and Ally could feel a blush heating her cheeks.

Cruz tucked the covers warmly around her, caring for her as she imagined a father would, even though she'd never had a father who'd cared. Cruz would be a good father someday; he knew how to care. She bit her lip against the pain. Cruz would know how to be a father, but she had no idea how to be a mother. She wouldn't know where to start. She loved him, she had made love to him, but she was the wrong woman for him.

"Ally." Cruz turned her face to him with a gentle fingertip. There was warm concern in his dark eyes when he looked at her, but she knew he'd misinterpreted her distress. He kissed her forehead and lowered her gently against the pillows.

He switched off the bedside lamp, but the glow from the hallway outside still dimly illuminated the room. The mattress dipped as he sat on the side of the bed.

"Cruz, what are you doing?"

"Taking off my shoes." She heard one thud to the floor. "And my shirt." There were soft rustles and quiet movements, and then he pulled back the covers again. "Come here."

He slid into the bed beside her, and Ally turned into his arms as if they slept that way every night.

Cruz settled her comfortably with her head pillowed against his chest. His chest rose and fell with his even breathing, his heart thumped a steady lullaby beneath her ear, and she breathed the scent of his skin mingling with the fragrance of the lilac sachet she kept tucked in her linen closet.

"Comfortable?" His voice was a rumble under her ear.

"Mm-hmm." She nodded, her cheek brushing over soft hair. Lying in his arms like this, she felt more secure than she'd ever been in her life. As a child she'd known there was no one to comfort her in the night, so she'd pulled the covers over her head and waited for dawn to push back the terrors of the dark. She'd never known what it was to be protected, comforted, secure, and until Cruz had pulled her into his arms, she hadn't known that was what she needed tonight.

"Go to sleep."

In his arms, warm and safe and secure, she slept.

Long after her breathing had deepened and slowed, Cruz lay with his face against her hair, his eyes open, watching the patterns of light and shadow on the ceiling.

Clay Williams got up early when he had to, but he didn't have to like it. He slouched in his chair, scowling at the pre-dawn murk outside his dirty office window and sipping from the Styrofoam cup of police-station coffee he held. It was strong, the way he liked it. With the coffee percolating through his system, he turned and focused his narrowed gaze on the two people awaiting his verdict.

"Your midnight caller said the same things that were in the letter?"

Ally nodded. "In almost the same words." Cruz gave her hand a comforting squeeze, and she smiled quickly at him. She could feel warmth flowing through her from their clasped hands.

"I think your guess is right," Clay said to Cruz. "It sounds as though our drug thief is responsible."

"What should I do?" Ally asked.

"Nothing unusual. Pay attention to what's going on around you and act as if you never saw that note. The thief can't be sure you found it. If he thinks you didn't see it, he may be frustrated enough to tip his hand."

"But what about the phone call? He'll know I got that."

"Yeah, but if you don't react, that takes the wind out of his sails." He paused and drank his coffee to the dregs.

Watching him, Ally shuddered. She'd tasted some of that mud and set it aside.

"You said 'he,'" Clay went on. "Was it a man who called you last night?"

"The voice was muffled, like there was a cloth over the phone. I can't be sure if it was a man or a woman, but I seem to think of this person as a man."

Clay nodded. "Since you can't tell if it's a man or a woman, we'll assume it could be either. Don't tell anyone about that phone call. Not a word. We'll see if we can't push our drug-stealing friend into making a mistake.''

''Okay.'' Ally looked up at Clay, her jaw set. ''I don't like being threatened, and I don't like being framed. I want this guy to get what he, or she, deserves.''

''He—or she—will. I think the threats mean the thief is getting worried. I want him to worry. That's when he'll make a mistake, and we'll have him.'' He leaned forward, and his dry smile held real warmth this time. ''If I thought there was any danger to you, Ally, I'd put a guard on you.''

Later that morning they arrived at the hospital separately. Ally concentrated on acting normal, but she was primed and ready for action. She waited for someone to mention letters or phone calls, waited for *something* to happen, and when absolutely nothing happened that day or the next, irritation began to take the place of fear and nervous anticipation.

''It's driving me nuts!'' she muttered to Stacy at suppertime on the third day. ''I'm waiting for the other shoe to drop—and it won't!''

They were in a remote corner of the cafeteria, having supper in the brief lull before Ally went back to work. She was on call that night and Stacy had a class to teach at seven, so the meal was a hasty one.

''I would think,'' Stacy said around a bite of something the cafeteria had optimistically called Chicken Supreme, ''that you'd be happy to be left alone, considering what the note and the phone call said.''

''I know.'' Ally stared glumly at the bowl of her usual extra-hot chili with peppers. ''It's the waiting that's getting to me.''

''That's understandable, but don't buy trouble. I'd be a lot happier if nothing else happened at all.''

''I'll only be happy when it's over.'' Ally sighed. ''That's all I want.''

''I want you to be safe! And I don't like the idea of you playing detective. You're a *doctor*, for heaven's sake. Speaking of which, who's on call with you tonight?''

"Somebody named Millsap from the medicine department. Do you know who it is?"

"If it's Jack Millsap, you'll be all right. He's third-year, and he's a nice guy. He's built like a battleship, too."

"If I have to work all night, it's nice to know I'll be working with a guy who's not only nice but also bigger than the patients."

"I don't envy you. At least I get to go home and sleep after I teach."

"Think of me when you're tucked in bed and I'm still up to my—" She was interrupted by the insistent beeping of her pager. She pressed the button that silenced the signal and rose. "So much for peace and quiet. Want my dessert?"

"Thanks." Stacy took the cupcake from Ally's tray. "I'll save this for my break. Have a quiet night!"

The page was STAT, so Ally took a shortcut through one of the oldest and seldom-used underground tunnels. Earthquake activity had cracked the wall in one spot, and the floor was damp. It was dank and cold and creepy, and she was reminded anew of why so few people came this way. She quickened her pace.

She was halfway to the end when she heard running footsteps behind her. The runner was out of sight around a bend in the tunnel, but her uneasiness blossomed into the beginnings of fear.

The unseen runner was moving fast, footfalls and the sound of rapid breathing echoing hollowly through the concrete tube. Ally hesitated, then quickened her pace toward the ER, but it was already too late.

The pounding feet, the labored breathing were close, then closer, and then they burst around the corner. With escape impossible, Ally turned to face her pursuer.

She saw a blur, a flashing glimpse of a white lab coat and an upraised arm as it struck out at her. There was a blinding flash of light and pain, and then there was nothing at all.

Chapter 13

Cruz stopped just inside the cafeteria doors and scanned the room.

"Excuse me," said a nurse wearing a protective gown over her greens.

Cruz stepped out of her way with a quick apology and resumed his survey of the room. Stacy Alexander was sitting in a far corner. She looked up as he neared.

"Hello, Cruz." Her smile lit up her face. "You're here late."

He greeted her and took a chair. "I have a reason."

She eyed him curiously, her smile teasing. "Would that reason, by any chance, be Allison Schuyler?"

Cruz's smile was rueful. "Since she's on call tonight, I'm going to stick around. I thought she might be here."

"She was, until about two minutes ago. She got beeped."

"So she's back at work?"

"She headed for the ER. Would you like her cupcake? She didn't get to eat it."

"A cupcake again? Did she at least get to eat—"

"Dr. Schuyler," a tinny voice blared from a speaker above their heads. "Dr. Allison Schuyler to the Emergency Department. Dr. Schuyler to the Emergency Department."

"That's funny." Stacy frowned. "She's had time to get to the ER by now."

"How long ago did she leave?"

"Five minutes or so. Long enough to walk over there." Stacy shrugged. "Maybe she went to her locker."

"Maybe." Cruz took a bite of the cupcake and smiled at Stacy. "Why are you here late? Big night in the library?"

"Big night in class. I teach a course in Medical Library practice at City College at seven."

"You do a lot of teaching, don't you?"

"I teach a couple of classes a year. I like it."

"I do, too." He glanced at the clock on the wall. "Do you think Ally's there yet?"

"She must be."

"Dr. Allison Schuyler," the loudspeaker contradicted. "Dr. Schuyler to the ER, STAT."

Cruz met Stacy's eyes. "She should be there by now."

"Yeah. Even if she stopped somewhere on the way." Stacy frowned at her watch. "It's been ten minutes."

"Something's wrong." There was a hard urgency in his words. Cruz shoved his chair back and picked up Stacy's dinner tray. She grabbed her cane and hurried after him as he strode away.

"Which way did she go?" he demanded as they reached the doors.

"I don't know. She was in a hurry."

"So she might have taken the tunnel." His lips thinned. "She does sometimes, when she's in a hurry. I'll look for her that way. You go through the halls." Stacy started in the direction of the main corridor while Cruz made for the tunnel. "And hurry!" he shouted after her.

Stacy hurried as fast as her cane and her halting gait would allow, cursing her injured leg under her breath.

Cruz simply ran, but he was also swearing under his breath. There could be a logical reason why she was late, but a knowledge that went beyond the five ordinary senses told him that something was wrong.

He dodged past people walking in the halls and nearly ran down a couple of technicians when he rounded a corner by the lab. "Sorry!" he called.

Someone shouted, "Watch where you're going, bud!" from behind him.

Cruz grabbed a handrail to swing himself around the last corner and thundered down the stairs to the tunnel. He took the flight of steps in four reckless strides and sprinted into the tunnel. It was as unpleasant as ever, cold and damp and dim, with half the ceiling lights broken or burned out.

Where is she? The question was a steady refrain in his head. *Where the hell is she?* The first long leg of the tunnel was empty. He turned the corner into the second section and looked ahead of him.

This stretch was as empty as the first, except for a shadow against the wall, halfway along. It looked like a crumpled bundle of some kind, and Cruz raced toward it with sickness rising in the back of his throat.

She had fallen awkwardly and lay slumped against the wall in an impossible position, her legs and arms tangled into unnatural lines. Her face was on the wet cement floor, her hair trailing in a dank puddle. For one endless moment, Cruz thought she was dead.

He flung himself on his knees beside her, swearing and praying in a tortured undertone as he touched her with shaking hands. He pressed his fingertips to her throat and breathed devout thanks when he found a light, rapid pulse. She was breathing, and he turned her over gently. A quick examination showed no broken bones, but she was unconscious, and her hair was matted and sticky with blood. He probed her scalp delicately and found a cut, deep and still bleeding.

He started swearing again as he parted her hair to see how bad it was. It was pointless. He couldn't see anything there in the dark, dirty tunnel, and he certainly couldn't do anything for her. He had to get her to the ER.

He gathered her into his arms, limp as a rag doll, her head lolling against his shoulder. How long? he wondered as he strode through the tunnel as fast as he dared. How long had she been unconscious? How hard had that blow to her head been? Hard enough to cause a concussion? There could be permanent memory loss after a concussion. Hard enough to cause bleeding inside her skull? That kind of injury could be life-threatening. His pace quickened to a half-run.

He kicked the staff entrance to the emergency room open violently, and ten people spun around to see what was going on. There was an instant of frozen surprise as he carried her inside.

"Get me a gurney!" he snapped, and the frozen immobility exploded into a burst of activity. Someone rolled a gurney up, and he laid Ally on it with tender care. The ER team swarmed around her, but Cruz didn't move away.

"Dr. Gallego, you'll have to step back." Cruz looked around at Hank Thomas, one of the ER staff physicians. "We've got to take her to a treatment room."

"Oh. Yeah." Cruz looked down at Ally's face again. It was dirty and frighteningly pale, with the beginnings of an ugly bruise beneath her right eye and blood streaked on her scraped cheek. And it was his fault.

"You'll have to let go of her hand," Dr. Thomas added, gentle amusement underlying his words.

Cruz looked down and was surprised to see that he was gripping Ally's limp hand tightly in his. Reluctantly he released her, and they rolled her away. He stood immobile until the gurney was out of sight, his fist tightly clenched. It was his fault. His fault. His fault.

The words echoed in his brain. Though he'd feared for her safety, he'd minimized the danger when he'd talked to her. He'd stayed at the hospital to watch over her, but he hadn't been there when she'd needed him.

His fault. An image of her bruised, pallid face swam in front of his eyes. His fault she was exposed to danger, his fault she was injured.

"Cruz?" Stacy touched his arm, her face pale and taut with concern. "What happened? All they'll tell me out front is that she's here. Did you find her?"

"I found her." He forced the words past stiff lips.

"Oh, thank God!" She pressed her hand to her mouth. "I looked through all the halls, and she wasn't anywhere."

"She was in the tunnel." Cruz looked at her then, and Stacy caught her breath at the anguish in his eyes. "Lying on the floor. Someone attacked her down there, Stacy, and I was too late to stop it. She's hurt, and it's my fault."

"How badly?" She grabbed his arm. "How badly is she hurt?"

"She has a head wound."

"She's going to be all right, isn't she? *Isn't she?*"

"Her pulse was steady when I found her. I don't think any bones are broken—"

"And she'll be all right?" Stacy whispered. "She's not going to—"

"No!" Cruz snapped. "She's going to be all right!"

It was several moments before Stacy spoke again. "What happened to her?"

"I didn't get there soon enough. She'd been hit over the head. She was unconscious when I found her." His voice shook, and Stacy tightened her grip on his arm.

"Cruz, don't do this to yourself." His muscles were rigid under her hand. "It wasn't something you could have prevented." She looked into his eyes, and saw wide, dilated pupils. He was nearly in shock; he hadn't heard a word she'd said. "Come with me." She spoke quietly and firmly as if to a child. "Come on."

He let her lead him to a seat in the staff lounge. She poured a cup of coffee. "Drink this." He took the cup and held it between his hands, staring into the brown depths. Stacy looked at his anguished face and closed the door.

"Cruz, it wasn't your fault."

He looked up at her, and his face tightened into a mask. "All my residents are my responsibility."

"Of course they are, but that's not the issue here." Stacy sat down in the chair facing his.

Cruz looked at the tall auburn-haired woman who sat with her well-used cane hanging on her chair. She'd known Ally for years, much longer than he had. She loved Ally and was as frightened for her as he was.

"You know." It wasn't a question.

"She's my friend." Stacy smiled a wan smile. "And I'm glad she has someone like you to care about her."

Cruz reached out for her hand, and they waited in silence.

Her skull was shattering into a million pieces.

"Can you hear me, Ally?"

The deep voice was vaguely familiar, speaking soft words that boomed and echoed painfully in her ears. Ally tried to turn toward the voice, then froze as hot lances shot through her head.

"She moved her head," a quiet female voice said.

"That's good, Ally." The male voice spoke again. "You're starting to wake up. Try it again and see if you can open your eyes for me."

With the sound of his voice still thundering in her head, she tried to lift her lids and was mildly surprised to find that she couldn't. The effort was excruciating, but the voice urged her to try again.

She gathered her strength and forced her eyes open a fraction. The overhead light stabbed at her, and nausea rose in her throat with the waves of pain in her skull. She squeezed her eyes closed, oblivious to anything else. When the pain began to ease, she could hear the quiet voice again.

"That's good, Ally. That's great. I know it hurts but it'll get better. We'll try again in a few minutes. Do you know where you are?"

She didn't shake her head; she was learning. She formed a soundless "No" with her lips.

"You're at Memorial. In the ER. You were unconscious when you came in."

The ER? She frowned. Pain must be confusing her. She was supposed to be working in the ER, but she was lying on a hard bed with gentle hands here and there on her body.

Why? She opened her eyes a fraction and saw a blur of light and movement. She raised a hand, reaching for her head. Someone caught the hand and gently lowered it again.

"Don't touch that, okay? You have a bandage on your head." She tried to focus blurry eyes on the speaker's face. "Don't worry," he went on, "we didn't have to shave your hair. We cut a little of it away to put the stitches in, but you can comb the rest over that. It won't show at all."

"Why?" She was surprised that no sound emerged. She moistened her dry lips with the tip of her tongue and tried again. "Why—here?" It was barely a thread of sound, but they heard.

He repeated her question. "Why are you here? You were hurt, Ally. We're trying to find out just how badly."

"What...?" Ally was pleased that the word came out on the first try.

"You don't remember?"

The question was gentle; its impact was not. She closed her eyes again. Remember? She didn't remember anything.

"No," she whispered. "No."

"Don't worry about that. It'll all come back soon enough. Let's try opening your eyes again, okay? I want to see if you can look at me now."

She opened her eyes, and this time she could keep them open. She blinked into the bright lights, forcing herself to wait out the pain. At first she could see nothing but blinding brightness. Then the rest of the room began to swim into view, people standing around her, blurry images that wavered in front of her, mocking her efforts to sort them into separate people.

"That's good." The male voice belonged to a large dark-haired man who bent over her with an ophthalmoscope in his hand. When she brought him into an uncertain focus she saw Hank Thomas, the ER staff physician.

"Hi." Her voice was a raspy whisper.

He looked at her and grinned. "So you know me, Ally? Good. Let me see your pupils." He examined one eye, then the other. "Not so bad," he said when he'd switched off the ophthalmoscope. "I think you have a mild concussion, but

I'll need some X-rays to know exactly what's going on. We're going to clean up your face now. It's not bad, just scraped up a little."

"What happened?" Ally asked.

"You don't remember?"

"No." It was a forlorn little syllable.

"I'll tell you what I can. You were paged to come see a patient down here. When you didn't come, they repeated the page a couple of times." He grinned, and Ally watched with interest as it became two grins, then merged into one again. "We were starting to get annoyed with you for being late when Cruz Gallego carried you in the back door."

"Cruz?" She jerked her head to look for him, then closed her eyes as a wave of pain and dizziness swept over her. When it had passed, she carefully opened her eyes again. Forming the words with great deliberation, she asked, "Where's Cruz?"

"I think he's waiting outside. Do you want to see him?"

"*Yes,*" she replied as emphatically as she could. "Please."

"Sure." He looked at someone on the other side of the little room. "Connie, get Dr. Gallego, would you?"

"Of course."

They'd begun to clean the rest of Ally's bumps and scrapes when the door flew open and Cruz burst in. He stopped short a foot from the treatment table. His stomach muscles clenched in protest as he looked at her. He took the last step and forced himself to smile at her as he spoke.

"Hi," he murmured. "How are you?"

She gave a rusty chuckle and lifted her hand. "I'm okay," she whispered as he took her hand. Her fingers curled trustingly around his. "You brought me?"

"Yes, I brought you here."

"What happened?" Her voice was still soft, but it was steadier than it had been.

"You don't remember?" Cruz asked.

"No."

"Cruz?" Hank Thomas interrupted. "We've got to get the skull X-rays. Can you wait until that's done?"

"Yeah, sure." He looked down at Ally. "You can talk to Clay Williams when they're done, all right?"

"'Kay." She was too tired from the effort of concentrating to protest. Cruz squeezed the limp hand he held in his and felt a slight answering pressure before he tucked her hand beneath the sheet. He could see her exhaustion, and he could imagine the pain in her head. And he knew it was his fault.

Cruz walked out of the room in silence. Stacy was waiting tensely in the hall. "Is she all right?" She caught his arm in a tight grip. "Cruz, is she all right?"

"Yeah." His voice was flat. "She's probably got a concussion. They're taking her down for some skull films. Did you make that call?"

"Mm-hmm. They said they'll send Sergeant Williams over here as soon as they can locate him. He's out in his car somewhere."

"Did they think it would be long?"

Stacy shook her head. "Fifteen or twenty minutes."

In fact Clay arrived twelve minutes later. "How is she?" he demanded without preamble after bursting into the staff lounge. "Well? Is she gonna be all right?"

"Yes, she'll be all right." Cruz waved toward a chair. "Sit down, Clay. Stacy, this is Sergeant Clay Williams. Clay, Stacy Alexander. She's the hospital librarian and a friend of Ally's." The detective greeted Stacy and dropped into a chair, which squeaked beneath his weight. "Ally may have a concussion," Cruz told him. "Beyond that, we don't know."

"When will I be able to talk to her?"

"I don't know. They've taken her up to X-ray, and it'll depend on how she feels after that."

"The sooner I talk to her, the sooner we can circulate a description of the assailant. Right now we're looking, but we don't know who we're looking for."

Cruz and Stacy filled the time by telling Clay everything they knew about what had happened. They gave him the beginning and the end of the story, but only Ally could fill in the gap.

"Cruz?" Vanessa Rice, a nursing supervisor and an instructor at the school of nursing, peered around the door. Her thick, dark hair was caught back with a tortoiseshell clip that accentuated the dramatic streaks of silver at her temples. The three waiting in the lounge rose at her appearance.

"What is it, Van?" Cruz asked tensely.

"Ally's on her way down from Radiology."

"Can I talk to her?" Clay demanded.

Vanessa glanced at him, one elegant eyebrow lifted at his rough tone. "I don't know, sir," she said coolly. "That will depend on her condition. Will you come with me, Doctor?"

He was gone before the other two could even move.

"What do we do now?" Clay asked Stacy.

"We wait. They'll come for us when the doctors are finished with her."

It was ten minutes later that a nurse summoned them to the ER office, which was being loaned to them for privacy. Ally was sitting in a wheelchair, with Cruz standing close beside her, one hand resting on her shoulder, as if he had to touch her to reassure himself that she was all right. Vanessa Rice was watching Ally closely for signs of fatigue.

The agonizing pain in Ally's head had settled down to a steady pounding. Van Rice had told her that would fade gradually over the next week or so, but for now the little man with the big hammer inside her skull was having a great time.

She looked up when Stacy and Clay entered the room, but it took her a moment to focus. "Hi, Stace." She wished her voice had a little more substance to it; she sounded like a wet kitten.

"Oh, Ally!" Tart-tongued, slightly cynical, unemotional Stacy limped across the office, flung her arms around her friend and burst into tears. "Allison Morgan Schuyler, you scared me to death!" When she'd regained some control, she leaned back to look into Ally's face. "Don't you ever scare me that way again!"

"Okay," Ally replied with a watery smile.

When Stacy stepped back, Clay took her place, crouching in front of Ally's wheelchair. "What happened, Ally?"

This was the moment Ally had been dreading. She'd been asked that question three times, and her answer remained the same. "I don't know."

Clay frowned. "You didn't see the person who hit you?"

"I don't know if I did or not." Ally shrugged, carefully, so she wouldn't move her head. "All I remember is having supper with you, Stacy. Aren't you supposed to be teaching?"

"I canceled the class," Stacy told her. "Do you remember anything?"

"I remember eating supper."

"You had chili, and you got a cupcake, but you got paged before you could eat it." Stacy watched Ally's face, willing her to remember. "Do you remember getting the page?"

A page. Ally wanted to remember; she needed to remember. She closed her eyes, concentrating. "I remember the chili," she said a few seconds later. "But after that—nothing."

"Nothing?" Clay looked into Ally's face. "Listen, Ally, can you go through everything you do remember?"

She told him how she'd finished work that afternoon and met Stacy in the cafeteria, eaten her chili and then—

"That's all. There isn't any more until the treatment room. Dr. Thomas was there. He said Cruz brought me in."

Cruz stroked her hair, and Ally looked up as he spoke. "I found you about halfway along the main tunnel."

"So we have to reconstruct the middle of the story," Clay said. "What happened between your bowl of chili and Cruz finding you in the tunnel. Stacy, tell her what you remember, okay?"

"Sure." Stacy recounted the events from the time Ally had been paged until she and Cruz had left the cafeteria to search for her. Ally listened intently, fighting to remember something, anything at all. She failed.

"Nothing?" Clay asked. His voice, rarely gentle, was harsh with frustration. Ally, feeling the same frustration, didn't even notice his tone, but Van did.

"Don't hector her, Sergeant!" Van said sharply. "She has a concussion. Short-term memory loss isn't uncommon after a head injury."

"Posttraumatic amnesia." Ally was glad she could remember *something*.

"Exactly. And badgering her won't help," Van reprimanded him sharply. Clay shot her a startled glance, and Ally almost laughed. Clay Williams wasn't used to being spoken to that way.

"How long will the amnesia last, Van?" she asked, distracting them from further hostilities.

"Anywhere from a few hours to a few weeks. There's no way to tell."

"Until you do remember," Clay said, "we'll go with standard forensic procedure. They took skin scrapings and fiber samples when you were brought in. It's not much, but we'll start the investigation with that. It doesn't look as if you struggled. Someone just conked you on the head and ran away." He scribbled in his notebook, then flipped it closed and stuffed it in his pocket. "You can give a statement when you're feeling better. Right now—" he grinned at her "—you look like you could use some rest."

"That bad, huh?" Ally smiled weakly at him, warmed by the concern in his eyes. "Thanks, Clay." She reached out for his hand and squeezed it briefly. "G'night."

"Night, Ally. Cruz. Stacy." He turned to Van. "Miss Rice," he said carefully.

"Ms. Rice." Her correction had an edge to it, and Ally looked at her in renewed surprise. Easygoing Van was practically hurling darts at Clay.

"Ms. Rice." He laid a subtle emphasis on the title. "Good night."

"Here are your pain pills," Van told Ally, ignoring Clay as he walked out the door. "They're labeled. Bed rest for at least twenty-four hours, and stay out of tunnels!"

"Don't worry," Ally chuckled. "Tunnels don't really appeal to me right now."

Cruz was laughing with her as he rolled her out of the office, but their laughter died quickly. Ally found that it made her head hurt, and Cruz didn't know if he'd ever laugh again.

Chapter 14

"Cruz, I can walk into the house!"

He reached into the car for her. "I'm carrying you, and you're going to shut up and like it."

"I'll shut up, but I'm not gonna like it." She tried to make it a joke, but it came out grumpy.

Cruz slid one arm behind her shoulders, the other beneath her knees, and eased her out of the car. Ally closed her eyes as he carried her from the garage into the house. The drive home hadn't done the pounding in her skull any good, and the accompanying nausea was a nagging counterpoint.

She didn't want to be brave right now, or even polite. She was dizzy and exhausted, and her head hurt abominably, and she wanted to crawl into her bed and stay there until all the awfulness was over. She dropped her head onto his chest and held still. She opened her eyes once, as he started up the stairs, but there was something unpleasantly dizzying about looking down from that perspective. She closed her eyes again.

She didn't look up until Cruz lowered her to her bed.

"You need to rest," he said.

"I've got to get these clothes off." Her skirt was dirty from the tunnel floor, and she plucked it away from her knees.

"Stay put." Cruz pushed her back down. "I'll take care of everything."

Too weary to argue, Ally gave herself up to his care. He stripped the dirty clothes off her passive body and slipped a nightgown over her head with a quiet, nonsexual economy of movement. Ally swallowed the capsules he brought her and was already sliding into sleep when he pulled the bedclothes up to her chin and kissed her lightly on the forehead.

She didn't know how much later it was when she drifted awake. The room was dark except for a wedge of light falling through the half-open door from the hall outside. She wasn't disoriented. She knew where she was, knew that she'd been hit over the head and had awakened in the ER. But everything between the cafeteria and the ER was still a blank.

She tried to relax and go back to sleep, but she was terribly thirsty, her mouth dry, her throat raspy and sore. She had to have a cool drink. She sat up cautiously and swung her legs over the side of the bed. Her head was still pounding, but it seemed to have abated a little. She could feel bruises on her shoulder and hip, and movement hurt, but the need for a drink outweighed the headache.

Moving like an old woman, she made her way to the bathroom and ran a glass of water. She didn't turn on the light, because she wasn't ready to face that blaze of brilliance. The first glass tasted wonderful, but two swallows into the second her stomach rebelled. She poured the rest down the drain and shuffled back to the bedroom.

She was climbing back into bed when she heard soft voices and music. She listened for a moment and recognized it as the television in her guest bedroom.

Bracing herself with a hand on the wall, she walked slowly down the hall and stopped in the doorway. The only light in the room came from an old movie flickering across the television screen. Cruz was slumped in the armchair opposite the bed, fast asleep.

Ally made her careful way over to him and touched his shoulder gently. "Cruz?"

"Huh?" He jerked upright in the chair and stared at her for one uncomprehending moment until he blinked and remembered. "Ally! What are you doing in here?"

"I could ask you the same thing." She swayed dizzily and put a hand on the chair to steady herself.

"Sit down before you fall down." He steered her to the bed, where he sat beside her, a supporting arm around her shoulders. "Are you all right?"

She smiled weakly. "I'm fine, except for the anvil chorus in my head."

"Why did you get up?"

"I was thirsty. I got a drink."

"You should have called me," he remonstrated. "I'd have gotten your drink."

She smiled wryly. "The way my head feels, I'd rather die of thirst than try to shout."

"Ah, querida." He folded her into his arms and kissed her forehead lightly. His voice was low and rough, his accent more pronounced than usual. "I am sorry. I blame myself for what happened to you."

Ally snuggled into his embrace, welcoming the warmth and comfort. He was stroking her back in a rhythmic caress that was marvelously soothing. She turned her head, brushing her cheek against his shirt, breathing the scent of his skin, sensing hard muscle beneath the soft cotton.

"Why should you blame yourself?" she asked in a drowsy murmur. "You didn't have anything to do with this."

"But I did!" He shoved himself off the bed to pace across the room. On the opposite side he stopped and turned to face her, his face dark with inner-directed anger. "It's my fault this happened to you! I should have taken care of you! I should never have let you walk around that hospital alone. I should have seen to it that you were protected!"

"Cruz, this was not your fault," Ally said firmly. "If you want to lay blame, lay it on me for taking that tunnel. It's the perfect place to get mugged. I should have gone through the halls.''

"Yes. You should have." Cruz paced along the prettily papered wall like a caged tiger. "But if I had been with you, you would have been safe, even in the tunnel. I blame myself."

"Well, *I* don't blame you. And I wish you'd give me a little credit. I'm an adult, Cruz, and I'm capable of making my own decisions."

Cruz scowled. "You're capable of making your own decisions, huh? Is that why you have a concussion this evening?"

"I didn't say all my decisions were good ones," Ally snapped. She wasn't sure why he was acting this way, but she didn't care much for this overbearing macho business. "Some of my decisions *aren't* good, Cruz, but they're *my* decisions, and that's what's important."

"A concussion isn't important?"

"Right now it feels pretty important." She touched the lumpy bandage with careful fingers and grimaced.

"You made a bad decision tonight, and now you have the concussion to show for it. I made a bad decision, too. I left you on your own, and this happened." He walked back to sit beside her, an arm around her shoulders to hold her close. "I'm going to make the right decision now."

"And what is that?"

"You must be protected. You *will* be protected."

"How?" she demanded. "By bodyguards? Cruz, I can't work with a bunch of cops following me around."

"You don't need to. Until the thief's caught you're not going to come back to work."

She jerked free of his arm and knelt on the mattress, staring at him. "Of course I'm coming to work!"

"No." His voice was flat. "You're not."

"I am." Her voice was as flat as his. "This is my training you're talking about, Cruz, my education. I'm not going to lose ground just because I happened to go through the tunnel at the wrong time."

"You will not go to the hospital."

"I will go where I damn well want." Her temper was rising, but she tried to keep it under control. The effort made her head pound. "And I resent you trying to tell me what to do."

"I will not allow you to come to the hospital. It's too dangerous."

"You can't stop me." She tried to keep her voice level. "I know the rules, and you can't force me to stay away from Memorial. What bothers me is that you would want to."

"Of course I want to keep you away!" He grabbed her shoulders and shook her slightly. Her head ached abominably. "I want to keep you safe!"

"I can understand that, but—"

"Then you'll stay away."

"No!" She had to close her eyes against a wave of dizziness. She wasn't up to the effort of arguing, but she had to make Cruz understand.

"What good would it do to stay away? This guy knows where to find me. He's put a note in my locker, he's called me on the phone." She flung out a hand, lost her balance and steadied herself on the mattress. "He can find me if he wants to, Cruz. Hiding here won't be any help."

"Going to the hospital won't be any help, either. At least you can be guarded here!"

"You mean I can be imprisoned!" Ally shoved herself off the bed and went over to look out the window. The cul-de-sac outside was deserted and silent in the glow of the streetlights. "Cruz, I've had enough problems because of this creep. I won't let him run my life for me." She turned to him, her face set and determined. "I'm going back to work."

"I can't let you do that!" He got off the bed as he spoke, caught her shoulders and pulled her roughly close. "You're my woman, and I can't let my woman walk back into danger!"

Ally gaped at him, shocked into silence. His woman? The claim of possession echoed in her ears. His woman? That wasn't possible. It was too much too soon.

"I'm not anybody's woman," she retorted, jangled nerves and insecurity making her words sharp and hard. "I don't belong to you, Cruz."

If possible, Cruz was even more stunned by his admission than she was. He had no idea where the words had come from, but they were true. He wasn't much happier about that than Ally seemed to be, but it was true. She was his.

"I don't want to own you, Allison," he said quietly. "I just want to keep you safe."

"I know you do." Her eyes were grave. "But I can't let you make me a prisoner, even to protect me."

She spoke with more regret than anger, and when Cruz reached out to her again, she went gratefully into his arms. He steered her to the bed and sat down with her across his lap. She turned her cheek into his shoulder and winced as her bruised cheekbone met hard muscle. Cruz lifted her face and traced a fingertip along the edge of the bruise, which was blossoming into a rainbow of livid colors. He brushed her hair off her face, taking care not to disturb her bandage.

"I worry about you," he murmured into her hair. "I want to keep you safe."

"Mm-hmm." Ally knew that, but all she wanted right now was to be held and comforted. She was warm and protected, his arms enclosing her in a safe circle. He stroked her hair in a slow, soothing rhythm, and if she'd been a cat, she would have purred.

She was glad that Cruz had accepted her decision to keep working. She didn't want to fight with him.

"I want to take care of you," he said softly, his breath ruffling the tendrils around her ear.

Ally felt the familiar melting begin. His slightest touch could start that reaction in her, and with the kind of fuzzy interest that fatigue and injury can produce she decided that there must be some scientific reason for it. Chemistry, wasn't that what they called it?

"I want to take care of you," Cruz repeated softly. "I want to marry you."

It took several seconds for that to register. When it did, the warmth and comfort drained out of Ally, leaving icy emptiness behind. She straightened and slid carefully off Cruz's lap.

"What did you say?"

"I said I want to marry you."

She looked down at her hands. "Why?"

"What do you mean, 'Why?'"

"Why are you asking me to marry you now?" She looked up into his face, her eyes dark with pain. "Is it because you want to protect me and you think if I'm your wife I'll do what you tell me to?"

"What are you talking about?"

"Cruz, it's obvious! You've spent the last hour trying to make me stay away from the hospital, and now you say you want to marry me. What am I supposed to think?"

"You're supposed to think I want to marry you!" Cruz reached for her, but she moved away. "What's so terrible about that?"

"Your reason! You're not supposed to marry somebody because you can't lock them in a closet."

"I *would* lock you in a closet if I thought it would do any good!" He rose to his feet and stood glowering down at her, his eyes black with emotion. He knew better than to touch her. If he did, the anger he could barely control would flame into a passion he would be helpless to contain. "But you'd probably hack a hole in the wall with a nail file to escape and then report me to the police. I don't want to cage you, Allison. I love you, and I want to protect you."

Ally shook her head sadly. "That isn't love, Cruz, that's possessiveness. Maybe you think you love me, but I have to tell you it would be a big mistake—for both of us."

He moved toward her, an involuntary movement she didn't think he was even aware of, any more than he was aware that his right hand lifted, reaching for her. She stepped back, steadying herself when the movement caused a moment's vertigo. His hand dropped back to his side.

"I'm going back to bed," she said quietly. "Which pills do I need to take?"

He hesitated for a moment before he answered. "The an-
algesics. They're in your bath, by the sink. Take two."

He held her gaze for several long seconds. There were
messages in his eyes that she didn't want to see, messages she
refused to read, but she couldn't make herself look away.
She forced herself to take a step back, but her gaze was still
tied to his.

"It wouldn't be a mistake, Allison." His voice was little
more than a whisper, like velvet on smooth skin. "It would
never be a mistake."

He looked away, and only then could she escape to the
safety of her empty bed.

Ally stared at the ceiling for several minutes, then rolled
over and groped for her clock. It was a few minutes past
eight in the morning. Someone with a severe concussion
would no doubt still be asleep, so she must not be as badly
injured as everyone had feared. The pounding in her head
had settled into a muted background rhythm, and she felt
infinitely better.

She maneuvered herself carefully upright, anxious not to
undo any of the night's progress, and assessed her condition. Headache: about the same. Vertigo: gone. Nausea:
gone so completely that she was actually hungry—for eggs.
Eggs, gently scrambled, and crisp bacon and whole wheat
toast and some thick tomato slices—Her stomach rumbled,
and she levered herself to her feet.

She tiptoed past the guest room, pausing only for a moment to listen outside the door. She heard nothing and as-
sumed Cruz was still sleeping. She'd wake him later. She
needed some time alone to think, anyway.

She moved quietly around the kitchen, scooping coffee
into the coffee maker, squeezing oranges and slicing toma-
toes before she began on the rest of the meal. As she
worked, she thought about things, and she reached the only
conclusion possible. Cruz wasn't going to like it, but he'd
have to live with it.

The bacon had begun to sizzle when he appeared. Ally
turned to take the eggs from the refrigerator and saw him

standing in the doorway, one shoulder against the doorframe, watching her. Her heart lurched against her ribs, then settled into a heavy, pounding beat.

"Good morning." She was pleased to find that her voice only shook a little. "How do you like your eggs?"

"Scrambled," he replied. "Do you have any salsa?"

"Sure. Do you want red or green?"

"Which is hotter?"

"The red's medium, the green's hot."

"I'll take the green."

"Okay." Ally took out eggs, milk and the bottle of salsa, then closed the refrigerator door with a swing of her hip. After all that had happened in the last twenty-four hours there was something surreal about standing in the kitchen discussing the relative merits of salsas. Perhaps, like her, Cruz wasn't eager to confront anything else.

She broke eggs into a bowl, added a splash of milk and began beating them with a fork.

"How do you feel?" She hadn't heard him move, but Cruz spoke from directly behind her.

She jumped, splashing a yellow streak of beaten egg onto the countertop. "I feel a lot better." He was too close, and she edged away from him, reaching for a cloth to wipe up the spill.

"How's the headache?"

"It's there, but not nearly so bad. I can deal with it."

"Nausea? Vertigo?"

"Both gone." She turned her back and took the bowl of eggs to the stove.

"Do you have an ophthalmoscope in the house?"

"Yeah. My black bag's in the den, off the living room."

While he went to get it, she put the bacon on a plate to drain and began heating another pan for the eggs. She was about to pour them in when he returned.

"Turn around."

She stared at his hair as he peered into her eyes, searching for evidence of further injury. Apparently she passed the test, because he said nothing until he'd clicked the ophthalmoscope off and replaced it in its case.

"What's the verdict?" She poured the eggs and listened to them sizzle.

"Your pupils are equal in size and reactive to light, and your retinas look fine."

"So I'm all right?" She concentrated on the eggs.

"That depends." His voice was low and grim. "What do you remember about what happened?"

She met his steady gaze. "The same as last night."

"Then you're not in the perfect shape you'd like to be in, are you?"

She wondered if the anger in his face was directed at her or at himself. She turned back to the stove, poking absently at the eggs. "I looked up posttraumatic amnesia this morning. It can persist for a few hours or a few weeks, and the length of time is not indicative of the severity of the injury. I don't remember yet, Cruz, but I will."

"That's what I'm afraid of."

"Of me remembering?" She spun around. "Why? I'd think you'd want me to remember."

"But when you remember—then what?" Cruz demanded harshly. "What's going to happen when you remember who attacked you in that tunnel?"

"I'm going to tell Clay Williams and he'll catch whoever it is and put them in jail." She studied his thunderous face and frowned, puzzled. "What else?"

"'What else' is that the the person who attacked you, the person you may have recognized, will try to get to you and shut you up before you can talk to Clay."

"You sound like a bad detective story." Ally turned back to the eggs, which had cooked past the stage of palatability. She shoveled them onto a plate anyway. She'd eat them, dry as they were. With brisk efficiency she put everything on the table, then sat down and began filling her plate without waiting for Cruz. "That stuff doesn't happen in real life."

"And people don't get mugged in hospital tunnels in 'real life,' either, do they?" he asked, heavily sarcastic. "Face it, Ally. Whoever this guy is, he wants you out of his way. He's tried once, so what's to stop him from trying again?"

"The police, I assume." She glanced at him, then away. "I know what you're getting at."

"What's that?"

"This is another way to persuade me to hide. You can't order me away from the hospital, and marrying me so you can force me to stay hidden away won't work, so now you're trying to scare me away." She laid her fork down and pushed her plate away. "It isn't going to work, Cruz. I know you mean well." She brushed aside the protests he wanted to make. "But the road to hell is paved with good intentions."

He rose when she did. "I did not ask you to marry me because I wanted to manipulate you." He bit the words out with steel-sharp precision. "I asked you—"

"No! I don't want to know! It doesn't matter why!"

"The hell it doesn't!" He caught her elbow and jerked her around to face him, and the speed made her dizzy. "I love you, Allison! That's the most important thing of all!"

"No, it's not!" She struggled against his grasp. She didn't want to say these things—it hurt to say them—but they had to be said. He had to understand. "There are a lot of other things that matter, like families and personalities and expectations. You may think you love me, Cruz, but you also think marriage would be a way to protect me. It wouldn't be, and marriage wouldn't work between us, anyway."

"How do you know that?" His fingers tightened on her arms. "How can you possibly know that?"

"Because it just wouldn't, Cruz. I *know* that." She reached up to touch his hands. "You're hurting me."

"I'm—oh! I'm sorry!" He lifted his hands away. "Ally, you don't know what you're saying."

"Don't tell me that!" She backed away, out of his reach. "Don't patronize me. I know exactly what I'm saying, Cruz, and I mean it! Stop trying to push me around. Just stop it! I told you before, I'm an adult, and I wish you respected me enough to treat me like one." She stared at him for a moment, her eyes wide with anger and hurt; then she turned on her heel. "I'm going to the hospital," she announced, and stalked out of the room.

She was surprised that he didn't follow her to her room and argue with her; she wasn't surprised to find him waiting in the living room when she came down again. She was dressed and primed for battle.

"I'm going, Cruz. Please don't try to stop me."

"I'm not going to stop you. We have to go see Clay at the station before we do anything else, and anyway, your car is still at the hospital."

"Oh." She deflated like a spent balloon. "Thank you."

"Don't thank me." His smile was more of a grimace. "Whatever you think of me, I'm not going to leave you stranded without a car."

Whatever she thought of him. She couldn't tell him that she admired him for his dedication and his talent as a physician. She couldn't tell him that she enjoyed his sense of humor, his quick intelligence, that she respected his integrity. She couldn't tell him that she loved his tenderness, his strength, his passion, or that she was hopelessly, helplessly, irrevocably in love with him.

Biting her lip, Ally followed him out the door.

Chapter 15

Cruz had telephoned from Ally's house, and Clay was waiting for them at the station. Cruz was coldly, furiously angry, and he escorted her into Clay's dingy office with icy courtesy. From the speculative way Clay watched them, she could tell that he sensed the tension between them.

The last time they had been in this office, Cruz had sat close beside her, holding her hand. He sat several feet away this time, his arms folded across his chest, his face closed and unreadable.

"I want you to talk to people," Clay was telling her. "Talk to everybody. Be sure to tell them that you don't remember anything about the attack."

"You want me to tell people I have amnesia?"

"For the time being, yes." He shifted his position on the edge of the desk, watching her closely. "If your memory does return, don't say anything about it. You can tell Cruz or me, no one else."

"But I ought to tell the people who treated me."

"Just tell Cruz. He can do whatever needs to be done, but you are to tell *no one else*. Your safety could depend on it."

He studied her for a moment. "There was another theft yesterday."

"There was?" She looked at Cruz, and he nodded.

"It happened sometime after the afternoon count."

"The person who attacked you," Clay said, "was probably running from the clinic, maybe even carrying the drugs. Ally, you'll be a lot safer if everyone knows you have amnesia."

"All right," she agreed. "I'll make sure everybody knows I don't remember a thing. Is there anything else?"

Clay nodded. "Two undercover officers will work in the clinic until this is over. They'll pose as medical students, with you assigned to 'supervise' them."

Ally mulled that over for a moment. "That might not be so easy, Clay."

He exchanged a glance with Cruz and grinned. "One is a paramedic, the other was a biology major in college. They both swear they're not squeamish."

"I talked to Clay about this," Cruz said, unsmiling. "We'll say they're second-year students getting an early look at clinical training. It will work."

"Will they carry guns?"

"Yes," said Clay.

"It won't work," she said, shuddering.

"It will," Cruz promised grimly. "I'll make it work."

Ally glanced at him, then dropped her gaze. As angry as he was about her insistence on returning to the hospital, as hurt and furious as he was about her refusal to marry him, he was still determined to protect her. She couldn't deny that she felt better knowing that he was watching over her.

When she saw the two undercover officers, she began to believe Clay's plan might actually work. In their early twenties, they were fresh-faced and intelligent, and when they were dressed in casual clothes, with white jackets and medical school name badges, they were remarkably convincing.

Anne was about Ally's own height, slim and wiry, with dark, pixie-cut hair and freckles sprinkled across a gamine's face. Chris was taller, five feet nine or so, stocky and strongly built, with curly reddish-brown hair and a blunt-featured, friendly face. Neither of them resembled Ally's mental image of the cold-eyed cop.

"I thought you were going to carry guns," she said after meeting them.

Anne smiled and turned her back. Tucked into the waistband of her skirt, beneath a heavy fisherman's sweater and the medical student's white jacket, was a leather holster containing a small, deadly-looking gun.

"Oh." Ally's eyes widened. She turned to Chris.

He grinned and turned in a circle, arms raised. "Can you see it?" Ally saw nothing resembling a weapon, but it was there, in his boot, concealed by his trousers.

"You win." Ally turned back to Cruz and Clay. "They could pass for medical students anywhere."

"As long as we don't have to answer any questions," Anne pointed out with a grin.

"Don't worry. We'll call this an orientation or something, and you can ask the questions."

Cruz pulled into a parking space near the rear of the hospital, but didn't kill the engine. "I don't want you to go in there. I still don't think it's safe for you."

His gaze was fixed on her face, dark and dangerous. Ally shivered in spite of herself. She'd seen the dangerous edge in Cruz before, but now he was making no attempt to conceal it. He looked as hard as any of the criminals Clay Williams dealt with, and twice as formidable.

"I'm going, Cruz. The police will be watching me." She spoke as firmly as she could, but her voice was high and nervous.

"I could stop you, but I won't—this time."

"Don't threaten me."

"It's not a threat, Allison, it's the truth." His voice was soft and cold, his eyes hard. "You say you're not my woman, that you don't want to marry me. You say I can't force you to keep yourself safe—"

"Cruz, I'm sorry I was so blunt, but—"

He cut short her little speech. "It's all lies. You can tell yourself that all you want, but you're lying, Allison. You're lying to yourself."

"I'm going in!" She jerked the door handle, but Cruz caught her arm and pulled her back. "Let me go!" In sudden panic she struck out at him, but he caught her other hand, immobilizing her with infuriating ease. "Let me *go*!"

"When I have made my point." His voice was caressingly soft, and his angry eyes were no longer cold. Ally began to shiver. "You can tell yourself you are not my woman, Allison, but when you do, I want you to remember something." He drew her closer with a steady pressure. "I want you to remember this."

His mouth closed over hers, hard and hot and demanding. All the love and longing she had tried so desperately to suppress came surging to the surface, making a mockery of her cool facade.

He didn't need to embrace her or caress her body. Touching her only with his mouth and hands, he seduced her. And when her surrender was complete, when her body was straining toward him in the awkward confines of the car, he pushed her away. He half smiled as he studied her face.

"Remember," he said very softly.

For a moment Ally sat stunned, staring at him. Then, in a burst of frantic movement, she flung the door open and scrambled out. Half running, she threaded her way between the cars, her fist pressed to her throbbing lips.

Fighting for composure, she ducked into a ladies' room. A few minutes alone, some cold water on her face and a touch of powder, and she could blame her wan appearance on her concussion. The ugly purple bruise on her cheekbone and temple gave credence to the claim and drew attention from the bleakness in her eyes.

She didn't blame Cruz for his anger. The things he said were true. It was just that two people as mismatched as they were could never have a workable relationship, much less a successful marriage. Eventually Cruz would realize that.

She'd done the right thing in refusing to consider marriage. So why did she feel this empty desolation, as if she'd thrown away something real and beautiful and rare?

She walked into the clinic shortly before the afternoon appointments began and was greeted with surprise, sympathy and the perfect opportunity to put Clay Williams's plan into effect. Most of the staff was gathered near the nurses' station, gossiping about her attack. She had an audience, ready and eager for her tale.

She didn't have to dissemble, either. She told the simple truth, that she remembered nothing of the attack or the events immediately surrounding it.

"That's terrible!" Barbara Clark touched her shoulder lightly in sympathy. "When do they think you'll get your memory back?"

"They can't say. It might be days or weeks, or it might never come back."

"Never? How awful!"

"Oh, I don't know." Ally grinned. "I'm not that anxious to remember being hit over the head."

"Do they think you'll remember everything sooner or later?" Charlie Parsons wanted to know.

"Maybe. There's no way to tell how much I'll remember. There's no telling how much I actually saw, either. I may not even have seen who hit me."

"But you won't know that until you get your memory back," Charlie concluded for her.

"And I may never remember, so I may never know." Ally shrugged. "They told me not to worry about it, since that won't bring it back any sooner."

"Sounds like a good idea," Barbara commented. "Just take things easy and don't worry about anything."

"I intend to." Ally smiled as Barbara moved away to get ready for the afternoon appointments.

"You're not going to work this afternoon, are you, Ally?" Karen Willis frowned in concern.

"I'm going to catch up on my charting. Just think—no more nasty notes from Medical Records about my unfinished charts!"

Cruz watched her from across the lobby. She was doing exactly what Clay had asked; everything she'd done and said had been perfect. He was probably the only one who could see the pain in her eyes.

He'd watched her run from his car, run from him. "Damn!" he muttered under his breath, flexing his right hand. It was bruised, from slamming his palm against the steering wheel. The anger and passion that fueled him out in the parking lot had drained away, leaving behind only emptiness.

He was a fool. Instead of talking reasonably with her, he'd come on like a caveman, browbeating her, forcing a kiss on her and scaring her half to death. He was furious that she was putting herself in danger this way, but that was no excuse for what he'd done. His temper had gotten the better of him, and instead of making the situation better, he'd made it infinitely worse.

His first mistake had been to demand that she marry him. She'd been shocked by that, and no wonder. He had given her no soft words, no gentleness, only that blunt demand. What woman in her right mind would put up with that?

The fact was that Cruz had been as shocked as she had to hear his lips form those words. He hadn't planned to ask her to marry him. He had no right to ask someone like her to marry him.

He knew he couldn't expect her to commit her life to his. She was accustomed to luxury and grace and comfort. All he could offer her was a tiny apartment, years of meager living as he repaid his college and medical school loans, and his love.

Love was a wonderful thing, but it didn't pay the bills. Cruz had spent too many years starving in a garret to delude himself that it was romantic. Poverty wasn't romantic; it was cold and unforgiving, and it could grind people down, drive love away, drive people apart. He'd seen it happen to others, and he wouldn't allow it to happen to Allison.

In five or ten years his debts would be paid, he would have his career established, and then he would be able to buy a house, make a home for a bride. Then, and only then, would he have the right to ask a woman like Allison Schuyler to marry him.

Of course she had refused him. He might have been a fool to propose, but she would have been a greater fool to accept.

She finished her conversation, and Cruz led the two undercover officers over to "meet" her.

"I have something else for you to do today."

Ally jumped when Cruz spoke from close behind her. She couldn't help it, and she took a deep breath before she turned to face him, smiling. Ally greeted Anne and Chris politely as Cruz explained that she was to introduce the two "medical students" to the clinic and its work.

When Cruz left them, she led the officers around the clinic, playing her part while she familiarized them with the physical layout. When she'd finished the tour she led them to the staff lounge.

"Do you feel all right, Ally?" Anne asked.

"I'm all right. Why do you ask?"

"You've been rubbing your temple, and I wondered if your head was bothering you."

"Oh." Ally lowered her hand. She hadn't realized what she'd been doing. "My head aches a little, but it'll get better." She turned back to the lounge door. "I'm going to get some charts, and I'll bring you each a copy of the orientation manual. It's got a floor plan and some other information you might be able to use."

"Should one of us go with you?" Chris asked.

She shook her head. "That would look funny. The chart room is off-limits to everybody but God. I'll just be a minute, and you can see me through the doorway."

Chris agreed, though reluctantly, and Ally quickly crossed the short distance to the desk. There was no one there, so she went into the chart room to pull her own records.

"What are you doing in here?"

Ally didn't need to look to know that Marsha Mott was standing in the doorway. Her temple began to throb again. She was in no mood for Marsha today.

"And hello to you, too, Miss Mott." She turned with two charts in her hands. "I'm pulling some charts, as you can see. I wouldn't be pulling them myself if there had been anyone at the desk to do it."

Marsha moved into the small room and let the door close behind her. "You're not on the schedule today," she snapped. "Why do you need charts?"

"To catch up on my notes," Ally replied, her voice dangerously quiet. "Do you have a problem with that?"

"Yes." Marsha shouldered her way past Ally and stared with deep suspicion at the shelf. "If you're not on the schedule, you can't take charts out."

Ally stared at her, speechless for a moment. "That's it!" She slapped the charts down with a clatter. "I give up! You know as well as I do that everybody comes in and does chart work on their days off. Why pick on me?"

"Dr. Schuyler, I'm *not* picking on—"

"Oh, come off it, Marsha!" Ally strode around the low shelf to stand face-to-face with the other woman. "You've had it in for me since the first day I set foot in this clinic. I've put up with it for too long, and now you're going to tell me what the problem is."

"Nothing!" Marsha blustered. "There's nothing wrong except that you're in the chart room and you shouldn't be—"

"Oh, please!" Ally stared at her. "Don't insult my intelligence. I want to settle this, *right now*." She took a deep breath and spaced her words for emphasis. "Why is it me you pick on? Why *me*?"

Marsha regarded her in silence for a moment, then let out a long breath. "You don't belong here," she said heavily.

"Why not?"

"Because you're rich. Because you're a Schuyler." Marsha's voice rose. "Because you're Ward Schuyler's daughter!"

"Because of my *father*?" Ally stared at her, dumbfounded. "What on earth does *he* have to do with it?"

"He has everything to do with it!" Marsha picked up a chart and studied the dented cover intently. "I went to nursing school at California Medical College."

Ally digested the apparent non sequitur for a moment. "That's where he went to med school before he dropped out."

"That's right."

"And you knew him?" Ally asked.

"Knew him?" Marsha tossed the chart aside. It struck the shelf and fell off, clattering to the floor. Her laugh was high and bitter. "Oh, yes, I knew him."

"Only it was more than that," Ally said very softly. "You were in love with him."

Marsha looked up, her eyes filled with remembered pain. "I loved him more than my life. I thought we had a future together. I dreamed about it—right up to the moment he quit medical school to marry Alicia Cordell."

"My mother," Ally whispered.

Marsha nodded. "She was everything I could never be. Tiny, blonde, pretty, rich." She glanced at Ally. "You look like her. When he married her, I knew how they'd live. Vacations on the Riviera, shopping in New York. For years I could close my eyes and see the two beautiful people, happy together."

"My mother committed suicide when I was two years old."

Ally's interjection stopped Marsha short. "She—" She faltered, shocked and staggered by the idea. "I didn't—I'm sorry, I didn't know that."

"I'm sorry, too," Ally said. She moved a step away, trailing her fingertip in the dust on a shelf. She looked at Marsha. "I'm sorry my father hurt you. He seems to be good at hurting people. I wish you could find some way to deal with your feelings about my father, though, besides taking them out on me."

Ally watched Marsha's set face for a moment, waiting for a response. She got none. With a sigh, she picked up her charts and turned to go.

"Dr. Schuyler, please wait."

Ally stopped with her hand on the doorhandle. "Yes?"

"You won't—you won't tell Ward about this, will you?"

Ally looked back at her and laughed, short and bitter. "There's not much chance it'll come up in light conversation. I haven't spoken to my father in eight years." She pushed the door open and walked out.

She didn't even see the nurses' station as she walked past it, lost in thought. Marsha Mott and her father? She couldn't even imagine it. She couldn't imagine her father, the man who was never without a woman in one hand and a drink in the other, with someone as intense and serious as Marsha Mott. Her flighty, careless, shallow father with Marsha? It defied imagination.

"Ally?" She jumped when Anne spoke to her. "Ally? Are you all right?"

"Yes." Ally blinked and came back. "Yes, I'm fine."

"Is something wrong?" Anne followed her into the lounge and closed the door. "You were gone a long time."

"Nothing's wrong." Ally dropped into a chair and set the charts down. "I ran into someone I had to talk to."

"The woman who came out crying?" Anne asked.

"Crying?" Ally jerked around. "A tall woman with gray hair?"

"Yeah. Gray hair pinned back," Chris elaborated. "She came out of that doorway a few seconds after you did and headed straight for the ladies' room. Did you two argue?"

"In a way. But I think we finally worked out an old problem." Ally managed a wan smile. "It's okay. Now, do you two want to learn about charting?"

They didn't of course, so while Ally was updating her charts they read the hospital orientation manual and compared the staff lists Cruz had given them with the faces of the staffers who came in. It was nearly five when Ally closed the last chart and stood.

"That's all I'm going to do today." She stretched and rubbed her head, which was starting to ache again. "Is there anything else you guys need to know?"

"Not tonight." Chris grinned. "We've had quite an education this afternoon. We'll escort you to your house, though."

"You don't need to do that," Ally protested, but they were adamant. Clay had told them to see her home, and see her home they would.

Ally had to give in gracefully. "I need to put these away and check my mail before I go, all right?"

That was no problem for Anne and Chris. They followed her to the nurses' station and watched as she signed the charts back in, then signed herself out of the clinic. Barbara Clark walked up, demanded an introduction and launched into an exaggerated, slightly racy and hilarious description of a "typical" day at the clinic. Ally abandoned them to Barbara's tender mercies while she studied her patient list for the next day.

Her mailbox was the last stop, a cubbyhole stuffed with professional journals, hospital staff memos, an invitation to the Residents' Association fall picnic, notes from other departments and health insurance forms. She sifted quickly through the bulk of it, then stopped at a plain buff envelope. It had only her name on the front, and it was sealed.

Ally stared at it for a moment, and her hand began to shake. A plain envelope with only her name on the front in a loose scrawl. Taking a deep breath, she fought off a wave of nausea. She held the envelope by one corner and tucked it between the pages of a journal.

"Anne? Chris?" She tried to keep her voice level, but it was too high, too thin. They turned, and Anne's eyes widened.

"What is it, Ally?" Anne spoke in a casual tone, but she could see what was in Ally's face. She moved to screen Ally from the rest of the room. "Is something wrong?"

Ally shook her head. "I have to see Dr. Gallego before I leave. Why don't you come along and see if he has anything else to tell you?"

"Sure." They fell into step on each side of her, for all the world like bodyguards. No one spoke.

Cruz swung his chair around at Anne's perfunctory knock and looked at them in surprise. "Ally?" He looked from her to the others. "What's going on? Anne? Chris?"

"We don't know yet." Anne gave Ally a little push toward the chair. "She got her mail out of the mailbox and then she had to come see you."

Ally slid the envelope out of her copy of *The Lancet*. "This was in my mail."

Cruz took it carefully by the edges and examined both sides of it. "Does it look like the other one?"

"Not really. But it's an envelope with nothing on it but my name...."

"Yeah." Cruz understood. He laid the envelope on his blotter and looked up at Anne and Chris. "Can we open it, or should we wait for Clay?"

"No, we can open it." Anne stepped forward. "Do you have some of those rubber surgery gloves?"

"Sure. Here."

Cruz rummaged in a drawer, then passed her a pair of thin latex gloves. Anne drew them on and carefully slit the envelope. She extracted one folded sheet of heavy notepaper.

"Here, Ally. Take a look at this and see if it's another threat." She unfolded the note and held it out.

Ally scanned the few lines quickly, half-afraid to read the words. She reached the end and blinked at the paper for a moment before she burst out laughing.

"What is it?" Cruz was around the desk in an instant, but she'd already taken the note from Anne, heedless of fingerprints. She read it through again, laughing helplessly at her fears.

"I can't believe I've become so paranoid!" she gasped. "It's not a threat. It's from Marsha Mott."

"Marsha Mott?" Cruz looked at the letter in her hand. "What's she doing writing you notes?"

"You wouldn't believe it if I told you!" She lay limply back in her chair, her laughter dying away. "It's all right, though. We had a little...talk this afternoon."

"Did she get out of line?" he demanded. "I'll make sure she doesn't say anything else—"

Ally stopped him. "Cruz, no! She didn't do anything wrong. We talked, and I think we worked some things out."

"With Marsha?" He found that hard to believe. "What did you work out?"

Ally smiled wryly. "It's between Marsha and me." She folded the note and stuck it in her pocket. "Come on, bodyguards. Let's get out of here."

She paused before she followed them out the door. She looked back to where Cruz stood watching her.

"I'm sorry we interrupted your work for something so stupid."

"It wasn't stupid." He moved a step closer, but stopped when Ally stiffened. "It was perfectly natural for you to worry. I'd feel better if I knew what was in it, though."

She shook her head, relieved that he hadn't touched her. She couldn't have borne that.

"It's between Marsha and me. I'm glad to have it solved, though." She grinned at him. "I wish the rest of this mess was as easy to solve. Good night, Cruz."

And she was gone.

Chapter 16

Cruz stared at the door for several seconds before he realized what he was doing. He was waiting, wishing, willing that door to open again and Ally to come back.

"*¡Dios!*" He struck a stack of journals with his palm and watched them slither to the floor. He stepped over them and walked around to drop into his chair and spin it around to the window. The sky was gray and heavy with low, threatening clouds.

She'd shown him no emotion at all. His face twisted. No emotion except fear of him when they were alone. She'd kept the two officers with her as a buffer, even when they had no longer been needed. When she'd left his office it had been clear that she was relieved to get away from him.

Cruz raked a hand roughly through his hair. He couldn't blame her for wanting to escape him, not after the way he'd acted. He wanted a chance to talk to her, but he knew anything he said now would be interpreted as another attempt to manipulate her. He wouldn't be able to really talk to her until the thief was caught and the nightmare was over. Soon, he thought. It had to end soon.

He was unaware of time sliding past as he gazed bleakly out at the darkening sky.

"Two weeks, Clay! Two weeks!" Tense as a coiled spring, Ally paced the short width of his office. He watched her from behind the desk while Cruz stood by the door.

"These two—" she indicated Chris and Anne, who were lounging against the wall "—have had to follow me around and listen to the dull details of my day, and all they've learned is a heck of a lot about paperwork! We're no closer to catching this guy and ending this than we were two weeks ago!"

Clay heard her out. "We're waiting for him to make a move."

"He's not moving, Clay!"

"I don't think that's true."

She dropped into the chair and regarded Clay with open skepticism. "What do you think he's been doing, then?"

"Waiting and watching, the same as us."

"Wonderful. So we're all peeking around corners and getting nowhere." She folded her arms and sighed heavily. "I'm sorry, Clay. I know I'm not being very mature about this."

"You're allowed. You've had a rough couple of weeks. Nobody's going to blame you for getting fed up."

Ally knew someone who might. She didn't look at Cruz; she wouldn't be able to read anything in his face, anyway. He had been politely indifferent to her for two weeks. When they had been forced to speak, they'd behaved with a punctilious courtesy that concealed any real emotion.

She hadn't wanted to hurt Cruz, but she'd been unable to avoid it. Though his wounded anger had frightened her, it was real emotion, and it had been better than this. She had no idea what was going on behind his distant, disinterested facade, but if they exchanged one more artificially polite word she was going to scream.

"You might like to know," Clay told her, "that I think it's time to quit waiting and take some action."

Ally leaned forward eagerly. "When do we start?"

"Don't you want to hear what it is first?" He grinned.

She shook her head briskly. "I don't even care. I just want to *do* something! What is it?"

"I want you to remember."

She frowned. "Remember what?"

"I want you to remember the night you were attacked."

"I've been trying to, and it hasn't worked. I don't remember any more now than I did that first night."

"And our thief is on pins and needles waiting for you to remember what happened in that tunnel. If you *pretend* that your memory is coming back, just in bits and pieces, and the word gets around, he's going to panic. And we'll get him."

Intrigued, she leaned forward. "Do you think—"

"Are you crazy, Clay?" Cruz demanded. "She can't do that!"

"Cruz, I can decide what I'm—"

"You can't set yourself up as bait for this sick—"

"I can decide what I will do!" Ally's voice was low and cold, the words falling diamond-hard into the sudden silence. She glared at Cruz for a moment, and though his face was impassive she could feel the anger simmering in him. She ignored the chill that slid down her spine and turned away. "Will it work, Clay?"

He glanced at Cruz. "I think it will break the stalemate."

"And what happens then?" Cruz's voice was very soft.

He was standing beside Ally's chair, and though a space of several inches separated them, she could feel him there. His protective, possessive stance was unmistakable, but she didn't mind that as much as she should have. She felt safer with him beside her.

This was her decision, though, not his. She stiffened her spine and looked at Clay. "As Cruz says, what happens then?"

"We watch and listen." He spoke to them both. "You won't be left alone. Anne will stay at your house, because we don't know which way this guy will jump."

"You're sure that he will, though?"

"As sure as I can be."

Ally could feel Cruz's almost unbearable tension. At his side, near her shoulder, his hand was clenched into a fist so tight that his knuckles had whitened. Ally couldn't forget the ways he'd touched her with that hand, comforted her, caressed her body. She wanted to forget, she was trying to forget, but . . .

She dragged her gaze away. "If it will help end this mess," she told Clay, "I'll do it."

After listening to all Clay's instructions and warnings she walked out of the office without once having looked at Cruz, and she was in the parking lot before he spoke her name.

"Yes, Cruz?" She leaned against a car.

He didn't stop until a scant six inches separated them. Ally, pressed against the car, could feel the heat of his body. She stood very stiff and straight.

"You know how I feel about this, Allison." He spoke softly, his voice almost a caress. "I don't want to see you in danger this way. You'll be used as bait for Clay's trap, like cheese to catch a mouse, only this is a dangerous mouse. He's hurt you once. How can you give him a second chance?"

"It has to end, Cruz." Her voice was as quiet as his. "I'm a prisoner right now just as much as anyone in a cell. I have to be guarded at the hospital. I can't relax in my home. I'm not living right now, I'm just existing. It's got to end, and I can make it end."

"And if you get attacked in the process?"

"I could get killed going home on the freeway tonight. Anne and Chris will be with me all the time, and there are uniformed cops in the hospital." She wasn't aware that she had reached out to him. "I'm not taking unreasonable risks, Cruz."

"Any risk is unreasonable. You should stay out of it."

"You're not telling Anne she should stay out of it."

"It's her job."

"Yes, and she chose that job. I wasn't given a choice. I'm stuck in the middle of this against my will. But I can help put an end to it. It's something I have to do."

His gaze dropped to her lips, and he placed his hands on the car, on either side of her. "And this," he said, leaning close, "is what I have to do."

She had time to turn her face away, but she waited, scarcely breathing, her heart pounding as his breath feathered over her mouth. And then his lips touched hers. Helpless, she let her head fall back, parting her lips to kiss him with all the passion and despair she'd been holding in check.

She didn't want to, but she reached for him, unable to stop herself. Her yearning body swayed toward his; her hands slid up, over his shoulders, around his neck. As their bodies met, heat seemed to flare between them, pulling them together, until she was pressed tightly against him. He pressed her back against the car, moving his hips against her until her movements echoed his, and the movements of their mouths mimicked what they both wanted so badly.

The kiss ended slowly, their lips drawing gradually, reluctantly apart, their breathing ragged. Cruz looked down into her eyes.

"I can't stop you from making your own decision, Allison," he murmured. "But I will do everything in my power to protect you." He turned on his heel and left.

"Cruz, what—" But he was already gone. She stared after him, fingertips pressed to her tingling lips.

"Ally, what's wrong?" Anne walked up from another direction and stared across the parking lot at Cruz. "Did you two argue?"

"Argue?" Ally's laugh was high and shaky. "No, we didn't argue, not this time. Actually, we had a nice, quiet conversation."

Anne looked at her face again. "I'm driving you to the hospital," she announced calmly. "My car's over here."

Ally was glad to be chauffeured; it gave her time to think. By the time she walked through the clinic doors, she was calm and determined, ready to put Clay's plan into action.

Anne walked in with her, asking about how to interview patients. With an acting ability she'd never suspected she possessed, Ally was telling Anne how she talked to nervous teenagers when they reached the desk and found Thea Stevens waiting there.

"Good morning, Ally. I was looking for you."

"Morning, Thea." Ally reached for the clipboard and signed herself in. "What's up?"

"I need some help." Thea held a folder stuffed with papers. "I've got to do an update of this slide program for new clinic patients, and I don't know where to start." She grinned. "I need a brain to pick, so I thought of yours. Do you have a free hour this morning?"

"Let me check." Ally scanned the schedule. "You're in luck. I don't have any appointments until nine. I guess they think I'm still too fragile to work a full day."

"Speaking of which," Thea said, concerned, "how are you?"

The innocent question gave Ally the perfect opening. She didn't like lying to Thea, but she smiled easily. "If you'd asked me that yesterday, I'd have had to say that everything was just the same, but today..." She let her voice trail off.

Thea took the bait eagerly. "Don't leave me in suspense. What is it?" People standing nearby turned to listen.

Play it carefully, Ally reminded herself. Clay had warned her not to reveal too much at once. It would seem more natural for her to pretend to remember in bits and pieces.

"It's my memory."

"Has it come back?" Thea demanded eagerly. Behind her, Barbara Clark gasped and echoed the question.

"No, no, only a little," she replied to them both. "I wish it would all come back in a rush, but I guess that only happens in the movies."

"Well, what do you remember?" Thea was practically hopping up and down with curiosity, and others were gathering around.

"Come on, Ally," Karen urged her. "Don't drag this out!"

"Okay, okay! All I could remember before was sitting in the cafeteria with Stacy, eating supper, then waking up in the

ER with people standing around asking me if I remembered anything.''

"And now?" Thea prompted.

"Now there are bits and pieces. I know I got a page. I don't remember leaving the cafeteria, but I can remember deciding to use the tunnel because it was quicker."

There was a quick babble of congratulations.

"Anything else?" Thea asked when it died down.

Ally shrugged. "I'm afraid that's it."

"Well, I'm glad it's coming back, even if it's only a little bit. Anyway," Thea said, smiling brightly, "if some is coming back, the rest can't be far behind, right?"

"That's what they tell me," Ally replied. When everyone had congratulated her, she led Thea to the lounge, and they worked until nearly nine. Ally was glad to help, but she also wanted to repay Thea for her inadvertent help in spreading the news of her "regained" memory.

It had worked, too. Not ten seconds after she said goodbye to Thea, Ray Walcott hurried up to her.

"Hi, Dr. Schuyler. How are you?"

"Good morning, Ray." She smiled at his eager interest. "I'm fine."

"I heard you're startin' to remember things." He trotted along beside her, watching her face.

"It's not much. Just little bits."

"That's something. What have you remembered?"

"I can remember eating dinner and getting a page, and the fact that I went through the tunnel."

"You don't remember who hit you?"

"No. But I'm glad I'm starting to remember something."

"That means the rest of it could come back any time, huh?"

"I hope so. They can't make me any promises, but it's a good sign." She smiled brightly, and after a moment his rather sullen face lightened into a weak grin.

"Yeah. Well, congratulations, Dr. Schuyler."

"Thanks, Ray." She waved an absent goodbye and walked into the first examining room.

It was a busy day, with its share of problems. At 2:30 Ally sent Anne and Chris to have a cup of coffee while she examined a three-year-old with a history of fever, sore throat and general malaise. Jeffrey Connors had a straightforward streptococcus infection and needed nothing more than penicillin to fix him up. The problem was the boy's mother.

Barely twenty, she was shy and withdrawn, and Ally didn't have much confidence that she would actually give Jeffrey the full course of medication. Like many parents, well-meaning but misinformed, she would give him his "medicine" until he felt better, then abandon the strenuous task of getting medicine into an uncooperative preschooler. The medicine would sit on the shelf, and Jeffrey's infection would recur, probably worse than ever. There was another way, though.

"He has a strep infection, Mrs. Connors." Ally kept a firm hand on Jeffrey. He kept trying to climb off the table and make a break for it. "I'll give him a shot of penicillin today, and you can bring him back in a week for another, all right?"

"Yes, ma'am." Mrs. Connors peered timidly at her through lank dark-blond bangs.

"Can you hold him still for the shot, or would you rather I got someone to help me?"

"Oh, no, ma'am!" Mrs. Connors's pale face pinched in distress at the idea. "I don't like shots and things."

"That's all right. I'll get a nurse to help."

Ally smiled and handed Jeffrey back over. The little boy's bold curiosity contrasted with his mother's timidity, but she was clearly proud of her adventurous son. Perhaps he brought to her life the eager fearlessness she'd never known. "I'll just be a moment," Ally said as she stepped out of the exam room.

Cruz was at the desk, writing in a chart. He'd kept his word to watch over her. Every time she looked up, he was a few yards away, watching her. Whenever she sent Chris and Anne away for a break, assuring them that she'd be fine, Cruz appeared, always in the background.

She didn't need a guard now, though, she needed assistance, and with a sense of déjà vu she saw that Marsha Mott was free. Ally glanced at her and started to walk past, looking for someone who would help.

"Dr. Schuyler?" Marsha's oddly diffident voice stopped her and she turned around slowly.

"Yes, Miss Mott?"

"Can I help you with something?"

Ally was so surprised that it took her a moment to respond. "Yes, you can," she said after a moment. "I have to give a shot to a three-year-old, and his mother doesn't want to hold him."

"I'll do it," Marsha said decisively, walking out from behind the desk. "I'm a good holder."

"Thank you." As Ally turned back toward the exam room she saw Anne and Chris returning from the cafeteria. She waved at them. "I'll be done here in a few minutes, all right?"

Anne nodded, and they took up positions on the far side of the room with a view of everything. Ally and Marsha went the other way. Marsha glanced back at the two of them, neat and official-looking in their white coats.

"They're nice kids, aren't they?"

"Yes, they are." Ally carefully signed out a prefilled syringe of penicillin.

"Their school gives them a lot of time off for observation. Will they be here much longer?"

"I don't think so," Ally replied, thinking fast. "They're on a rotating course system, and each month a few of the students have observation or research instead of regular classes." She smiled as naturally as she could. "They have to write a paper about what they've observed." For a spur-of-the-moment lie it sounded plausible enough.

"I hope they've observed something worth writing about. It's been pretty dull around here."

"I think they're interested. It's all brand-new to them." That was the truth. Even Chris, the former paramedic, had been surprised and interested by what he'd seen.

It was a brief business to give Jeffrey his shot and return him, wailing furiously, to his mother. Ally wrote out an appointment request.

"Give that card to the clerk at the desk," she told Mrs. Connors, "and they'll set up an appointment for Jeffrey's second shot." Mrs. Connors whispered her agreement and carried her son out. He was leaning over her shoulder, trying to grab charts off the wall racks.

"He got over his shot quick enough, didn't he?"

Marsha was actually smiling as she watched him. Ally stared at her, stunned by the transformation. Beneath that severe hairstyle and grim expression was a woman who could be beautiful. Marsha turned back again and caught Ally watching her.

Her smile faded. "I have a lot to apologize for, don't I?"

"You apologized in your note. I appreciated that."

"It was little enough, after the way I behaved." Marsha bent her head, studying the doorframe as if fascinated by the chipped paint. "Have you heard from your father?"

"No." Ally was curt, but Marsha seemed to understand.

"I see. Well—" she straightened, her voice brisk now "—is there anything else you need help with?"

"Not right now." Ally smiled. "Thank you."

Marsha hesitated, as if about to say something else, but she was prevented by the jangling ring of the desk phone. She hurried to answer it, then turned to Cruz.

"Dr. Gallego, it's Sergeant Williams for you."

"Thank you." He glanced across the room at Ally, his face grim. "I'll take it in my office." As he passed he nodded to the officers, and Anne moved closer to Ally's examining room.

Ally went back into the small room and bent to pull a tray of instruments from the cupboard at the rear. Her next patient was a carpenter who needed an infected splinter removed from his arm. She didn't know how bad it would be, but she wanted the instruments ready, just in case.

She was kneeling in front of the cupboard, searching for tape, when the door squeaked open. "Anne, you don't need to stay in here if you don't—"

"It isn't Anne," said a male voice.

She looked around to see Ray Walcott. His face was more sullen than usual, and he held a tray of instruments.

"Hi, Ray." Ally smiled, but he didn't smile back. "Thanks for bringing that, but there's already a tray in here."

"Oh." The tray clattered slightly as he set it down. "I thought you needed it."

"You can leave it here anyway. I may need it before the day's out." She rose and took the tray, but he stayed, standing just inside the door. She stooped again to search for sterile drapes.

"How do you feel?" he asked abruptly.

"Fine." She pulled out a folded green cloth, then thrust it back with a mutter of annoyance when she realized it was the wrong size. "I haven't had a headache in days."

"And your memory? How's that?"

"About the same."

"All you remember is going into the tunnel?"

Ally glanced over her shoulder, wondering at his interest. She'd told him her story this morning, but maybe he got a vicarious thrill from this kind of thing. He'd probably spread gossip, though, so she'd tell him what he wanted to hear.

"That's all," she said. "But they tell me that my memory will keep coming back a little at a time."

"And you'll know who it was?"

"Eventually. And the police are looking for him, too. They may catch him before I get my memory back, but one way or another, they'll catch him."

"They will, huh?"

Ally couldn't have said what it was, but something in Ray's voice was wrong, like a missed chord or a sour note.

She blinked and had a sudden flash, like a glimpse through a camera lens, of the tunnel and someone running toward her. Fear slid down her spine in a cold trickle. She rose slowly, a bundle of folded drapes in her hands, and turned to him with a carefully bland expression on her face.

Her nonchalance dissolved when she saw the scalpel gleaming in his hand.

"It's not gonna be *that* easy, Dr. Schuyler." His face was twisted, his voice a low, feral snarl. "You been playing your game all day, telling everybody you only remember a little bit, but I know better."

Ally swallowed with difficulty. "Ray, I don't know what you're talking about."

With an effort, she kept her voice level. The door was only a short distance from her, but she was trapped at the back of the exam room by the big examining table, which was solidly bolted to the floor. The only path of escape was the narrow space between the table and the counter. Ray stood there, the scalpel gleaming, small and deadly, in his hand.

"Don't give me that," he spat. "You say you only remember a little, but you remember it all, don't you?" He eased closer, his eyes alight with desperate cunning. "You remember. You know who was in that tunnel, and you remember what happened. You've just been trying to make me sweat, playing Miss Detective, setting your little traps."

"Ray, I don't remember. I don't even remember going into the tunnel." She rocked her weight onto the other foot, judging the distance to the door, wondering if she could get past him.

He followed her glance and grinned with relish, showing his yellowed, uneven teeth. "Don't lie to me, Doctor." He turned the title into something obscene. "And don't even think about makin' a break for it. You tried to spring your little trap, but it didn't go off. You're the one in the trap now, and you're gonna be my ticket out of here."

He held the scalpel low and slightly to his side, like every knife fighter in the movies. Ally couldn't look away from that blade. It gleamed bright and deadly in the harsh overhead light, and watching it was hypnotizing her. She focused on Ray's face.

"I'm not trying to trap you, Ray." She spoke soothingly and edged along the side of the table. His reply was an obscenity. She slid another half step closer to the door, the bundle of folded drapes clenched in her hands, the shiny steel edge of the tabletop against her side.

"You know you won't get out of here this way, Ray. The best thing to do is to talk to Sergeant Williams and—"

"Shut up, bitch! You don't think I'd—"

Ally swung the drapes at his face with all her strength and hurled herself at the doorway. She almost made it.

Ray knocked the drapes aside and whirled with the agility of a striking snake. He caught her arm and hauled her roughly back into the room, twisting her arm behind her back. He pulled it painfully up between her shoulder blades, holding the scalpel at her throat with his other hand. The small blade touched her skin, and Ally felt a cold sting as it drew blood. She froze.

"That's good," he whispered, his breath hot and foul on her cheek. "That's real good. Now we're gonna walk out of here, real quiet. Aren't we?" He jerked her arm higher and laughed softly at her gasp of pain. "Let's go, bitch."

Chapter 17

Ally hung back, but he forced her forward. The searing pain was a red-and-gray mist in front of her eyes for a moment, but as it cleared she saw the rolling stand beside the doorway. It was metal, a pedestal on a three-wheeled base, with a tray on top for instruments and supplies.

No one out in the clinic had noticed what was happening, but she could change that. Ignoring the pain, she leaned back until she could hook a foot beneath the base of the stand. When Ray tried to push her forward she kicked out and up, toppling the stand with a resounding crash.

"Damn you, bitch!"

With vicious force he shoved Ally out the door. Everyone in the lobby had heard the noise and was looking curiously to see what had happened. Curiosity changed to horrified shock, there were gasps and shouts and someone screamed, but they could all see the blade and the warm, wet trickle that Ally felt on her throat. No one dared approach too closely.

Her gaze swam around the room as Ray held her. Barbara Clark stopped short in the doorway to the waiting room, gasping "Ally!" She heard Charlie Parsons swear from somewhere behind her, and from the corner of her eye she could see Karen staring at her in openmouthed shock. She was facing the desk and saw Marsha Mott reaching slowly for the phone.

Unfortunately, Ray also saw her. "You! Don't touch that phone!" he snarled. "Yeah, you!"

Marsha froze.

"Drop it over the side."

Slowly she lifted the receiver and dropped it over the front of the desk to dangle from its cord.

"That's right," he said in a soft voice that made Ally's skin crawl. "Everybody just stay right where you are and the pretty little doc won't get hurt."

His back to the wall, he began to sidle slowly toward the door. Ally stared wide-eyed at the horrified faces passing in front of her. Behind them, she saw movement. Anne was slipping through the crowd, looking for a clear shot. Chris had to be doing the same, though Ally couldn't see him, but with the knife at Ally's throat, neither of them could chance shooting.

"I said don't move!"

He'd seen Anne to the left of them. She straightened but kept her hands, and her gun, out of his sight. As Ray watched Anne, he pulled Ally another step closer to the door.

"Stop right there!" Chris snapped from their right.

Ally jerked her head around to see him in the policeman's half-crouch, his gun trained on Ray. Ray started, and the scalpel nicked Ally's throat again. She pressed her head back, away from the blade, staring at Chris. His gun was level and steady, but he couldn't shoot. Ally's body shielded Ray.

"Don't try it," Ray snarled, "or she gets it."

Ally stared at Chris, waiting for some kind of signal. She was damned if she was going to let herself be dragged meekly out the door, but with that cold blade touching her neck she could do nothing. She had already decided that when they reached the doorway and Ray had to use one hand to pull the door open, she would throw herself to the floor, knife or no knife.

Then she saw movement.

Off to the left, by the hallway to Cruz's office, she could see people moving, making room for someone. Anne was looking at those moving people, but then her gaze shifted fractionally to something behind them.

"Let her go, Ray!" Anne shouted suddenly.

Ray swung Ally around to the left to face Anne, yanking cruelly on her arm. Keeping Ally in front of him, he started to pull her back to the other side, toward Chris and his gun.

"You know this won't work!" Anne shouted, drawing his attention back to her.

As Ally was pulled from side to side she could feel the effect things were having on Ray. He was starting to panic. He was trembling, breathing rapidly, and his grip on her twisted arm tightened. The scalpel blade shook against her throat, stinging as it drew blood again. She pressed her head back against his shoulder, away from the blade.

"You're just making it worse for yourself," Anne yelled at him. "You know you are!"

"Shut up!" Ray screamed at her, near hysteria. "Just shut up or I cut her!"

Behind her, Ally heard the soft sounds of stealthy movement. Ray didn't seem to notice, but she began to hope. She let her knees buckle, her weight dragging her down against Ray's grip on her arm. It hurt abominably, so badly that her vision blurred for a moment. Ray was screaming abuse at Anne; he didn't even seem to realize what Ally had done.

The careful movement behind her became a sudden rush of footsteps. At the last second Ray noticed and tried to haul her around. She resisted, dragging her weight against his grasp. She got a blurred glimpse of a body hurtling toward them, and then she was knocked violently to the floor.

The clinic was a madhouse of shouting and screaming. Heavy bodies thudded to the floor beside her, and she scrambled away from them. Something, a fist or a foot, struck her ribs. Gasping for breath, she jerked herself farther from the center of the maelstrom. Hands reached out to grab her and pull her to safety, dragging her across the linoleum until she could turn and sit up and stare in horror at the men a scant two yards away.

Ray's face was a blur of blood. Cruz had him pinned to the floor with his fist drawn back to hit Ray again. As she watched, Chris stuffed his gun into his belt and grabbed Cruz's arm, holding him back before he could beat Ray to death. Cruz's chest heaved with his labored breathing, and the fury in his face was frightening. Ally could believe that if Chris hadn't stopped him, he would have killed Ray with his bare hands.

With Charlie Parsons's help, Chris pulled Cruz away. Charlie held Ray while Anne trained her gun on him and Chris snapped handcuffs on his wrists.

With Charlie standing between him and Ray, Cruz watched the man who had caused them so much agony being handcuffed and read his rights. Gradually the red haze of rage cleared from his eyes, his breathing slowed, and the terrible tension in his body eased.

Ally could see what it cost him to control himself. She tried to stand, but could only manage to push herself to her knees, swaying dizzily. Further effort was beyond her.

"Ally, sit down." Barbara Clark took her shoulders and tried to push her back to the floor, but she resisted.

"No." She batted at Barbara's hands. "Let me up...." She looked up into Barbara's face. "Please, Barbara."

Barbara hesitated, then sighed. "All right." She took Ally's arm and helped her struggle to her feet.

When Ally was standing, swaying slightly with the effort, she lifted her head and looked across at Cruz. He was watching as Chris and Anne, with the help of two uniformed officers, led Ray out of the clinic.

Ray looked small now, pathetic, his hands cuffed behind him, a burly policeman on each side. Ally knew she should feel anger or hate or disgust, but all she could feel now was sadness, pity for a broken human being. He couldn't hurt her now; he couldn't hurt anyone anymore.

Cruz's palms still itched to close around that animal's neck and choke the life out of him. It was an effort to stand

and watch in silence as Ray was led away. The door closed behind the police officers, and Cruz drew a deep, cleansing breath.

Forcing his face into impassivity, he turned to the ring of staring faces around the lobby.

Ally's was the only face he saw. Pale and strained, she was staring at him, wide-eyed. As he started toward her, she lifted one hand to reach for him, swaying on her feet as a roaring filled her ears and the world went dark.

She would have fallen if Cruz hadn't run to catch her. He scooped her into his arms when her knees buckled and lifted her against his chest. Her head lolled limply on his shoulder.

"Let me get her to the ER!" he barked, and the crowd parted before him as he strode down the hallway.

"Cruz!" Vanessa Rice gaped as he walked into the ER. "And Ally? Bring her in here." She pulled back the curtain of the first treatment cubicle. "What on earth is going on? There were police, and—"

"It's all over now." Cruz laid Ally gently on the table. "We've got to take care of her." He smoothed back her tumbled hair, caressing the side of her face.

"Her throat!" Van gasped as she saw the series of cuts bleeding onto Ally's collar. "Let me get some help in here!"

She hurried away while Cruz loosened the neck of Ally's blouse and covered her with a blanket. Ally muttered something and moved. Cruz bent over her.

"You're okay, Allison. You're all right."

"Ray..." Her voice was a hoarse whisper.

"The police have him. He's gone."

She blinked at him, then grabbed his arm in a desperate grip. "Cruz?"

"Yes, Ally. I'm right here."

"You said...he's gone?"

"He's gone. The police took him away."

She laid her head back. "Oh, yeah. I saw them take him."

"Mm-hmm. Right before you fainted."

She looked up at the big treatment light. "Is this the ER?"

"Yeah."

"You seem to be bringing me here a lot lately."

Cruz grinned at the observation. "More than I'd like to, you know. All this getting-hit-over-the-head-and-taken-hostage business is getting wearing."

"I shouldn't mess up your work like this."

"And it's rude, too..." He dropped his voice. "...to frighten me like that." He took her hands in his as he spoke. "I have never been so afraid in my life. When I saw he had hurt you, when I thought he was going to—" He broke off and turned away.

Ally could see him trembling. She looked at his bent head, at his rigidly set shoulders, at his hair gleaming blue-black under the light, and she loved him so much she ached with it. "Cruz?" she whispered.

"Yes?" He didn't look around.

She swallowed. "I just—"

"What have you been doing to yourself this time?" boomed Hank Thomas as he threw the curtain aside and strode in. He lifted the sterile towel Cruz had placed over the cuts on her throat and clucked reprovingly. "You're gonna have to adopt a quieter life-style, Ally. You're wearing me out."

She laughed hoarsely as she laid her head back and let him get on with his work.

Cruz took her hand as Hank began cleaning the cuts. She could tolerate the discomfort as long as Cruz was there, holding her hand, and she clung tenaciously to him as she suffered through the treatment, the tetanus booster and finally Clay's interrogation. When it was all over, dusk had fallen and she was reeling with fatigue.

Ally waited in a straight chair in the ER lobby while Cruz sat beside her and talked to Clay in an undertone. She caught the occasional word of their conversation, "statement" and "station" and "tomorrow morning," but none of it seemed real. Reality was Cruz's hand, hard and strong, enclosing hers.

Clay touched her shoulder and murmured something as he left, but he was unreal, too, seen through a haze of exhaustion.

"Come on, Allison." Cruz raised her to her feet, supporting her with an arm around her waist. "It's time to go home."

She let him lead her to the car and belt her into the passenger seat, but as they drove, the mist in her brain began to clear.

"It's over, isn't it?" she asked wonderingly.

He glanced at her and smiled. "Yeah. It's over."

She dropped her head back against the seat and closed her eyes. "Why?"

It wasn't more than a whisper, but Cruz heard. "Why what?"

"Why did he do it? Why steal the stuff, and why try to get me blamed?"

"Money. Clay said that's all he would tell him at the station. He's been selling the stuff to people in his neighborhood."

"Do you think that was all? Just money?"

"That's part of it, but I think the thrill was part of it, too. He's the kind of guy who got picked on in school, never got chosen for the team, who was a scapegoat for the bullies. I figure this was his way of getting back at all the people who made his life miserable."

"But why me?" She was unaware of the hurt in her voice. "Why should he try to get me blamed for it?"

"You were convenient."

"And that's all?"

"And you were new in the clinic. There was already gossip about you. You were an easy target, and when you didn't have an alibi for the first theft, it was simple for him to wait until he thought you were around before stealing again."

Ally shivered, remembering how terrible that suspicion had felt. She hoped she'd never feel anything like that again. "Will he go to jail?"

"Maybe. Or to a hospital. Everyone in the clinic saw what he did. He won't be out on the streets for a long time."

Ally sat in silence for several minutes. "I think I'm starting to believe it." Her smile started slowly and spread as she absorbed it all. "I can go to the hospital without guards. I don't have to look over my shoulder anymore."

"That's right." He changed lanes for the exit to her house, but Ally reached over and flipped the turn-signal lever off.

"I'm not ready to go home just yet," she said in reply to his questioning look. "Can we go to the beach first?"

He glanced at her. "It'll be cold."

"I don't care. I want to feel the wind. I think about how the wind blows, all the way across the ocean, with nothing to hold it back. This thing has been holding me back for weeks, Cruz. I want to go out there where everything is free."

"Then we will." He changed lanes for the freeway that would carry them to Malibu.

The clean, cold, salty wind slapped at Ally as she stepped out of the car. She tasted the sea on the air and lifted her face to the wind, letting it whip her hair into a pale flag in the dim light of the falling dusk.

Cruz walked around the car, and she looked up with an eager smile. "Can we walk?"

"Sure." He reached into the back seat to pull out a battered leather bomber jacket. "Put this on so you don't freeze."

He put it on her, then turned her around and zipped her into it. It was far too big, reaching below her hips, with shoulders that drooped and sleeves that covered her hands. The knit cuffs turned back, though, and the pile-lined leather bulk was wonderfully warm.

"Don't you need a jacket?" She looked at his cotton shirt and thin sweater.

He slammed the car door. "I'm okay. Ready to walk?"

She ran ahead of him, scrambling down a steep bank to the deep, soft sand and striding out along the beach, head lifted into the wind. She walked fast for several minutes, until she reached the pile of boulders where they'd picnicked. She scrambled onto one and patted the stone beside her.

"Come on up. This is as good as a sofa."

Cruz climbed up beside her and draped his arm around her shoulders, pulling her close. The breaking waves foamed on the beach, silvered by the rising moon, then slid down into the water again. Ally folded her legs and tucked herself against Cruz, her cheek on his chest, and gazed out at the water.

He linked his hands behind her, holding her safe. After a moment she felt his face come down to rest against her hair. As she sat in Cruz's arms, Ally felt her tension and fear seeping away.

It was all over. The shadow that had been hanging over her had been lifted. By tomorrow the whole hospital would know that she had never stolen any drugs, that she wasn't guilty of any crime. She was free.

She was free to feel again. She was playing with fire, but she didn't care. She leaned back to look into Cruz's face and brushed his windblown hair off his brow.

Fire. It was there, deep in his eyes, as she traced her fingertip lightly over his face.

Playing with fire. She could feel the fire, heating her blood. She tugged gently on his lower lip, and he nipped at her fingertip, then pulled it into his mouth.

A wave of pure heat flowed through her, followed by another when he kissed her palm. He tightened his arms around her, sliding her onto his lap and bringing her mouth to his. His touch was light, then lingering as the heat built in them both. Then the fire took over and Cruz crushed his mouth onto hers.

Ally clutched his shoulders, holding him close, wanting him closer, as close as a man and woman could be. She twisted across his lap, feeling his legs shift beneath her and one arm tighten around her as he cupped her head in his hand. She returned his kiss with all the wanting and love she'd been suppressing, seeking his lips with blind questing movements when he took his mouth away to kiss her cheek, her jawline, and the soft, thin skin of her throat, beside the bandage that covered her cuts.

She shuddered and sighed, and he kissed the sensitive spot just beneath her ear, the curve where her shoulder began, then slid the jacket's zipper down a few inches and pushed her sweater aside to kiss the delicate line of her collarbone. He stopped there, with his lips pressed against her skin, her subtle fragrance filling his senses.

"Allison."

She let her hand drift over his hair. "Yes?"

He looked into her eyes. "I want to take you home."

Ally felt her heart leap, then begin to pound. She wanted that as much as he did. "Yes." She touched his face, marveling at the beauty of him. "Yes."

Afterward she remembered little about the walk back to the car and the drive to her house except for the fact that she kept some kind of contact with Cruz the entire time. Whether her arm was linked with his or her hand was resting on his thigh, she was touching him all the time.

She stood in the center of the living room while he carefully locked the door, closing the world out. Impatient, she didn't wait for him to walk to her, but ran into his arms. Her sudden movement broke the tight rein he'd held on himself, and Cruz wrapped her in a crushing embrace, drinking the sweetness of her kiss, running his hands over her back, her hair.

When he pulled the leather jacket off, Ally tugged clumsily at his sweater. He released her long enough to whip the sweater over his head and throw it aside, then dragged her into his arms again. He stroked her back, and her wool sweater slid against her skin; then he shaped her shoulders with his palms, drew his thumbs along her collarbone and trailed his fingertips down and over her breasts.

Ally gasped and hid her face against his neck. Her bloodstained blouse had been left at the hospital. Beneath the thin wool she wore only a silk camisole, no barrier at all to his touch. Her nipples tightened to aching nubs as he circled his palms over her breasts, and she arched her back, pressing up into the curve of his body. They were close, but not close enough. Only the ultimate closeness would be enough.

She squirmed against him, giving a little murmur of protest at the impediment of their clothing. Cruz muttered something she didn't understand, then bent and hooked an arm behind her knees, lifting her effortlessly against his shoulder to carry her up the stairs.

Ally had never realized how powerfully exciting a man's strength was, but she reveled in Cruz's easy ability to carry her weight, in the power beneath his gentle touch.

He set her on her feet beside the bed, then stepped back, his hands on her shoulders, gazing at her in the soft glow of a small lamp.

"You are so beautiful." His voice was a ragged whisper. "So very beautiful."

Ally's cheeks warmed, but she didn't look away. "I want to be . . . for you."

Her sweater closed down the front with a long row of tiny pearl buttons. When she lifted her hands to open the first one, Cruz breathed something she didn't understand.

He pushed her hands away and opened the next one himself, brushing a fingertip over the little triangle of skin he exposed, making Ally shiver with delight. One by one he undid them with a careful deliberation that was designed to drive her to distraction. When at last he'd finished, he pushed the sweater off her shoulders and let it slide to the floor. One ribbon strap slid off her shoulder as well, and the camisole clung to the curve of her breast, covering just enough to tantalize.

Cruz started to unbutton his shirt, but Ally took over the task for him, her trembling hands clumsy and unwittingly seductive. When the shirt fell to the floor she stroked her fingertips down from his shoulders, running them over the heavy muscles of his chest, brushing them through the crisp hair, following its narrowing line to the point where it disappeared into his waistband. He sucked in a quick breath, and she felt a thrill of feminine power at the tensing of muscles beneath her touch.

His patience fraying, he stripped off her slacks more quickly. In her tiny panties and lacy camisole she felt no shyness, for in his eyes she was beautiful. Too beautiful. When she impatiently unbuckled his belt, Cruz could wait no longer. He stripped off his remaining garments, then pulled her into his arms and off her feet as he turned and fell onto the bed.

Ally relaxed and went with him, barely knowing when they came to rest. She was floating in his arms, floating on a tide of love she could no longer hide. Cruz rolled onto his back and she rolled with him, sprawling across his body, their legs entwined. He tangled his fingers in her hair, bringing her face down for his kiss, then slid his palms the length of her torso to stroke the soft curves of her derriere.

Ally quivered and gave herself up to the magic. There was no gentleness now, only urgency and need and demand meeting demand. His hands and mouth sought the secret places, the places only he knew, the places that drove her to madness. She tried to work the same magic for him, but she was helpless, lost in a swirling, flooding torrent that carried her away from any reality but him.

This was a strong man, but she matched his strength with hers, matched his passion with hers. He pulled at the camisole, and she felt a strap break before the silk was tossed aside. Then there was skin against skin, her breasts brushing across his chest, teasing, tempting. Cruz bore it for a moment, then groaned and pulled her beneath him.

They fit together perfectly. Their bodies matched, soft to hard, curve to hollow. Cruz sought all her curves and hollows with his lips and hands, kissing, stroking, teasing and arousing until she twisted beneath him, her head tossing on the quilt. She was melting and burning and dissolving inside, all her being concentrated on the river of flowing need.

When he touched the center of her need she gasped and cried out, and when he moved his body above her and bent his head to take her mouth, she arched beneath him, demanding more. And then she clutched his shoulders as he made them one. The waves came in a rhythm that built and quickened until the world whirled and spun around her and she was engulfed in heat and light and release.

Ally came back to earth in a haze of exhaustion, lax, sated, dazed. She was only dimly aware of Cruz pulling the covers over them both, tucking her warmly against his side and kissing her hair as she slid into sleep.

It was dark when she awoke. She was curled snugly against Cruz, her arm across his stomach, her head pillowed on his shoulder. She should have felt warm and content.

Instead she felt hollow and empty, frightened and cold and already alone. She eased herself away from Cruz, holding her breath when he stirred and muttered. She waited until he was still again, then slipped carefully out of the bed. She covered him warmly, pulled on a robe and padded away.

Chapter 18

The kitchen was dark and cold—or was it simply that she was cold? Ally switched on one dim lamp, which cast enough light for her to fill the coffee maker. She flipped the switch and sank into a chair while she waited, elbows on the table, listening to the hiss and gurgle as the machine began to drip.

This was the end. The end of waiting to catch the thief, and the end for her and Cruz. As long as the investigation had been going on they had been unavoidably thrown together, but that was over now. It was time for her to tell Cruz.

She admired him for his courage, for his talent as a physician, for his unshakable integrity. She wanted him as much as he did her, maybe more. She loved him with all her heart and soul and strength, and she was going to tell him that she could not see him anymore. It was going to be the most difficult thing she'd ever done.

He wouldn't want to hear it, nor to believe it. He'd asked her to marry him, and once she said the things she had to say, he would ask her again, would insist and argue. She wasn't entirely sure why he wanted to marry her, but he would be adamant.

Perhaps because she'd been a virgin. He was her first lover, her only lover. Somewhere deep inside him the voice of honor was telling him that he owed her marriage, the traditional price of a "good" woman's virginity. Well, she didn't want a husband that way, bought with her body.

The only husband she wanted, the only one she would have, would be a man she could make a life with. And there was the thorn in the rose garden.

Much as she loved Cruz, how could she be the kind of wife he had every right to expect? He would want a mother for his children, a woman to make his home comfortable, to care for him. Ally wasn't that kind of woman.

She wasn't domestic, though she tried. She could cook, courtesy of a gourmet cooking course at her Swiss finishing school, but the other mysteries of housekeeping were beyond her. If not for Toni, who cleaned her condo once a week, she knew she'd have drowned in clutter or been poisoned by toxic fumes from some deadly household cleaner by now.

She'd tried vacuuming, but the vacuum hadn't closed right after she'd put in a new bag, and all the dirt that had gotten sucked up by the wand had sprayed out the back of the machine. Toni had laughed until she'd cried when she'd arrived to clean and found dirt stuck to the walls and ceiling.

Ally shook her head. Good grief! She couldn't even vacuum a floor, so how could she pretend to be a wife to Cruz?

Visions of children swam before her eyes, dark-haired children with Cruz's midnight eyes, his intensity and his gravity and his courage. They would be beautiful children, but they wouldn't be hers. She knew less than nothing about raising children. It was the most awesome responsibility imaginable, and it was one she wasn't equipped to deal with.

Cruz wouldn't like what she had to say, but he'd have to listen. She would make him listen. Ally stared fixedly at her hands, which were knotted together on the tabletop. A tear splashed onto her fingers, then another.

"No!" Angrily she blinked the tears away. This was the right decision. There was no reason to cry over it. She flung her head back, staring out the window at the city lights dotting the blackness, but the lights blurred and smeared across her vision.

"No, what?"

She whirled around in her chair. Cruz stood in the doorway, watching her. He wore only his slacks, pulled on but not belted. Ally's gaze skipped quickly over the wide expanse of his chest, over the dark hair and the smooth skin that gleamed in the dim light. His face was in shadow, so she couldn't read the expression in his eyes. She blinked quickly, fighting back more tears.

"I don't know." She pushed herself up and went to take down cups and saucers. "I guess I was just talking to myself." She closed the cabinet door with a bang. "Do you want milk in your coffee? I don't have any cream."

"Black is fine." He stood in the doorway, watching as she poured coffee and added a splash of milk to her cup.

"Here." Her hand trembled, and the cup she handed him had coffee spilled into the saucer. She turned quickly away and leaned against the sink, staring blindly out the window as she sipped her own coffee and scalded her tongue. The silence stretched, hanging in the air between them.

"Why did you come down here?"

She tensed at the sound of Cruz's voice and turned slowly to face him. "I woke up." Her voice was thin and too high. "I wanted a cup of coffee."

Cruz glanced at the coffee can. "If you couldn't sleep, why didn't you make decaf?"

Ally glanced guiltily at the telltale can. "I wasn't paying attention, I guess. It doesn't matter." She held her cup near her mouth, enjoying the warmth and the fragrant steam, using it as a shield to hide her face and her emotions.

It did no good, of course. He knew. When he moved, it was to prowl into the kitchen. The large room seemed to shrink around him, and Ally forced herself not to flinch when he neared. If she was going to say her piece and make him believe it, she couldn't afford to show weakness. She felt Cruz's gaze on her like a physical touch and shifted her shoulders uneasily.

"What's wrong, Allison?"

There was no point in trying to deny it. "I needed time to think before I talked to you."

"And have you thought?"

She lifted her head to gaze into his eyes. "Yes."

"What is it you want to tell me?"

"That this is the end."

"Well, of course it is." He frowned in confusion. "The investigation is over and we can get on with our lives now."

"Yes. We can." She set her cup on the countertop. "Our separate lives, Cruz."

He watched her for a moment, his eyes dark and opaque. "How do you figure that?" he asked very softly.

"It's over. It's over!" she repeated more loudly as she turned away. "The investigation, this whole horrible mess, is finally over. Oh, we'll have to give statements and maybe testify in court, but the waiting and watching are over now. I won't even be in the clinic much longer. I start another rotation in two weeks, and you and I won't even see each other at the hospital. It's over."

His voice was soft and certain. "I asked you to marry me. You haven't answered me yet."

She hid her pain. She didn't know how, but she managed not to let anything show when she looked at him. "I said no."

"I won't accept that."

"You don't have a choice!" Her agitation broke through. "I said no, Cruz. That's the end of it."

"It isn't—"

She cut him off. "And anyway, we both know you only asked me because you thought that would give you the right to tell me what to do. You'd have kept me away from the hospital, and what would that have accomplished? What?" she demanded angrily. "You'd have locked me away somewhere in the misguided belief that it would keep me safe, and this mess wouldn't be ended yet, would it?"

"We would have caught him in the end." Cruz moved toward her, and she stepped back.

"You think so?" Ally asked with bitter sarcasm. "I'm not so sure. Nobody had any idea who it was. He only gave himself away because he talked to me this morning about my 'returning' memory. If it weren't for me, he wouldn't have felt desperate enough to make a mistake."

"A mistake that damn near got you killed!" Cruz retorted.

"A few scratches." Ally touched the butterfly bandages on her neck. "Trivial."

"But it could have been—"

"It could have been a lot of things, but it wasn't! You didn't *need* to protect me, don't you see? And you don't need to marry me, either." She turned away, watching her fingertip trace patterns on the countertop. "There's no point in it."

"I love you!" Cruz grabbed her elbow and whirled her around. "Isn't that enough?"

"Oh, Cruz." She shook her head sadly, wearily. "You think you love me because you feel responsible for me."

"You can't believe that!"

"Hear me out, will you please, Cruz?"

Ally could see the tension in him, the urge to shout her down, to overwhelm her with his strength or his kisses or the simple force of his personality. He could do it; they both knew that. Ally could only hope that his sense of fair play would force him to listen to what she had to say.

"Please?" she asked.

His chest lifted and fell in a deep breath. "All right. I'll listen."

"You're attracted to me," she began hesitantly. "I'd be a fool not to know that. I'm attracted to you."

"Then why—"

"Please, Cruz!" She waited, and after a moment he nodded. "Thank you. We're attracted, but that's not love—and neither is feeling responsible for me. You know that I—" She looked down at the floor, her face flushed. "You know you were the first...man, and somehow it makes you feel responsible for me.'' She faced him steadily. "I absolve you of that responsibility, Cruz. You didn't seduce me. You didn't take anything I didn't want to give. You don't have to marry me.''

"I know I don't have to. I want to.''

For the first time Ally looked directly at him. "Why?''

Cruz shook his head. He felt a totally inappropriate urge to laugh, but he controlled it. "Because I love you,'' he replied as calmly as he could, "and because I believe that you love me.''

Ally closed her eyes against the stab of pain. "Cruz, can't you just accept my no?'' There was a note of desperation in her voice, but he followed when she moved away, trapping her in the corner between the cabinets and his body.

"Look at me, Allison.'' The soft words were a command, not a plea. Slowly she lifted her face. "Good. Now tell me why you made love with me, and then tell me you don't love me.''

"Cruz, no!'' She pushed at his chest, but he was as immovable as a stone wall.

"Tell me.'' His voice was hard, his face implacable. "Tell me why you gave yourself to me.''

"Because I wanted to!'' she retorted defiantly. "Lust, Cruz, simple lust.''

"Oh, no. I know better than that. You're not a woman who'd feel simple lust and act on it. You waited all those years, and you must have been waiting for something. I think it was love.''

"You do, do you?'' She glared.

"I do.'' He took her shoulders, pulling her closer. "You love me, Allison. Why are you denying it?''

Ally's gaze slid away. This was so much harder than she'd feared. "Because it doesn't matter.'' She didn't care that she'd given herself away. She would have to make him understand anyway. "Because you and I are *not* getting married.''

Cruz shook his head at her obtuseness. "We *are*.'' He leaned against the counter and pulled her between his knees.

"I love you, and you love me. That's why people get married."

"No!" She jerked her shoulders against his hold, but he wouldn't release her. "People get married because they can make a life together."

"And we can't?"

"No." She spoke with absolute conviction. "We're too different."

So that was it. Cruz felt something in him chill and die. If he had any pride, he would leave right then, but he needed to hear her say it. "I see. I can't give you the things you're accustomed to." His voice was quiet and cold.

Lost in her own misery, Ally didn't understand at first. "What are you talking about?"

"The difference between us. The difference between old money in Pasadena and no money in East L.A." His words were harsh, biting.

Ally stared at him, her confusion evident. "What on earth? It's not you. It's *me*. I'm not the kind of woman you need. I can't be the kind of wife you want."

"What?" It was his turn to stare.

"Think about it." Ally's face twisted in pain, and she dropped her head. "You're used to a big, loving, happy family. I don't know anything about families, Cruz. I don't cook much, and I can't clean house or take care of babies. I can't be a wife like that."

"Be a wife like what?" He took her shoulders and shook her lightly. "And what do you mean, you aren't the kind of woman I want? You *are* the woman I want!"

"But I'm not the kind of woman you need!"

Cruz's fingers tightened painfully on her shoulders. "You are exactly the kind—" his voice dropped, and his face lowered to hers "—of woman I need." And then he kissed her.

The touch of his mouth was like a match to a fuse. Ally whimpered low in her throat and kissed him with helpless abandon. She wound her arms around his neck and clung to him desperately, tears running unnoticed down her cheeks.

It was Cruz who realized she was crying. "Tears?" He touched her cheek with a gentle fingertip. "Allison, don't cry. Please don't cry over me. I promise you I'm not worth it."

Ally scrubbed the tears away angrily. "I'm not crying." She sniffed. "I'm not!"

"There's no reason to." He stroked the tumbled hair off her face, his touch inexpressibly gentle. "But tell me, please, why you think you aren't the woman I want, when you're the *only* woman I want."

"Because of your mother," she whispered.

"My mother? What does my mother have to do with?"

"She's the kind of woman you need for a wife. The kind of woman who can keep house and raise children and take care of a husband. I'm terrible at cleaning house, and I never had a family, and I don't know anything about children!"

"Ally, I don't want a clone of my mother!" Cruz pulled her close. "I want the woman I love more than my life itself, and that woman is you."

"But what about children? Don't you want children?" Her eyes were wide and worried.

"I hope to have children, but my life doesn't revolve around that one ambition. Why does that worry you so much?"

"I don't know anything about children! I don't know how to change diapers or teach them to ride a bike or anything."

"That doesn't matter. We'll learn how to change diapers together, and we can run on either side of the bike. It's you I want, Ally, not a robot programmed for child care." He pressed her face into his shoulder, where her lips met smooth, warm skin. "I didn't plan to ask you to marry me," he murmured into her hair. "I didn't think you'd want me."

Ally jerked her head up. "You thought *I* wouldn't—"

"I have nothing to offer you, Allison. No nice home, no nice furniture, nothing but a pile of debts."

"And your love." Her eyes were as soft as her voice.

"And my love." He cupped her face in his hands, gazing down at her. "I don't know if that's enough."

"It's more than enough. Money—" She shrugged, thinking of her wealthy father. "Money is worthless if there's no love." She reached up to touch his face, hardly daring to believe he was real. "Cruz?"

"Yes?"

"Is this really happening?"

He chuckled. "If it isn't, the caliber of my dreams has improved lately." He looked down at her breasts, barely concealed by her loosely tied robe, at the lines of her body, veiled yet revealed by the clinging fabric. "This—" he traced a fingertip along the lace that edged the robe, over the gentle swell of her breast "—is a particularly beautiful dream." Ally caught her breath as desire settled low and heavy in her belly. He smiled. "Do you love me, Allison?"

"Yes." It was a whispery thread of sound.

"And do you believe that I love you?"

"Yes."

"Then we don't have any problem we can't work out." He bent to kiss the spot below her ear, but she pushed him up so she could see his face.

"You don't mind a working wife?"

He bent again, murmuring against her skin, "Not as long as that working wife is Dr. Allison Schuyler Gallego." His fingers slid the silk off her shoulder so that it clung precariously to her breast.

Ally pulled his face up again. "You don't mind that I don't know anything about children?"

"We'll buy a book."

He bent to kiss the shadowy valley between her breasts. His hand moved again, and the silk fell down her arm, baring one high, round breast, its rosy tip tight with arousal. "The only thing that would bother me is if you didn't love me." He covered the taut bud with his hand, stroking it as he kissed her mouth.

"But I do love you." She gasped the words against his lips, her body arching up to that sweetly stroking hand. "I do love you."

"Then you'll marry me?" The robe slid off her other shoulder and fell to her waist. Cruz pulled her fully into his arms, her breasts flattening against the solid wall of his chest. His hands slid seductively over her back, from her shoulders down the graceful line of her spine to the narrow span of her waist and the soft curves below it. Ally's breathing was shallow and shaky. Her legs no longer wanted to hold her up, and she wound her arms around Cruz's neck for support.

"Yes," she whispered.

"Next week?"

Her eyes opened wide. "Next week?" she squeaked.

"I don't want to wait for you, Allison."

"But next week?"

His hands moved again, tracing the line where her robe clung to her hips, held there by the loosely tied belt. His fingertips dipped beneath the silk, and Ally gasped. "Next week?" Cruz asked, caressing her again.

"Next week," she replied breathlessly. "That's not fair."

"I know." Cruz was unrepentant. "I don't intend to play fair." He pulled her up to kiss her again. Ally shivered, and he lifted his lips. "You're cold." He pulled her robe back onto her shoulders, the front open, baring her breasts to his loving gaze. He drew her into his arms again. "We'll be married next week," he said with deep satisfaction, then kissed the curve of her shoulder.

"But what about your family?" Ally was still worried. "Won't they want a big wedding for you?"

Cruz lifted his head to gaze into her eyes. "I'm not getting married for my family, Ally. We'll have any kind of wedding *you* want. Do you want a big one?"

She thought about it, then nodded. "You know, I think I do. I want to show the entire world how much I love you. Do you think you can wait a few weeks?"

"If I have to," he conceded with a mock pout. "Will there be a lot to plan?"

"Oh!" Her eyes widened, and she bit her lip. "I don't know how to plan—"

"Would you like my mother to help you?"

"Do you think she would?"

"She'll be thrilled. She loved planning my sister's wedding."

"That would be wonderful."

"Then it's settled. Now, where do you want to go on our honeymoon?"

A slow smile spread over her face. She wriggled her body closer against his. "How about here?"

Cruz looked around him. "The kitchen? Why not?"

"Here in the house, silly." She ran her palms over his chest and around his flanks to clasp them behind his back. She traced little circles with her fingertips at the base of his spine. "We can unplug the phone and lock the doors and pretend the world doesn't exist."

"It sounds perfect." He buried his face in her hair. "Perfect."

"Thank you." He slid his hands inside the robe, and she moved seductively with his caress. "Cruz?"

"Yes?" His voice was rough with desire.

"I know we're not going to get married for a few weeks, but can we—start the honeymoon now?"

He was very still for a moment; then, with a low laugh, he swept her into his arms and lifted her against his shoulder. "Oh, yes," he said as he strode toward the stairs. "We can start now." The silk robe fell to the floor and was forgotten.

* * * * *

*...and now an exciting short story
from Silhouette Books.*

*

HEATHER GRAHAM POZZESSERE

Shadows on the Nile

CHAPTER 6

Jillian," Alex repeated. "I love you."

He *loved* her. She didn't know which meant more, which touched her more deeply: the husky timbre of his declaration, or the sweet and passionate hunger of his kiss, which was drawing her more and more deeply into a musk-scented world of ecstasy.

She tasted his lips, and his fingers played along the length of her spine, swift and erotic. He breathed in the fragrance of her hair and held her very close to him, and then, when he touched her, it was to remove what remained of her rumpled clothing. He whispered to her as he went, breathing soft fire against every inch of exposed flesh. "Jillian, I love you."

She locked her arms around him, smiling and causing him to stop in his sensual assault. Her eyes were as blue as a clear sky, as honest, and as warm. "Alex, I haven't felt like this since ... I've *never* felt like this. Never."

"You've never felt like you're going to, either," he promised her, then proceeded to prove it. His lips fell against the pulse at her throat, while his hands stroked over her breasts, soft and provocative. Then he cupped the full weight of one breast and teased her nipple with his thumb, before circling it with his tongue, the pressure growing hot-

ter and harder. His body shifted against hers, a caress in itself. Her fingers curled into his hair, then into the muscles
of his shoulders, and she began to writhe beneath him, alive
and explosive with sweet sensation.

"Alex..."

He fell to his knees and stripped away the dark bur-
noose, then his shirt, and she smiled, awaiting his return. In
seconds he cast away his trousers, and when he returned to
her, she whispered to him that *he* was the beautiful one. He
laughed raggedly; then his laughter caught in his throat as
she tasted the flesh of his shoulders and chest with fevered
kisses.

The scent of roses surrounded her, along with the sleek
feel of the silken sheets. Soft pillows cosseted her head, but
all she knew was Alex. He made a promise, and he kept it.
She was loved exotically from head to toe, kissed and caressed until she could barely breathe, throbbing and alive
with wanting him. Then she was part of him, or he was part
of her. It made no real difference; they were simply fused
together. She felt that she rode the wind, that she touched
the sun, and she burned with the greatest splendor, reaching to the sky for the stars. And when ecstasy burst through
her, it was the most shattering moment of her life, deep and
erotic, and as magical as the ancient mysteries she had come
to see.

Perhaps, she thought idly later, as he held her close and
stroked her hair, she had discovered the true secret of the
ancients. Love itself was ancient, and a mystery. It could not
be forced, yet it could bloom and grow in the driest desert.

They held each other in silence for a long time; then Jillian touched his cheek and murmured, "You have to admit, you aren't the average Egyptologist."

He exhaled slowly. "I never lied to you about that. I *do*
work for the museum. I was in the special services in the
Marines for several years, and I did some intelligence
work." He hesitated. "John is an agent with a special

branch of the Department of State. Our relations with the Egyptians are very important.''

He rose on one elbow, watching her with a rueful smile. Drawing a line down her cheek with his finger, he continued it to the valley between her breasts, and she trembled. "It's not the best start in the world, is it?" he murmured wistfully. "The lies. But this is the greatest truth, Jillian. Every minute meant more than the one before. Falling in love is so strange. I'm not sure what kind of a bargain I am, but I'd like to give us a chance, Jillian."

"Alex—"

"Don't!" He pressed a finger against her lips. She felt the heat and passion in his gaze. "Don't answer me now. Give me tonight. Please, give me tonight."

She had no power to deny him. He touched her again, and she marveled at the magic.

He was awake and dressed when she woke up the next morning. She smiled, drawing the covers around her. He came over to her, then bent to kiss her on the forehead. "You'd better get dressed. Achmed Jabbar is coming to see you."

"Alex?" The call came from outside the tent. Alex responded, asking for a few moments. Jillian flushed and quickly scrambled into her clothing. When she was dressed, Alex went to the entrance to invite Achmed in. He wasn't alone; John was with him.

"We just wanted to let you know that Ali Saud is in custody and the government will be taking over now. Last night we went back out and brought him in. It's over, Miss Jacoby, and we're very grateful."

"I'm glad that everything worked out all right," she murmured, casting Alex a glance that was only slightly reproachful.

Achmed cleared his throat, bowed and spoke to her with dramatic appeal. "Miss Jacoby, you are a fair rose in our desert. Please, stay with us a while." He reached out a hand to her. "Please? I will see that you eat well, that you enjoy fine music, and—"

"And a bath? Please? I'd really love a good bath."

"Ah, surely! With the finest rose oil!" he promised her. "We shall make a very fine day of it, I assure you."

It was indeed a fascinating day. Jillian drank rich Arabic coffee and sampled goat cheese, as well as delicious breads, dates and fruits. She watched a display of horsemanship and applauded for the men. She laughed with Achmed and John—and with Alex, whom she watched covertly with her heart hammering against her chest. Could it really be forever? For a lifetime?

After a late luncheon of delicious marinated lamb, she had her bath in a steaming tub of hot water, perfumed with attar of roses. She washed away the dirt and sand of the desert, luxuriating in the cleansing steam.

Achmed gave her a stunning emerald silk caftan, softly embroidered in gold, and a pair of jeweled sandals. Once she had dressed in her new clothes, she was anxious to see Alex again.

He was in his tent, lying on the bed, his fingers laced behind his head, staring at the canopy overhead.

He noticed her quickly, though, and rose on one elbow. "Jillian...?"

She walked over to the bed very slowly, and when she reached him, she smiled.

And then she let the caftan fall to the floor.

Night came, and shadows fell. Alex held her close, and Jillian felt her heart take flight again.

"We barely know each other," she reminded him.

"I thought we were fast becoming intimate friends," he protested, his eyes glittering in the dimness. He curled his fingers around hers and grazed his tongue over her flesh. His touch sent a swift river of yearning sweeping through her.

"Alex," she whispered breathlessly.

"Jillian."

"You said not to answer you before. I'm not—I'm not sure what you were asking me. I . . ."

He released her fingers and pulled her against him, then smiled down at her. "I want you to marry me."

"How can you be so sure?" she asked huskily. "We haven't had much time together."

He kissed her. "My time is your time, love. Whatever time you wish." He smiled, running his palm sensually over the silk sheets beneath him. "Do you like the feel of silk?"

She laughed, smiling curiously, warily. "I love the feel of silk."

"Then let's stay right here for a while. Let's take the time to get to know each other."

She hesitated for a moment. Then she slipped her arms around his neck and pulled him down to her. "I do so love the feel of silk," she assured him solemnly.

Two weeks later they were married. Achmed found them a small church near the Nile. He was there for the wedding, as was John. It was small, but it was very beautiful. Achmed had arranged for wonderful flowers, as well as a champagne reception on a colorful barge out on the river.

Jillian studied the dusky currents, and she shivered. She had longed to come to Egypt, and now she wondered if some instinct had promised her that she might find a modern treasure, as well as the masterpieces of the ancient world. Shadows on the Nile had haunted her; she had been threatened with violence and death.

But the Nile, she thought whimsically, had always been known as the river of life. And, in the end, she had indeed been given life. A new life, with Alex.

A warm, strong arm slipped around her waist. Alex smoothed away the tiny wrinkle in her forehead. "What were you thinking, love?" he asked her softly.

She shook her head, her eyes sparkling and kissed him. "I'm just glad I came to Egypt," she said, smiling.

Then she kissed him again, and they both forgot the conversation entirely as they sailed down the river to their new life—together.

*   *   *   *   *

The passionate saga that brought you SARAH and
ELIZABETH continues in the compelling,
unforgettable story of

Catherine

MAURA SEGER

An independent and ambitious woman earns the disap-
proval of Boston society when she discovers passion and
love with Irishman Evan O'Connel.

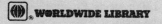

Silhouette Romance™

Legendary Lovers Trilogy

BY DEBBIE MACOMBER....

ONCE UPON A TIME, in a land not so far away, there lived a girl, Debbie Macomber, who grew up dreaming of castles, white knights and princes on fiery steeds. Her family was an ordinary one with a mother and father and one wicked brother, who sold copies of her diary to all the boys in her junior high class.

One day, when Debbie was only nineteen, a handsome electrician drove by in a shiny black convertible. Now Debbie knew a prince when she saw one, and before long they lived in a two-bedroom cottage surrounded by a white picket fence.

As often happens when a damsel fair meets her prince charming, children followed, and soon the two-bedroom cottage became a four-bedroom castle. The kingdom flourished and prospered, and between soccer games and car pools, ballet classes and clarinet lessons, Debbie thought about love and enchantment and the magic of romance.

One day Debbie said, "What this country needs is a good fairy tale." She remembered how well her diary had sold and she dreamed again of castles, white knights and princes on fiery steeds. And so the stories of Cinderella, Beauty and the Beast, and Snow White were reborn....

Look for Debbie Macomber's *Legendary Lovers* trilogy from Silhouette Romance: *Cindy and the Prince* (January, 1988); *Some Kind of Wonderful* (March, 1988); *Almost Paradise* (May, 1988). Don't miss them!

SRT-1

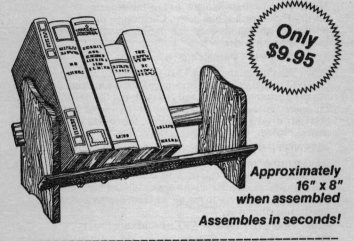